THE WOMAN
IN THE
PHOTOGRAPH

Also by Dana Gynther

Crossing on the Paris

THE WOMAN
IN THE
PHOTOGRAPH

DANA GYNTHER

Gallery Books

New York   London   Toronto   Sydney   New Delhi

G

Gallery Books
An Imprint of Simon & Schuster, Inc.
1230 Avenue of the Americas
New York, NY 10020

Copyright © 2015 by Dana Gynther

First Gallery Books trade paperback edition August 2015

GALLERY BOOKS and colophon are registered trademarks of Simon & Schuster, Inc.

For information about special discounts for bulk purchases, please contact Simon & Schuster Special Sales at 1-866-506-1949 or business@simonandschuster.com.

The Simon & Schuster Speakers Bureau can bring authors to your live event. For more information or to book an event, contact the Simon & Schuster Speakers Bureau at 1-866-248-3049 or visit our website at www.simonspeakers.com.

Interior design by Robert E. Ettlin

Manufactured in the United States of America

1   3   5   7   9   10   8   6   4   2

Library of Congress Cataloging-in-Publication Data is available.

ISBN 978-1-4767-3195-7
ISBN 978-1-4767-3196-4 (ebook)

For my mother, Ruth,
And my daughters, Claudia and Lucia.
Headstrong beauties,
All three.

THE WOMAN
IN THE
PHOTOGRAPH

PROLOGUE

———

"Hold it. Good. Now just one more." Edward Steichen looked through the lens, then back up at the statuesque blonde.

Lee leaned against an antique table in the Park Avenue penthouse; she was nearly holding her breath, affecting aloofness. From the corner of her profiled eye, she watched the photographer purse his lips and squint. He left his tripod to adjust her evening wear.

"The sleeves on this jacket would make a geisha girl jealous," he said, pulling the fur collar up on one side and letting it tumble down the other shoulder.

"Imagine eating soup in this thing." She jerked her arm to make the thick satin swing, then quickly resumed her pose. Her smileless profile faced a soft light cast by the crystal chandelier hanging overhead. It was as if she was observing an elegant gathering a few steps away, but not able to take part. Odd for someone so used to being in the center of things.

He snapped the last shot—"At ease, Miller"—then motioned to his assistant to pack up the equipment.

Lee slipped off the unwieldy jacket and reached for her cigarette case. "I'm going to miss you, Colonel."

"I'll miss you, too." He lit her cigarette, then his cigar. "When are you leaving?"

"Next week." She threw her head back, blowing out smoke, and stretched. "I can't wait. I spent almost a year in Paris when I was eighteen, and I've been itching to get back to Europe ever since."

"Is Paris your first stop?"

"No, I'm starting off in Florence. I've been hired to collect Renaissance patterns for a designer. You know, so he can copy bits and bobs from the sixteenth century and have everyone think it's the dernier cri." They shared a smile; both had an ample understanding of the fashion world and all its ironies. "I'm traveling over with Tanja Ramm."

"The dark-haired model with the perky little nose?" He scrunched up his own in demonstration. "Huh. I had her pegged as a real goody-goody."

"With her, at least I'll have the guise of respectability." Lee laughed, but there was some truth to what she said. They were so different—Lee often scandalized the shy brunette with her flippant attitude toward partying and casual affairs—that Lee often thought of Tanja as the Good to her Bad. "Really, she's lovely. Funny and bright. We've been close friends for years. We'll spend a month or so together in Italy, then she's off to visit relatives in Germany. That's when I'll head up to Paris."

"It *is* the center of the universe, after all."

"Absolutely! The language and cuisine, the art scene, the fashion—I love all of it. I can't believe four years have gone by since I was there."

"When you get there, you should look up Man Ray."

"Is that a person or a robot?" She smiled behind her cigarette.

"He's the best photographer in Paris, though he's actually a New Yorker. He's extremely innovative. He does abstract work, surrealist art, portraits, film . . . but he's been known to lower himself and do fashion shoots from time to time. I'm sure he'd love to use you."

With his cigar clamped in the corner of his mouth, Steichen began riffling through his briefcase. He pulled out a well-worn copy of *French Vogue*, opened it to a marked page, and handed it to her.

"This is his. It's called *Noire et Blanche*."

She took the magazine in both hands and sat with the image on her lap. In it, the oval head of a woman lay on a table, an African mask stood next to her chin, held upright by her hand. Lee studied the juxtaposition of the two faces. Their eyes were both closed, their surfaces smooth, the hair shiny and still. Their features—both the ebony mask and the pale woman— were honed down to the bare essentials of beauty.

"It's incredible." The words came out in an awestruck whisper.

How different this was from her modeling jobs, a variety of poses meant to set off fashionable gowns, striking accessories, the latest hats. This was bold—though she couldn't quite decide if it was sophisticated and sensual, or primitive and slightly terrifying. The nearly disembodied head, the nude shoulders, the serious stoniness—it was as if the woman was asleep, in a trance, or a mask herself. She wondered what the man who took the shot was like, who the woman was. Were they a pair?

"I could write you a letter of introduction if you'd like," Steichen suggested.

Lee Miller looked up at him; her slanted blue eyes were shining, her full lips parted with excitement.

"What am I saying?" he said with a laugh. "With that face, you don't need any letters."

"Don't be so sure, Colonel." She winked at the older man. "Looks like your Ray Man might prefer a voodoo doll or an Egyptian death mask to a mug like mine."

LEE & MAN

1929 – 1932

I

——

Lips pressed together in concentration, Lee sat under a gas lamp at a wooden table, tracing over a penciled design in India ink. With deliberate strokes, she colored in the dark spaces around a stylized artichoke, the central detail of a High Renaissance hat. She was finishing off her first batch of fashionworthy patterns—sketches made in the dim light of the Uffizi Gallery and Pitti Palace, then inked over at the *pensione*—and was eager to send it to New York and be rid of it.

"Hello there." Tanja breezed into their room, a knitted shopping bag over her shoulder, a fresh loaf of *filone* sticking out of the top. She peeked down at Lee's drawing. "What are you working on?"

"A hat I found yesterday in Perugino's *The Lamentation over the Dead Christ*. It made me laugh." She carefully blew on it, then picked it up to show Tanja. "I mean, look at it! More than a hat, it looks like the tattooed skull of a sailor, like the head of Ishmael's buddy in *Moby-Dick*." She set it back on the table with a small snort. "I thought it was funny—imagining the chic ladies of Manhattan strutting around in hats like these—until I started tracing it. It's a pain in the neck! I can't believe I agreed to this ridiculous job."

"You need a break. Are you hungry? I bought some of that chicken-liver pâté you like. The one with capers and anchovies."

"Wonderful."

Lee stood up to stow away her things, to make room at their only table. Slowly guiding her finished drawings into the cardboard portfolio, she knocked over the ink. Deep black seeped across the oak like an evil spirit, onto her cigarettes and over her sketchbook. "Damn it to hell! Grab a towel, a rag, something—"

Tanja snatched the *Guardian* off her bed, one week old and twice read, and handed it to Lee, who crumpled it to soak up the ink with newsprint.

"Shit, I think I've got some on my dress."

"Who wears ecru to work with India ink?" Tanja muttered, a loud aside.

"Who comes to Florence to work at all?" Lee pitched the soggy newspaper into the bin, then rinsed her hands in the basin in the corner. She examined her knee-length dress, staring down at the spattering of tiny black flecks on the hem of pale brown chiffon. She shrugged—"Not a bad look"—then turned back to Tanja.

"Let's get out of here and get a drink. I'm desperate for some air."

They left their dark *pensione* on the via Porta Rossa and strolled over to the sunlit Piazza della Signoria, the city's beating heart. In the two weeks they'd been in Florence, they had become habitués of a few local cafés, where the flirty barmen and waiters remembered their names and preferences. Heads always turned as the two slender, short-haired models—one dark, one fair—walked by.

"Lee, Tanja! *Le bellissime ragazze!*" The awkward youth, his hair slicked back with pomade, his waist cinched in by the strings of a white apron, was quickly joined by an older waiter, whose smile was equally large.

"Sit, sit! Chianti, no?" The older one asked, his limited English the better of the two. "Cold?"

"*Si, grazie,*" Lee answered. She had picked up a handful of phrases since they'd been in Italy, but was looking forward to being back in France, where she could truly speak the language and not just pretend.

Sitting back with closed eyes, her bare arms soaking up the sun, she tried to think of ways to get out of her research assignment. Would the seven completed drawings be enough? Maybe she could claim tuberculosis, malaria, the plague? Or that she was kidnapped by gypsies? Perhaps Tanja could write a letter for her, saying she'd lost all the feeling in her hands?

The older waiter ceremonially served the wine as the younger one slid a generous plate of almonds to the center of their table. "For you," he managed.

Lee raised her glass to them with a tired smile, then took a long sip.

"Oh, Tanja, I'm so fed up with these stupid designs."

"I have some news that might make you feel better. I've seen Mr. Porter this morning—"

"Hooray," Lee broke in, her deadpan voice oozing sarcasm.

Before their departure, Tanja's grandfather had somehow procured a letter of introduction to an elderly art dealer, Bancroft Porter, one of Florence's fin de siècle English expatriates and a lifelong bachelor. Since their first meeting the week before, they'd been saddled with him every day; he'd insisted on showing them every last monument, statue, painting—hell, every last rock in the city. Mr. Porter fancied himself their guide and chaperone, but Lee suspected what he really liked was the good-looking boys they attracted.

"Really, Tanja, not Mr. Porter again," Lee continued, pouring herself another glass. "He reminds me of that art history professor back at the League. What was his name? Dr. Rowell! Remember him, with his jowly drone and never-ending lists of dates?" Lee affected a whiney monotone, "And this master, from 1443 to 1497, used walnut oil to—"

"Oh, Lee, he's not that bad," Tanja began, then giggled. "Well, almost. But today he told me that he's managed to get us into Bernard Berenson's salon this afternoon." She beamed at Lee with expectation, but was met with a blank stare. "You know, the historian and critic, the man museums turn to if they're not sure a piece is authentic? Mr. Porter says Berenson is the leading expert on Renaissance art in the world."

"Not more Renaissance art! Tanja, I've had it up to here." Tipsy, she flung her hand over her head, nearly hitting a passing waiter. "All of these old expats are the same. Stodgy, self-satisfied, and, well, boring. Like characters out of a Henry James novel. I'd rather spend the afternoon on my own than with them."

"Working?" Tanja threw her an incredulous look.

"Of course not."

Feeling the wine move from her empty stomach straight to her head, Lee scooped up a handful of almonds and tipped them into her mouth. Crunching, she gazed around the large

10

square: a horse-drawn cart laden with tomatoes clopped along the ancient brick pavement, past grandiose palazzos and tall, narrow houses; young men lounging under the arcades called out to a trio of girls scurrying off to mass with heads covered in black lace; two clusters of plump, pink tourists—British? or Germans, more like—studied the open-air statues. One lot was peeking up at a marble woman being violently abducted, shading their eyes with Baedeker guidebooks while trying to ignore the hopeful beggars orbiting around them with shy, half-opened hands; the other, at the foot of an equestrian Medici, was swatting away a persistent souvenir vendor. He turned around in frustration and caught Lee's roving eye. With a professional smile, he made a beeline toward her. He rushed across the square, his arms stretched out to unfold an accordion of cardboard photographs tied together with a glossy red ribbon.

"*Signorina.*" Nearly breathless, he thrust the clumsily sewn book of picture postcards before her. "*Bellissime fotografie.*"

Lee glanced down at the gray churches, towers, and panoramic views and shook her head.

"*No, grazie.*"

"*Cinque lire. Molto economico,*" he insisted, pushing the photos toward her again.

The older waiter bustled over and growled at the vendor and—after a few staccato hand gestures—he left.

"That's what I'll do today." Lee's mood lightened swiftly. "Take some photos. Unfold the ol' Kodak. See if I can take one original shot of this place, find one angle that hasn't been made into a postcard."

"Well, it's up to you. I'm going to go meet Bernard Berenson."

Lee grinned at her friend. "Have fun, sweetheart."

That afternoon, after a heavy siesta, Lee pulled her camera down from the shelf on the wardrobe. She hadn't taken any photos since their crossing; a roll of six of the two of them—drinking cocktails on deck chairs, hamming it up with lifebuoy rings, peeking into funnels—had come out overexposed and slightly out of focus. Maybe the martinis were to blame? She put in a fresh roll, determined to do better this time around. Her father, an engineer, had a passion for photography—he even had his own darkroom—and Lee knew she'd inherited his tinker's soul.

With one last glarc at the worktable—the empty glass bottle sat next to the ink stain, innocent as poison—she checked herself in the mirror, adjusted the brim of her crinoline sun hat, and headed back to the square.

Now the buttery light came down in a slant, casting interesting shadows. Looking for inspiration, she studied various statues, hoping she didn't look as slack-jawed and dull as the morning's Germans. Her camera at her chest, she peered into the viewfinder: David, Hercules, Perseus, Neptune. Each time, she found her gaze drifting down to their groins. Lee hadn't been with a man since the night before they boarded ship in New York: she missed the heat, excitement, adventure. Looking down at the camera, her face safely hidden by her hat, she smiled to herself, comparing these bronze and marble bodies to ones she had known, tempted to make a photo series of Renaissance penises.

On the pedestal of the Hercules statue, heads of wild beasts adorned every corner. Lee noticed that, from an angle, the wolf's head looked like it wanted to bite a statue in an arcade behind it. Thinking it a clever shot, she tried to focus, but when the foreground was sharp, the background looked blurry. Sure her father would have known how to fix it, she grudgingly took the shot anyway. Maybe the figure would look like he was running away?

Lee went around the square and took more close-ups of statues from unusual positions: Neptune's horses seemed to spit, Perseus's winged sandals became hideous birds. Looking back at the sandals, she wondered whether *those* might make a splash in New York. Poolside languid ladies, poised to take flight at any moment. Should she draw them, as well? Or, perhaps she could just send the photo? Suddenly, it dawned on her. There was no need to spend hours making tedious sketches or tracing fine lines with that treacherous ink. She could let the machine do the work!

Lee held up her camera and kissed it.

For the next two weeks, Lee tinkered with taking photos in art galleries. It was much easier than drawing, but it was still a challenge. Capturing details—the Florentine patterns, the jewelry, the belts and ribbons—with low-speed film in gloomy, windowless rooms required a level of skill far beyond that of the typical Kodak Girl. But it was a challenge she enjoyed. She bought a tripod, which proved so flimsy that she had to anchor it down with an umbrella, and stationed herself in front of canvases like Botticelli's *Primavera* and Titian's *La Bella*, adjusting the light and toying with distance until she got it right. Finally, she had amassed enough successful prints to satisfy any employer.

Though still a novice, Lee had decided that photography was the art for her.

"Tanja, do you really want to spend our last night in Florence with Mr. Porter and his lot?"

Lee was sitting on her packed trunk, buckling her shoes.

"It's a soirée in our honor. I think it's sweet." Tanja screwed on a pair of earrings, then gently powder-puffed her face. "And we haven't met anyone else we can have a proper conversation with—"

"*Proper* is the word for it. What I'd give for a few dirty jokes."

"I'm sure you'll get plenty of that in Paris. Those bohemians in Montparnasse should keep you entertained." Tanja smiled at her. "Have you decided yet what you're going to do there?"

"I'll think of something."

That evening, in Bancroft Porter's nineteenth-century dining room, Lee barely listened to the discussion about servants and other local riffraff, but glanced around at the three other guests. Lord Rukin dominated the table with his loud voice and pre-war mustache while Lady Rukin, at Lee's side, sat silently, pulling her shoulder blades forward with the determination of a footbinder, trying to make her ample bosom as concave as possible. The other guest, a Mr. Larsen from Copenhagen, pale and effete, was a newcomer to Florence. The obliging Mr. Porter would surely take him under his wing; hiding a smirk behind her napkin, Lee supposed he would prove a much more satisfactory protégé than she and Tanja had.

At the end of the meal, the company made their way to the salon, where the much-discussed Italian maids laid out a variety of after-dinner options—fresh figs and apricots, crunchy biscotti, grappa and amaretto—and disappeared.

"Since it is Tanja and Lee's last night among us, I have hired some entertainment. A string quartet to play the highlights from *Tosca*." Mr. Porter, delighted with himself, swept an arm toward the door, where the black-tied musicians were waiting to enter. "My poor girls, after you leave Italy, you'll be hard pressed to find music like this."

Preferring Puccini to vapid conversation, Lee settled back in the fussy armchair with a glass of grappa, but as the musicians launched into an instrumental aria, her mind began to wander. Her eyes flitted around the room, from the antiquated guests to the gilded harpsichord to the ceramic figurines and shadowy landscapes; she wondered how difficult it would be to take photographs in there. Her eyes returned to rest on the pear-shaped violinist, whose back was to her. Lips curling into a smile, she thought again of Man Ray.

Ever since Edward Steichen had shown her *Noire et Blanche*, she'd been intrigued by him. After that shoot, back at the *Vogue* offices, she'd asked staffers if they could lay their hands on any more of his work. The image they'd found floored her: an armless woman whose back was pierced with the f-holes of a violin, her curves becoming those of the instrument. Another clean shot, both beautiful and utterly disturbing. She narrowed her eyes, trying to imagine the body of this bottom-heavy musician transforming into his violin. She let out a sigh. This stale old room just didn't have the Man Ray magic.

During that last week in New York, she had taken advantage of her good-bye dinners and parties to try to get the scoop on him. She found that most of the artists and writers she knew (and even some of the café-society elite) had heard of him, but they only had the barest facts: Mr. Ray was from Brooklyn but had lived in Paris for nearly a decade; he was one of those avant-garde (or "gaga," according to one source) Surrealists: artists so fascinated by the subconscious, they tried to paint their dreams. And the woman in the photographs? Most everyone agreed she was his lover and muse. One man identified her as a cabaret singer named Kiki. Just Kiki.

Lee had had the vague notion that, once in Paris, she would meet him or even model for him. That maybe she could pose for one of his brilliant ideas. But in the last two weeks, she'd begun to wonder if it was time to step behind the camera. Not only was she bored of having her picture taken, but she'd enjoyed the innovative headwork of taking photos, even of dull design details made under adverse conditions.

Listening to the swell of voiceless opera, she felt inspired. Man Ray could teach her how to be a real photographer. She was interested in his aesthetic—so creative and sexy—but also his technique. By all accounts, he was the most interesting, the most influential, the most daring photographer in Paris. Why learn the craft from anyone else? She quietly toasted the idea with a healthy sip of grappa.

Walking back to the *pensione* after the soirée, Lee took Tanja's hand in her own. "Well, that was worthwhile."

"You enjoyed it? I can't believe it. The ongoing woes of Lord and Lady Bumpkin and that scaredy-cat Mr. How-terribly-frightful?" She gave Lee a sidelong glance. "During the music, you looked like you were in a trance. I thought the voice of my dead Aunt Mabel was going to come out of your mouth."

Lee laughed. "I *was* in a trance. I've finally decided what to do when I hit Paris."

"What's that?"

"I'm going to take photography lessons from Man Ray."

"The Surrealist? What makes you think he's going to teach you?"

"Well, why wouldn't he?"

II

—————

Turning left off the boulevard Raspail, Lee took another look at the scrap of paper half-crumpled in her hand: 31 bis rue Campagne-Première. She walked slowly down the street, past a café and a neighborhood grocery, eyeing the numbers on the buildings: 35, 33, 31. When she found the correct address, she tilted her head back to take in the façade.

Unlike the other buildings on the street—all constructed of stuffy stone with narrow iron balconies too little for even a woman's feet—this one had enormous windows separated by tile designs, geometric towers of roses, buttons, and pyramids small enough to fit in a coat pocket. It was topped with ateliers, artists' greenhouses. The glass panes reflected a soft July sky, flimsy clouds floating on blue, which managed to make the huge place (was it the biggest building on the street?) seem airy. A new style, befitting the times: open, modern, full of possibilities. She'd seen nothing like it in Florence.

She stared up at the oval window over the doorway, topped with the sculpted head of a mythical woman (who might have resembled Lee herself, had the chin not been so sharp), formulating the right words to say to the concierge. Four years earlier she'd been fluent in French, but was now quite rusty. She pulled her cloche hat around her ears, practicing the words out loud, whispering formal inquiries and earnest requests, trying to remember the grammar and decide on the most charming approach. Finally, opting for simplicity, she rang the bell; a stout older woman answered.

"*S'il vous plaît, madame,*" Lee said. "*L'appartement de Man Ray?*"

"*Non, mademoiselle.*" The concierge looked genuinely disappointed for her. "*Monsieur Ray n'est pas là. Il est en vacances. Il est parti ce matin.*"

Lee's face fell. "*Ah, bon?*" She wavered a moment, staring back at the woman before accepting the fact she wouldn't be ushered in. "*Merci, madame.*"

As she turned back to the busy boulevard, she heard the heavy clink of the door closing behind her. What blasted luck! How could he be on vacation? It rankled her that she had missed him by only a few hours. Would he be gone long? She hated to think that her plan, as tenuous as it was, had already fallen through. It was time for a drink.

She went into le Bateau Ivre, a Montparnasse café near his studio. She'd heard it was popular with the avant-garde set— and Man Ray himself—and, even now, around noon, it was packed; every table was filled with young, intense-looking sorts engrossed in lively discussions. Lee skirted past loud, smoky tables, their numbers doubled by the mirrored wall, and went straight to the bar.

"A glass of Pernod, please, with lots and lots of ice." She was pleased to find the French vocabulary for ordering drinks came back to her without a hitch.

A pair of ice tongs in his hand, the bartender gave her a

quizzical look—"*Beaucoup, beaucoup?*"—but she nodded firmly. Lee knew only Americans took such stock in frozen water, but didn't care. She paid for her drink, then scanned the room for an empty table. Pushing off from the bar, she went up the spiral staircase, away from the crowd, to think.

She fell into a chair, then took a quick sip of the icy anisette before taking off her jacket and lighting a cigarette. Blowing the smoke out in a long sigh, she tried to decide her next step. Should she find a different teacher? Or go back to modeling and wait for Mr. Ray to come back to Paris?

A man emerged from an office there on the mezzanine and headed toward her. His thinning hair was carefully parted in the middle, his well-tailored suit made his waist look narrow, almost womanly. His eyes on hers, he straightened his bow tie. An overused gesture, she thought, self-satisfaction masquerading as nerves.

"I couldn't help but notice you come in, *mademoiselle*. This is my place," he said in French, with a slight sweep of the hand. "I'm—"

Lee didn't catch his name—an unfamiliar jumble of foreign syllables—but didn't care enough to ask him to repeat it. She offered him a patient smile as he sat down, arranging his chair as close to hers as possible, and began to prattle on about himself—but Lee scarcely listened. Her looks attracted men like bears to honey, and she usually found their motivations as empty and superficial as their chatter.

By the second round of drinks, restless and bored, she was waiting for a pause so she could make her excuses and leave. When the circular staircase creaked with the weight of a newcomer, she turned her full attention to it. A man seemed to be rising up through the floor, floating in a spiral. When he reached the top step, she saw that he was short and stocky yet somehow light, elegant in a loose pair of white flannels. He had a roman nose and, under dramatic pointed eyebrows, his heavy-lidded eyes were large and round. A voyeur's eyes.

Unlike the garden-variety bore beside her—a promising candidate for one of Mr. Porter's dinner parties—*this* man looked interesting.

Following Lee's gaze, the bar owner drew near her, his mouth almost touching her ear, his voice filled with self-importance: "That's Man Ray," he whispered. "The photog——"

Lee jumped up with a gasp, nearly overturning the drinks. What luck! He was still in Paris! Steadying herself with the back of her chair, she stared at the dark older man, tempted to call out to him. The startled bar owner stood up next to her with an uncomfortable chuckle.

"I'd be happy to introduce you, *mademoiselle*," he said, pleased at the opportunity to show himself as a man about town. He took her hand to lead her the three steps. "May I present Monsieur Ray?"

"Hello, Mr. Ray," she said. Reclaiming her hand, she stepped away from the bar owner, marking the distance between them, and stretched it out to the famous photographer. She was surprised to find she was nearly a head taller than him. Somehow, this made her bolder. "I'm Lee Miller. I'm your new student."

"I don't take students." His voice—the Brooklyn accent unchanged by years in Europe—was gruff and faintly sarcastic, but his eyes were all over her. Amused, she watched as they flickered around her face and then moved down, making a complete inspection: the short blond hair tucked under her hat, the clear blue eyes, the elegant neck. Her perfect flapper figure, slim and boyish, accentuated by a crocheted dress that hugged her slight curves and showed snippets of skin. "And anyway"—his voice lingered; was it regret?—"I'm leaving Paris this afternoon. I'm off to Biarritz on holiday."

Lee couldn't lose him so quickly, not right after finding him. He was here alone, with no woman on his arm; she decided to take the chance.

"So am I," she said, still holding on to his hand, staring into his dark eyes.

"Is that right?" he said, taken aback. The photographer threw a sympathetic glance at the man behind her. Although the bar owner obviously didn't speak any English—he stood at the side, mute, as the two Americans spoke to each other—he did understand the visual equivalent of "better luck next time." Man's thin, straight mouth curved into a smile. "Well, then. Shall we be off?"

Lee shot him a grin, nearly giddy, and grabbed her jacket. She took his arm, the attentive bar owner completely forgotten. The man with the wasp waist watched them disappear down the spiral staircase, his brow crumpled in disbelief, then turned and walked back to his office, straightening his tie.

III

—

"Don't be late," Man grumbled, then slammed the door of the cab.

With arrangements to meet at the Gare Montparnasse at four o'clock, she rushed back to her small hotel to retrieve her trunk. Checking in the day before, Lee had told them that she would be staying indefinitely; in this case, that turned out to mean less than twenty-four hours. As she repacked the few things she'd pulled out since her arrival, she decided against changing clothes; it seemed Man Ray had approved of her new dress. As she reapplied lipstick and powder, she grinned at her reflection, beside herself with excitement. Everything was falling into place. She was off on a whirlwind holiday to Biarritz with the very man she'd been wanting to meet: the photographer whose work had captured her imagination back in New York. All she had to do now was convince him to be her teacher.

By half-past four, she and Man were facing each other by the windows of a first-class railway car. His hat rested on the empty seat next to him, but he left his dark glasses on. The afternoon sun streamed in as the train jogged along; Man Ray looked out at a vanishing Paris—the buildings were becoming sparser—as they headed for the southwest corner of France.

Marveling again at how things had worked out, Lee stole a glance at him. Although he wasn't conventionally handsome, she liked his looks. The high forehead, the black widow's peak, the hawk nose. His dark, manly features made the Yalies she'd gone out with in New York seem like little boys. He was also surprisingly quiet in her company—not what she'd expected from someone famous—though she wasn't sure if he was nonchalant, aloof, or shy. He turned back toward her and caught her staring.

"Well, Miss Miller," he said with a slight smile. "Here we are."

"Call me Lee."

"What kind of name is that for a woman?"

"My name's Elizabeth but my father always had an assortment of pet names for me. When I left Poughkeepsie, I settled on Lee. I think it suits me." She shrugged, striving to be casual. He was completely unlike the flatterers she was used to, and she didn't quite know what to make of him. "But tell me, what kind of name is Man for a man?"

"Touché." He laughed but made no revelations. "So, you think you're interested in photography. Have you ever even held a camera?"

She pulled her folding Kodak out of her bag, determined to make an impression. Although Lee had no qualms about a beach holiday with an affluent, well-known artist, she didn't want their relationship to end after a few weeks of sunshine. She wanted him to see her as a promising student, a valuable assistant.

"It's not the greatest, I know, but it does the trick. I've just spent the last few weeks in Florence, in and out of museums and galleries, copying Renaissance designs for a New York couturier. I was drawing them until it finally occurred to me that I could take photos instead. With this camera, it wasn't exactly simple—the light was bad, and I had to take detailed shots, as close to the canvases as possible—talk about your trial and errors!—but, in the end, I got some swell shots. When I finished the assignment, I decided to study photography properly." Lee stretched her legs out, grazing his knees with her own. "With you as my teacher."

Man cleared his throat and shifted in his seat.

"Photography," he pronounced, "is just light and chemistry. And a camera is, I don't know, an old shoe. You can draw? Wouldn't you rather study fine arts? I'm also a painter, you know. That's my real work."

"Painting and drawing." The second word came out of Lee's mouth in a vindictive arch. "They're too damn slow. Really, I can't think of anything more excruciating. Besides, I think I have the knack. My father is an amateur photographer. When I was a kid, he converted a bathroom into a photo lab and has been developing his own pictures ever since. I've been around cameras and chemicals as long as I can remember."

"Some people think it's the equipment that matters," Man said, "but they couldn't be more wrong. It's the person who pushes the button."

"*I'm* that person," Lee said, in the most commanding tone she could muster.

She tried to see his eyes behind his dark glasses, to read his expression. Giving up, she picked up her camera and looked at him through the viewfinder; Man turned away. He was obviously far less comfortable in front of the lens than he was behind it. As he pretended to scan the horizon, she focused on his profile, his best angle. Funny, after seeing countless photos of herself over the years, she preferred her own face in profile as well. She imagined them as two cameos on a wall, facing each other, perpetually in profile.

Still looking through the camera, she moved down his shirt buttons to the sturdy hands on his lap, past his groin hidden in flannel, then down to his wingtip softly tapping the carpeted floor. The more she studied him, the more attractive she found him: his long, slender fingers, his sense of style. He turned back to her and she lowered the camera. The train was too shaky for picture-taking anyway. She pulled out a pack of Lucky Strikes and offered him one.

"Thank you," he said. He flipped open his lighter and lit hers before his own. "You know, kid, it's nice to be with another American for a change."

She grinned at him. "Don't get used to these, bud. I only have one pack left. We'll be back to Woodbines soon enough."

They smoked in silence and, again, she felt him looking her over. Was it professional interest? Or was he attracted to her? He finally took off his sunglasses; his dark brown eyes looked into hers.

"I've had a few assistants—apprentices, you could call them—since I've been in Paris. Two men and a woman. I find they quickly move on and become my competitors."

"I would never—"

"Not that I really blame them." He sighed. "You say you want me to teach you. Why me, Lee?"

"Edward Steichen told me all about you. Your inventions, your success—"

"Steichen!" He looked at Lee in surprise. "He's the highest-paid photographer in the world. You'd have done well to stick with him."

When modeling for him, Lee had occasionally asked Steichen about his techniques, and he'd been kind enough to show her a few tricks in the darkroom. But she'd been too restless in New York to pursue it. Hell, she hadn't even realized she was interested.

"He showed me *Noire et Blanche*," she said, staring back at him. "I'd never seen anything like it."

Man nodded, his expression softening into a smile.

"That is a good piece," he said, seemingly surprised that she knew something about him besides his name. He sat back in the seat, combing his hair with his fingers. "So, tell me. How do you know Steichen?"

"I modeled for *Vogue*," she said, slightly self-conscious about how frivolous that might sound to a serious artist. "The whole thing was just dumb luck, really. A couple of years ago I was on my way to a party on Park Avenue, running late as usual, and I wasn't paying any attention to the traffic. I stepped out in front of a motorcar. There was a loud honk and a whoosh of hot air, but before I was hit, a stranger grabbed me. In shock, I fell into his arms and started babbling in French." She laughed at herself. "The stranger was Condé Nast, the owner of *Vogue*. And just like that, he asked me to work for him."

"I've worked for Nast myself. I've done fashion shoots and taken portraits of all the aristocrats in the French Republic," he said, with a small snort. "But that's not what interests me."

"I know. That's why I'm here."

Her tone was persuasive, her eyes even more so.

"All right, then. You can be my assistant, Lee Miller, and I'll teach you the ropes. But it would be foolish to have a woman with your looks always on the wrong side of the camera. I'll want you to pose, too."

"Of course!" She nearly popped out of her chair to give him a hug but, with uncharacteristic self-restraint, contented herself with excitedly jostling his knee. "You won't regret it."

Her crazy plan had worked; she would be living in Paris, learning from the master. Man Ray—with his unique, unsettling aesthetic and impeccable technique, his fascinating friends and colleagues, his client list that read like a Who's Who—was to be *her* teacher, *her* mentor. Looking into his face—his bemused eyes, his lips rounded as they formed a smoke ring—she wondered what else he might be.

"I'm sure modeling for you will be much more interesting than for *Vogue*," she added, then lowered her voice. "African masks, violins; I'd be happy to do whatever you want."

His eyes darted to hers as he choked on tobacco smoke. Quickly recovering, he nodded. "Don't worry. I won't have any problems thinking of poses for you."

Over dinner in the dining car, they talked easily, Man's cool reserve nearly gone. They talked about New York and discovered a few common haunts and acquaintances; they discussed the overrun expatriate scene in Paris, the embarrassing Americans living large on the cheap. On their second bottle of wine, their talk became intimate, passionate. Art and jazz. Poetry and beauty. He lit her cigarette, his dark eyes glistening, then lingered at her hands; she shivered as he gently stroked her skin. His touch—soft, warm, and magnetic—was subtle, but not unclear. By dessert, she was lightheaded.

As he spooned a bite of his chocolate soufflé into her open mouth, she caught a glimpse of the two of them in the mirror behind the bar. Although she felt the smoldering intensity between them, she saw that, from the outside, they looked like opposites: old and young, short and tall, dark and light, serious and gay. But that night in the sleeper car, in his arms, she thought they made a perfect match.

IV

—

The next morning, the porter followed them down the platform and out the door of the small train station. Lee was stretching in the sunshine, wondering how far they were from the sea, when she heard Man whistle. He was waving at a man with a handlebar mustache and a chauffeur cap.

"Our ride is here," he said to Lee, motioning the porter to a long silver car.

"Jeez," Lee said, her eyes wide. "I just realized I have no idea where we're going."

"We're off to Emak Bakia," he said, offering her his arm.

"*Emak* what? Come on, that doesn't sound French."

"This is the Basque country, kid." He turned to the chauffeur. "*Bonjour*, Aitor."

"*Bonjour, Monsieur Man Ray, bonjour, madame.*" The chauffeur tipped his cap with a gloved hand and opened the back door.

She slid across the leather seat, still pleasantly confused, and Man made himself comfortable next to her.

"I usually drive myself down. This time, though, I had something better to look at than the road." Man took her hand in his. "So I sent a wire saying we'd be taking the train."

"Do you mean to tell me what we're doing? Or is it a surprise?"

"How about a bit of both?" He jiggled his eyebrows playfully. "Emak Bakia is the name of a house. In fact, I shot a film there three years ago and used the name for the title. It's Basque for 'leave me alone.' Really, it was too good to pass up."

"Have you rented the place?" she asked.

"No, some friends of mine have. An American couple, Arthur and Rose Wheeler. He made a killing on the stock market—the lucky bastard's younger than me and already retired—and they come down every summer."

"I can see why," Lee said, peeking out the windows. They were leaving the chic resort town and heading up a hill; the ocean shimmered to their right, the Pyrenees loomed in the distance.

"You'll like them," he said. "I met them when I took Rose's portrait. Afterward, they insisted on financing a Man Ray film. I told them I'd be happy to make one on their dime if they wouldn't interfere. And they agreed."

"What was it about?"

"It doesn't tell a *story,* for God's sake. It's a *ciné-poème.* It's a Dada film with surreal elements."

"Right." Lee nodded with a slight blush, not entirely sure what the difference might be.

"I used a lot of new techniques—my rayographs, double exposures, stop-motion, soft focus—and put it to Django Reinhardt, tango, and Strauss. It did surprisingly well for a jumble of disconnected images."

Lee squeezed his hand, excited all over again about being his student. Working with him, she'd be on the outer edge of avant-garde. And cinema!

"Do you think you'll make more films?" She tried not to gush. "I'd love to help you. Really, on either side of the camera—"

"I'm through with film." Man cut her off. "Sound has killed cinema. Everyone now just makes talking pictures. Before you know it, they'll be in rainbow colors. Or in relief! Who the hell wants to see real life up on screen? No, cinema's dead and there's no use mourning."

Unsure how to respond, she gave him a pretty half-smile. Lee just couldn't understand his point of view. Rudy Valentino, Louise Brooks, Charlie Chaplin—she loved movies with stories and thought the new talkies were just grand. After two years in New York City, was she still just a hayseed with old-fashioned ideas about art and cinema? She had too much to learn to argue.

The chauffeur shifted to a low gear and the car began chugging up a steep slope. Man crouched down to see out the front.

"Here it is," Man said, pointing out the window. A butter-colored mansion with various chimneys was coming into view. "'Leave me alone,' here we come!"

The driver passed through the gate and slid the car next to a shiny blue Speedster, parked in front of the door. Before the chauffeur had a chance to open the door for her, Lee popped out of the car to get a better look. The enormous house was riddled with arcaded balconies, offering vistas on every side.

Suddenly a petite woman in a lace dress and long strands of pearls burst through the large wooden doors.

"Man, darling!"

She gave him four Continental kisses, then turned to Lee.

"Rose Wheeler. *Enchantée.*" Young and perky, she kept her eyebrows cocked in studied elegance.

"I'm Lee Miller. The pleasure's mine."

"Welcome to our home. Arthur's out on the terrace," Rose chirped, ushering them inside. "We usually like to greet our guests with dry martinis, but at eight in the morning, that seems a bit much."

They passed through a hallway filled with paintings and went straight out into the soft light of the large balcony. The Atlantic shone through the yellow columns, creating the illusion that they were at sea, on the highest deck of an ocean liner. Lee breathed in, nearly feeling the roll of the waves, and gazed around at the plants and flowers. In the corner, a boyish man in white jodhpurs was arranging pastries on a plate.

"Ah, here you are!" Arthur quickly licked a finger before offering his hand to Man. "Wonderful to see you. And who might this be?"

"This is my new assistant, Lee."

"Your assistants get better looking every year." He shook Lee's hand. "I'm Arthur. I like to call myself one of Man's patrons. Sounds better than a retired broker, doesn't it? More Medici of me." He gave them a wink. "But you must be hungry. I think Aitor bought out the bakery down the hill."

Two uniformed maids appeared; one poured coffee while the other passed around plates of cream puffs, fruit tarts, and chocolate éclairs. Hands full, Lee sat back on satin pillows and smiled.

"It's wonderful here," she said, gesturing around the terrace with an éclair. "Just magnificent."

"It'll be even better once we get a few of Man's new photos on the walls. Such talent and imagination! I'm sure you're learning a lot from him. How long have you been his assistant?"

"Since yesterday afternoon," Lee said demurely.

Arthur's mouth dropped open, then he turned to Man and winked again.

After breakfast, they were shown to their quarters—a large pair of adjoining bedrooms, with balconies facing the sea—to freshen up and change. Lee looked around her room: the French windows, the fresh flowers, the bedroom set in the latest design, sleek wooden pieces fanning out at all angles. Her trunk was already propped open, her dresses hung in the closet, her toiletries were aligned on the vanity. She went to the balcony and sighed in satisfaction. Man popped his head out.

"Did I hear a lusty moan? Am I needed in Room B?"

She pulled him to her and kissed him. "I don't know what I was expecting from this trip or from you. But in a few short hours, both of you have outdone yourselves."

"It's always wise to keep your expectations low," he said.

"Ah, but mine were extremely high." She kissed him again, then led him into her room, onto her perfectly made bed. She put her hand on his crotch. "And yours are rising."

When they had thoroughly settled into their sumptuous rooms, they decided to go to the beach. Lee put on her bathing costume—a sky blue one-piece suit—then pulled on a pair of loose-fitting trousers. Man came in through the balcony, exuding insouciance in a Breton shirt and a beret, a cigarette dangling from his lips.

"Hello, sailor," he drawled seductively, pressing a button of her high-waisted pants.

"O Captain, my captain." She pulled the cigarette from his lips and took a puff. "You ready?"

They found the Wheelers on the balcony, lounging on deck chairs, perusing the *Times*.

"I'm terribly sorry we can't join you for a beach excursion. We have a thousand things to do here," Arthur said, shaking his head regretfully. With all the hired help, Lee couldn't imagine what. "But Aitor will drop you off at the Grande Plage."

"I'll have Cook prepare you a basket with sandwiches and wine in case you get hungry," Rose said. "For this evening, I thought we'd dine at the Hôtel du Palais. They have the most exquisite Basque cooking. Heavens, their seafood dishes are to die for. Then we could hit the casino or go dancing."

"Or both," said Arthur, peeking around the newspaper.

The long, sandy beach was tucked inside a large crescent with a quaint lighthouse perched on one tip and the town's most fashionable hotels lining the stretch in the middle. Curious rock formations rose up from the water; waves rolled in to greet bathers. Lee looked around, nearly purring with contentment, while Man spread a cotton blanket out under a large striped parasol.

"Let's take a dip." She kicked off her trousers. "Maybe we could swim out to that rock—the one that looks like a half-sunken bridge."

He twisted his lips to the side, doubtful. "To tell you the truth, Lee, I swim like a typewriter."

She threw her arms around his neck and gave him a quick kiss—he said the most impossibly charming things. "We can just stroll, then."

He rolled his pants up to his knees and took her by the hand. They walked along the shore, playful as children. They kicked at the water, splashing each other's legs and making silly faces to get the other laughing. Their absurd conversation centered around implausible conjectures about the other tourists: "In his hometown, that man is known for his ability to hypnotize chickens." "You see that little girl with the yellow pail? She speaks in tongues." Man often stooped down to pick up small treasures—shells, sponge, driftwood—and stuffed them in his pockets.

Back at the blanket, they lounged in the sun. To Lee's delight, Man strung his finds onto a strand of seaweed to make her an ephemeral charm bracelet, a mermaid bangle, and hung it precariously on her wrist. She was just about to fall asleep when she heard him grumbling beside her. She opened an eye and peeked at him through her sunglasses. His brow was furrowed.

"Is something wrong?" she asked, propping herself on an elbow to look around.

"Every damn wolf on this beach is staring at you," he said.

"Your legs, your bust. Hey! *Va-t'en, mec!*" Man barked at one. "Scram!"

"Oh, who cares about them?" She took her champion's hand, touched by his protectiveness.

"I do!" He continued, obviously still piqued.

"Come here, you," she said. She wrapped him in her arms and kissed him hard, breaking the little bracelet in the process. "That should make things clear. Now, relax. You're the only man I'm interested in."

As she said it, Lee realized with surprise that it was true.

That night, after a flawless dinner at the palace, the foursome strolled over to the casino. The ceilings dripped with chandeliers, stained glass and mirrors decorated the walls, and palms and statuary set off the solid-oak playing tables. The international crowd was impeccably dressed. Man, comfortably elegant in a midnight blue suit, and Lee, at her ease in a sleeveless burgundy gown with long black gloves, fit in beautifully. With a hint of apology, the Wheelers abandoned them for the baccarat tables.

"Are you a high roller?" Lee asked, wrapping her arm around his.

Unlike most of the men she'd been with, she knew very little about Man's background, his habits, his financial situation. It was obvious that he was affluent. His tailored clothes, his leather trunk, his address—as well as his reputation—guaranteed a certain amount of money. She had no idea, however, whether he was generous, tight-fisted, or a spendthrift. Not that it mattered.

"A highbrow, high-class high roller, that's me. Say, would you care for a highball?"

"Sure thing."

Armed with a bourbon and ginger, they meandered around the tables, then stopped at the roulette wheel.

"How old are you, kid?" Man pulled a few chips out of his pocket.

"Twenty-two," she said.

He raised his eyebrows—was that younger or older than he'd expected?—and put the chips down on the number.

"And you? Aren't you going to bet on your age, too?"

"The wheel doesn't go up *that* high," he said with a crooked smile.

The croupier spun the wheel. "*Et le nombre est . . . trente. Noir.*"

Man shrugged. "Ehh, forget it. With you on my arm, I'm the biggest winner in here."

They collected the Wheelers, who had run out of chips, and the two couples moved on to the ballroom, where the orchestra was playing a quickstep.

"Shall we?" Man led her out onto the floor and, with perfect rhythm, smoothly swept her into the dance.

Lee was bowled over. Man had the body of a bull, solid and compact, yet he was light on his feet, as graceful as he was natural. She'd rarely had such a good partner—and the ones she'd had could hardly rival him for wit or talent.

"Damn, Man," she said, with a laugh. "You are a fabulous dancer."

"Just add it to my list of accomplishments," he said drily.

And what a list, indeed.

That night, wide awake, Lee lay against Man's warm sleeping body and peered out the open French windows into the night sky. She couldn't stop smiling. Lee had often mixed with wealthy socialites in New York, she'd met writers and actors and dated men of accomplishment. But here, she was completely intoxicated by this combination of seaside, Frenchness, and the avant-garde, personified by Man Ray himself.

They spent a month in Biarritz with the Wheelers, sometimes socializing with their hosts and other guests, but most often on their own: at the beach, dancing, or on picnics in the hills. They went on drives in the two-seated Speedster, racing through the back roads, laughing and shouting as they skirted past herds of sheep. They took long siestas in the afternoons, clinging to each other, hardly ever sleeping. They were content together; they needed no one else.

On the northbound train, they sat in the restaurant car side by side, legs pressed against each other's. Lee let out a sigh, drowsily full, and pushed away the last of her lemon mousse.

"I can't remember a better holiday," she said softly. "But you know what? I'm really looking forward to being back in Paris. To starting my lessons and working at your side." She picked up his hand and stroked his open palm with her fingertips. "This is only going to get better."

He shivered next to her.

"I've been thinking, Lee. Since we're going to be spending so much time together, workwise and . . . otherwise." He raised his pointy eyebrows suggestively, then broke into a grin. "Well, why don't you just stay at my place?"

She dropped his hand and stared into his eyes. "You mean, live with you?"

"Until you find something better." He looked at her nervously. "That is, only if you want to. It's pretty small but——"

"Oh, Man, I'd love to!" She kissed him on the mouth.

The thought of a new place in Paris—a boardinghouse or a hotel? Left or Right Bank?—had been in the back of her mind for the past week, but it was a problem she'd been avoiding. And now it was solved! She could stay with him—learning the craft, meeting his friends, going out on his arm: the two of them together, at work and at play—until she found the perfect place. Which, of course, could be never.

"Wonderful," he moaned, kissing her back. "You'll love Montparnasse."

"I don't know how you get any work done, surrounded by all those cafés and bars."

"Oh, there'll be plenty of work to do when we get back. After a vacation, there's always a backlog of sitters and developing, too. And, along with the photography work, I'll need you as my secretary and receptionist. Are you still up for it?"

"Of course I am." She beamed at him, then turned to the waiter. "*Garçon! Une bouteille de champagne, s'il vous plaît.*"

She raised her glass to him. "To the new boss of me."

Man laughed. "I can't see that anyone could be the boss of you, Lee Miller. You're headstrong, impulsive, hedonistic . . ." He tweaked her knee under the tablecloth, then let his hand glide upward a few inches, inside her skirt. "And I'm absolutely crazy about you."

With a light frisson, she kissed him again, but slowly. "And I, you."

By the time they arrived back to Paris, tanned and rested, they were more than lovers. They were a couple.

V

On Campagne-Première, Lee and Man walked together to his large Art Nouveau building, the one where she had stood at the door, so disappointed, just a month before. Hand in hand, they passed through the iron and glass gateway, under the muse, and into the courtyard. He unlocked the door and, with a dramatic sweep of his hand, invited her inside.

Lee looked around the well-lit salon. The walls were covered with his esoteric oil paintings and extraordinary photographs, and every available space—except for the somber corner with the posing chair, backed by a white screen—was filled. Mannequins, masks, chessboards, gramophone records, arrangements of cubes, cones, and pyramids, a grown-up's building blocks. Near the door, a steep, narrow staircase led up to the bedroom.

"These studios are some of the best in Paris," he said, watching her look around. "We've got gas, electricity, telephone, radiators, a toilet—pretty high-class for the art world. The darkroom's in here." He showed her a nook that used to be a balcony.

Although Lee was surprised to see his darkroom was so small—was her father's bigger?—she could see he kept every-

thing in meticulous order. This was where those magical trans-
formations took place: chemical light painting.

"It's swell, Man," she said, putting her arms around him
tightly. "The whole place. I love it. You're an angel for having
me here."

"You're welcome to stay as long as you want." He slid his
hand up her bare back—she was wearing a halter in the Parisian summer heat—up to her neck, clasped her short hair, and
kissed her. "Let's go to a café. I want to show you around your
new neighborhood."

"I'd like that. When I lived in Paris before, I hardly ever
came to this part of town."

"Are you kidding? It's hard to imagine anyone—anyone
worth knowing, that is—living in Paris without spending most
of their time in Montparnasse. Where were you, then?"

"Here and there. When I was eighteen, I had a Polish countess as a chaperone. That may sound grand, but she was completely broke, which was why she was with me. She booked us
rooms in the Place Clichy, and from the very first day I thought
there was something fishy going on. I mean, every time you
passed through the hall, different men's shoes were lined outside all the doors, innocently waiting to be shined. It took the
countess a full week to realize we were staying in a whore-
house!"

Man burst out laughing, prompting her to grin. She loved
the rich sound of his laugh, the way his eyes half closed.

"Afterward—when I'd ditched my chaperone—I spent
most of my time in Montmartre, studying lighting, costume,
and stage design with László Medgyes. We'd go to the big

theaters on the Right Bank, too, mostly to criticize their old-fashioned ideas. In the world of stagecraft, Medgyes is a genius."

"I've heard of him. Hungarian, isn't he? They say he's quite the ladies' man." Man glanced over at Lee, then nonchalantly picked up his hat.

"Medgyes claimed to admire my intellect," Lee breathed, "but what he really liked were my tits." She watched as Man's brow began to furrow, then clapped him on the back with a laugh. She'd discovered his jealous streak at the beach and sometimes liked to tease him. "Oh, come on, lover boy. Let's go."

They took a right and began strolling toward the boulevard, Lee hanging on his arm. Thrilled to be staying with him, she was delighted to find Man every bit as pleased. Giddy as a child, he was eager to both impress her and show her off. He pointed out the small flats of poets and painters she'd never heard of, and then, as they neared the end of Campagne-Première, he stopped quite suddenly.

"This is where the bistro Chez Rosalie used to be," he said, gesturing to a pair of boarded-up windows. "She was a real Italian mamma, a hot-tempered old softie. She'd feed poor artists for sketches that she'd tack up on the wall. Of course, she'd feed stray dogs for nothing. Rats, too, for that matter."

Lee scanned the splintery wooden planks, just as happy they wouldn't be eating there, landmark or not. When they rounded the corner, Man paused again. This façade was covered with stylized cowboys and Indians whose faded paint was chipping.

"And this is the Jockey Club," he said with a flourish. "It was the first real nightclub in Montparnasse and was jam-packed every night. We spent a lot of time here, Kiki and me."

It wasn't the first time Man had mentioned his former lover, the woman in the photographs that had mesmerized Lee. They'd been together for six years before splitting up the year before, and she still played a role in his life—though *what* role was unclear. At the Wheelers, her name had come up often in nostalgic conversations about summers past and the film *Emak Bakia,* which she appeared in: driving his car, dancing, stretching on the beach. In the last few weeks, Lee had also learned that, apart from being Man Ray's muse and main subject for years, Kiki was famous in her own right. She was a singer, a model, an actress, an artist—hell, she'd even published her memoirs earlier that year. And for her magnetic personality—endearingly provocative, upbeat and saucy, generous to a fault—she'd been crowned the Queen of Montparnasse.

As Man's former girlfriend, Lee knew that Kiki had been extremely passionate. Over cocktails in Biarritz, they'd told hilarious anecdotes about her smashing plates, screaming obscenities, and awarding brisk slaps; privately, Lee guessed that it was also thanks to Kiki that Man was so well schooled in bed. On the whole, Lee found her legendary predecessor intimidating. Not only was Kiki beautiful and versatile and the leading lady in scads of charming stories, but she was an important part of the Paris that Man loved. An essential player on the Montparnasse scene. Whenever he mentioned her name, Lee made a point of appearing cool and unruffled while, on the inside, she deflated a bit.

"So, is the Jockey Club still a good place for a night on the town?"

"Not really. People go to bigger, flashier restaurants and bars nowadays: le Dôme, le Select, la Coupole . . . They're open all night with food, music, and dancing. You never know who you might see there — sometimes the most interesting folks in town, sometimes just poseurs or tourists. So, what are you up for? Seafood? Eggs? A steak?"

At a cramped table on a terrace, they shared two dozen raw oysters and a bottle of white wine, watching the passersby squeeze between the outlying café chairs and the busy street: women in elegant hats and sleeveless pastel shifts, men overly warm in three-piece suits, stray cats stalking scraps. Man Ray occasionally said hello or nodded to people—local artist types or wealthy Americans—but invited no one to join them save a striped cat. He set a few oyster shells on the ground, watched it lick them clean, then turned back to Lee with a thoughtful wrinkle on his brow.

"When we get back to the studio, I'd like to take some photos of you. I've been looking at your face far too long without doing anything with it."

"What do you mean?" she protested. "You took dozens of snapshots of me at the beach."

"Those holiday pictures don't count. No, I want to do some serious work. Portraits. Just your head." His voice trailed off as he gazed at her, reaching out to touch her face, her neck. "Nothing else for now; it's not necessary. Some poets—the bold ones—can see a woman's sex in her eyes," he said in low tones; Lee shivered in delight. Man sounded like an inspired gangster when he whispered. "You realize," he continued, "the head has more orifices than the rest of the body combined. The head is a complete portrait."

She took his hand, still lingering around her shoulder, and brought it to her mouth, grazing it with her lips. After oysters and wine, only a trace of lipstick remained, which left thin, uneven trails on his skin.

"I can think of other things we could do, back in the studio," she said, her voice low and sensual.

She enjoyed making him squirm. Man Ray was clearly one of those men who had been unable to attract women when he was young. Now in his late thirties, a celebrated American artist with at least one explosive relationship under his belt, she could tell that part of him still saw himself as that short, funny-looking boy that girls found unappealing. Every time he looked at her, he seemed amazed at his good luck. Lee found it touching. For her, appearance had never been the most desirable quality in a man. She was attracted to character, creativity, renown, charm, confidence, affluence. And besides, she quite liked Man Ray's looks.

Blushing, he immediately called for the check. But back at the studio, both the photographer and his subject were too engrossed in each other to bother with tripods, lighting, and focus. The official photo session was forgotten.

Her lessons began the following day. He brought Lee into the red light of the darkroom and, with calm control and patient movements, went through each step. He meticulously showed her how to insert glass plates into holders, dip them in the basin, then rinse them once fixed. He taught her how to use the enlarger, to print on his favorite eggshell paper, to retouch with a triangular blade, ironing out any wrinkles. Lee loved being privy to his preferences and methods—watching a genius at work—and was moved by his openness in the darkroom. He wouldn't share his professional secrets with just anyone, would he? It must be a sign of his feelings for her; surely he hadn't taken such care with his other apprentices.

All the fragments she'd been shown before—rudimentary notions from her father and Steichen's odd tricks—came together under his generous instruction. It was intuitive to her, and she learned quickly; Man was encouraging, almost proud.

Soon they were working together like a four-armed creature, absorbed by the task, both intent on perfection. Sometimes, however, in the night-heat of the darkroom, pressed against each other in the tiny space, they would become distracted by an accidental touch, the feel of warm breath, and they would remember the body beside them. In the shadows of the amber light, their hands and mouths would find each other again, their clothes wrenched aside. More than one photograph was left forgotten, overdeveloping to nothingness.

Their seclusion was broken nearly every day—and sometimes more than once or twice—by a steady procession of portrait sitters. *Tout Paris* wanted to be done by Man Ray, and Lee, as his receptionist and assistant, helped him with this multicolored parade of aristocrats, wealthy foreigners, artists, and novelists. Although she was fascinated by many of them—from Barbette, the female impersonator, to the mannish writer Gertrude Stein—she was never starstruck, but warm and welcoming. A pleasant contrast to Man, who was always businesslike with clients, cold and monosyllabic.

"Hello, there. Let me take your hat and coat." She smiled at a chubby British earl. "Mr. Ray will be out in a moment. Would you like a cigarette?"

She held out her silver case, and he accepted one. Blowing out smoke, the earl took in the unusual décor, wide-eyed, as if he were on an adventure holiday to the heart of bohemia. Man strolled in with a gruff hello, stationed himself behind the tripod, and crossed his arms over his chest.

"You can take your seat, sir." Lee gestured toward the portrait chair.

The earl frowned at the bare corner where he would pose, fingering the burlap backdrop as if it had been worn by a leper. He sat down stiffly and eyed the camera, set up across the room, and tried to get a good look at the photographer beyond it.

"Say, there," he said nervously. "I don't fancy a full-length portrait. Just, you know, the head and shoulders." He stroked his paunch as if to iron it out, then looked up at Lee. "Doesn't he need to move the camera in? Toward me?"

"Don't worry, sir," she said. "He knows what he's doing." Man always preferred to keep his distance, then crop his shots into portraits in the privacy of his own darkroom. "Now, just relax."

After a few minutes, the session was over.

"He's done?" the earl whispered to Lee, obviously disappointed.

Man disappeared as Lee wrote down the earl's address, made another appointment with him to view the prints, and ushered him through the door.

"You can come out now," she called to Man, half-joking. "No more sittings today."

"Excellent." He smiled. "Let's take some real pictures."

In their spare time Man photographed Lee, which was all he wanted to do anyway. Sometimes she would wake up to find him staring at her through the viewfinder, a light set up next to the bed. He would smile sheepishly, but she liked being at the center—the very seed—of his creative process. With his warm, silky hands, she let him place her body in position, set it up for a shot as if it were a still life. She watched the ideas whirring in his head and his eyes roaming over her body, taking in every inch. Besides the portraits that merely emphasized her beauty, he took shots that reflected his feelings for her, the depth of his emotion. Moving or motionless, in shadow or light, she was his subject. And Lee thought he captured the complexity of her nature: her sensuality, but also her energy, her rebelliousness, her dark humor.

It fascinated Lee that, depending on the photographer's vision, she could change into something else entirely. As she watched Man taking pictures, she occasionally compared him to other photographers she'd worked with. They'd all liked to look. Photographers, it seemed, were Peeping Toms who used the viewfinder instead of the keyhole. At *Vogue,* Arnold Genthe had softened her features, giving her the face of an innocent schoolgirl, whereas Edward Steichen had made her look worldly and sophisticated. While her father . . . What had his unorthodox photos brought out in her? Her inner strength, her self-confidence, perhaps? And what might a self-portrait show?

"I've been thinking of a pose all day," he said, moving the posing chair out of the corner, then putting it back. "And, finally, those idiots are out of our hair."

"That's what you get for being so damn popular. Everyone wants a piece of you," she said with a little snort. "So, what's your plan? Do you want to work with the patterns from the window bars again?"

"No, my little Leebra. I'm done with stripes for now." He tapped his lips with his index finger, thinking. "Here, carry these lights upstairs. I'll take the camera."

In their small bedroom, he began arranging the tungsten lamps around the bed, contrasting light with darkness. "Take off your clothes, kid. I'll be done with this in a minute."

Lee pulled off her jersey with a little tingle in her stomach. She had done nudes before she began working with Man Ray, but most of those poses were chaste and romantic—classic art shots—compared to his. She liked these provocative sessions in front of the camera—the heat from the lamps, Man's gangster voice, his obvious excitement—which often ended in equally long sessions in bed.

"Now, I want you to curl up into a ball. All I want to see is your ass."

She got on the bed, her backside to the camera, and ducked down; he was immediately there, moving her arms, tucking down her shoulders, fiddling with her fingers. She went slack and let him manipulate her like a lump of clay. She liked his strong touch. He readjusted the lights and peered through the camera. The pads of her feet and her bodiless hands came forth from her perfectly round bottom; the rest of her was obscured in the dark.

"It's beautiful," he whispered. "You have become the perfect peach."

Man took several shots, shifting the tripod a few inches to either side to vary perspectives. Finally, he unscrewed the camera and took a shot closer up.

"What I really want to do, kid, is take a big bite," he said.

He tossed the camera onto the pillows and began taking off his clothes, fumbling with the buttons of his bulging trousers. She lay in wait, keeping her pose, and licked her lips in anticipation. She'd been with many men before Man Ray—she'd always been keen on her sexual freedom—but no one so consistently. She reveled in the variation and experiment; older and more experienced than most of her former lovers, Man enjoyed giving pleasure as much as taking it. Under the hot lights, he became one with the peach, grasping her, then slowly unwound her coil. She turned to him, ready. Ah, the seduction of being a muse.

VI

"Why don't we go out tonight?" Lee said, closing the door behind their last client.

Though she'd been in Montparnasse now for over a month, they'd rarely ventured out of the studio. Ever since she'd moved in, they'd been working in tandem—teacher and student, artist and muse—or rolling in bed together as equals. But they had been doing little else. Lee was beginning to get restless; she needed outside company, new faces, a bit of adventure.

"Let's! I could make you a toga and bring out the Greek goddess in you. Or cover your head in scarves and make you into a Turkish princess." With flashing eyes, he wrapped her hair with an imaginary turban. "Or do your makeup. I could shave off your eyebrows and paint new ones on."

He was studying Lee's features, his thumbs gliding down the length of her eyebrows. Lee stared back up at him, mildly entertained and slightly peeved. Kiki had allowed him that luxury, to alter her appearance for photos, films, or just a night out. But there was no way in hell Lee was letting him near her face with a razor.

"I don't think so," she said shortly.

"Just an idea," he said, backing off, slightly disappointed. "Not that any of you needs changing, of course."

She went upstairs to get dressed. Some of her clothes were still in her trunk; the others were bursting out of Man's small wardrobe. She pulled out a floral frock with a cutaway back and inspected it; it would do. When she was dressed, Lee added the black feathered skullcap Man bought her in Biarritz—the feathers framed her face on one side, making her look half raven-haired—then went through her jewelry box in search of bracelets. Inside, she found a long gold chain. Meant to be looped around the neck several times, it was at least two yards long. Lee smiled. In the absence of togas or turbans, perhaps this would satisfy Man's need for theatrics.

When they were both ready, Lee brought out the chain. She clasped it around her wrist, then attached it to his belt.

"What's this?" he asked, visibly pleased.

"I don't want my little lamb to go missing."

Once on the boulevard, they headed to la Coupole.

"For its opening night two years ago, they popped fifteen hundred bottles of champagne. What a night!" Man said, quickening his step. "It's been a popular place ever since."

Even from the outside, the nightclub radiated excitement. Two stories tall, it was brightly lit with neon, and automobiles stood in a line out front. Lee squeezed his arm as Man escorted her inside; the head waiter immediately appeared—*Bon soir, Monsieur Man Ray. Suivez-moi*—and led them to a table under the cathedral-like dome next to the center fountain.

Lee looked at the people at the nearby tables, crammed together among the painted pillars. A quartet of affluent Americans, swinging half-empty cocktails and long cigarette holders, was slurring loudly about the absurdity of nouns having gender, while a serious mustachioed man was delivering a sermon on writing to a group of young disciples. Next to them, a wide-eyed, provincial family sat ignoring their dinners and staring at those they presumed to be bohemians ("Papa, do you think those girls model *nude?*" asked the son, earning a smack from his mother).

Man barely glanced at the menu. "I always get the same thing here. Onion soup, then roast chicken. It's so good, I've never bothered changing."

"Sounds fine to me. And let's get some red wine."

When they'd ordered, they sat back, sipping wine and smoking.

"After dinner, we can go downstairs and dance," Man said. "They have great jazz combos and——"

He stopped short, his attention suddenly absorbed by a trio at the bar. Lee turned and immediately recognized Kiki's reflection in the mirror. From the dozens of photos in Man's studio, Lee knew her features well: the straight black bob, the milky skin, the dramatic eyes and bow lips. She watched her laughing at the bar with her two companions, a Japanese man with round glasses and a pasty-faced man in a white scarf and bowler hat. The barman and a few patrons looked on in amusement. The Queen was holding court.

"*La soupe à l'oignon pour madame et monsieur.*" The waiter served them ceremoniously, then disappeared at once.

"That's Kiki, isn't it?" Lee almost whispered, as if anyone could hear over the din of the crowded room. "Who's she with?"

"Foujita and Pascin. They're painters here in Montparnasse, and Kiki's modeled for both of them." He picked up his spoon and chipped at the cheesy crust floating on the soup while Lee stole another look at the artists. Foujita, short but fit, was wearing hoop earrings; Pascin was telling a story with such grandiose gestures, it was obvious he was talking about bullfighting. "They're serious painters," Man added, "but they're also very serious about parties, picnics, and masquerade balls."

Although nervous, Lee was curious about Kiki, the well-loved neighborhood royal who used to sleep on her side of the bed; she also wanted to meet some of the unconventional painters that made Montparnasse famous. "Could you introduce me to them?"

Man took a tentative bite of soup—it was still hot—and looked into Lee's expectant face. "Well . . ." he began slowly.

He took a glimpse back at the bar and saw that Kiki had spotted them in the crowd. She was heading toward their table, her friends close behind her. Man stood up and greeted her with a light kiss on the mouth. "Kiki," he murmured, then faced the other two and shook their hands. "Foujita, Pascin. I'd like for you all to meet Lee Miller."

Pascin swept off his bowler hat to reveal sparse, uncombed hair, then leaned over the table to deposit a sodden kiss on each of Lee's cheeks. "Lovely," he managed. Foujita bowed politely. "Delighted."

Kiki looked Lee over—her Nordic good looks and elegant style—and when she caught sight of the gold chain binding her to Man Ray, she raised a thin, pencil-drawn eyebrow. "Tell me, then," she said in French, turning to her former lover, "does she whittle a good pipe?"

Pascin broke out in drunken giggles, and the gasp from the provincial parents at the next table was audible.

Man's face clouded. "Kiki, that's enough."

"I'm sorry, I don't understand." Lee looked around uncertainly. Was she being insulted? She stood up to be on even ground with Kiki. "My French isn't very good."

Kiki turned back to Lee, her dark eyes filled with spiteful mischief. "I asked, honey, if you knew how to suck cock."

For a second Lee stood dumbstruck, but quickly curled her lips into a confident smile. "You'll have to ask Man that," she said sweetly, refusing to be browbeaten. "It shouldn't be too hard for him to remember. We had a wild rough-and-tumble first thing this morning."

Pascin twittered through his fingers, but Kiki looked at her with surprise. A waiter carrying a large tray filled with heavy plates tried to push his way through. "Excuse me. Yes, a thousand pardons," he said drily. "Perhaps you could all sit down?"

"I'll be singing downstairs later," Kiki said. "Maybe we'll see you then." With a painter on each arm, she turned and left.

Disappointed, Lee slid back into her chair and took a sip of wine. She'd hoped to be instantly accepted as one of them, not ridiculed in public. But when she looked up at Man's troubled face, she started to chuckle, shaking her head.

"She's really something else," Lee said.

Kiki had held up her reputation as bawdy and jealous, but Lee was not terribly impressed. Far prettier in photos, her looks were now passé. She was too full-figured—her fringed shift fit awkwardly around her big, maternal breasts and ample behind—and her makeup made her look more like a circus performer than a woman out on the town. Somehow, Lee felt relieved.

"Don't mind Kiki. She's all bark, no bite," he said. "I don't know why she acts like that. She's been living with her accordionist for months."

"I'm not worried. I can take care of myself." She pulled at the chain. "And my little lamb."

After dinner, they went down to Le Dancing in the restaurant's dark, smoky basement. To the beat of the loud band, chic couples were dancing a sweaty tango on the packed floor. Man and Lee danced a number, then stood to the side to cool off with whisky on ice. Lee's eyes flitted around the room and caught the gaze of a few hopeful young men; she smiled back at them, but when she raised her arm to smooth the feathers on her cheek, she felt the tug of the chain. She was with Man Ray for now; Lee took his hand in hers. They were on their fourth or fifth round—and a bit unsteady—when Kiki swept down the stairs with her entourage. The members of the band called out to her over their instruments, waving drumsticks and trumpet, and quickly finished the number they were playing. The crowd shouted "Sing, Kiki, sing!" as the clarinet player pulled her up on stage.

With a captivating smile, Kiki winked at the piano player, who began plunking out a simple melody. Swaying to the music, in perfect pitch, she belted out a risqué song.

The young girls of Camaret say they are all virgins but . . .

Lee nudged Man in the ribs, a bit harder than intended, and

slurred into his ear. "I think Josephine Baker's much better. I saw her once back when—"

"Shhh." He hadn't taken his eyes off the stage.

Lee frowned and glanced back up. While she sang, Kiki flapped her skirt, back and forth, lifting it higher and higher over her black hose, up and over her garters. At the end of the number, she twisted around and flashed her bare backside. The crowd whooped and cheered; someone threw her a rose, which she put in her teeth with a bow. "*Encore!*" they began to shout.

"I need some air." Lee pulled at the chain, tired of being a spectator. "Let's go."

As they filed past the stage, Kiki called out in swampy English, "Bye, bye, my little Man," then grinned at him, fluttering her fingers.

"This little Man is mine!" Lee called out. With a large smile and single wave good-bye, she took his arm and added, "See ya later, sweetheart."

VII

—

"Well, on the upside," Lee said, looking around le Dôme's quiet salon, "it's rather nice to be rid of all those affected loafers."

The stock market had crashed the week before. In a single day the world economy plummeted; fortunes were lost, lives ruined. The exodus of American expatriates, most of whose livelihoods depended on intangible investments, began almost immediately. In Montparnasse, the difference was striking. The restaurants and bars—packed to the seams just days before—stood half-full. No one ordered dry martinis; the Welsh rarebit went uneaten.

"Absolutely." Man nodded. "A lot of our charming compatriots seemed to be here just for the cheap, legal booze. And I don't miss them one bit. Here's to the Crash!"

Man and Lee touched glasses and exchanged the irreverent smiles of naughty schoolchildren caught in the act of adding cuss words to the Pledge of Allegiance.

However, in the weeks that followed, they realized that even though they owned no stocks, Black Tuesday had affected their lives as well. Fewer sitters came to call, long-standing appointments were canceled, and new projects abandoned. Portraits had long been Man's bread and butter—there was no money in Surrealism, rayograms, or art photography—and he began stalking the studio nervously, puffing on his pipe. He followed Lee around, unable to work, his bleak presence filling the entire apartment.

Another rainy morning, they sat at the tiny breakfast table in morning muteness. Lee sipped her coffee—slowly waking up—as Man made changing patterns with the tableware, a triangle of knives atop a white plate, an overturned cup in the middle, salt shakers toward the sides, then something new.

"We're going to have to tighten our belts a bit," he said finally, shooting her the worried look of a man afraid of losing his too-beautiful partner due to lack of funds or prestige. "The French call it *une période de vaches maigres*. A time of skinny cows."

"I'm sure they'll fatten up soon," Lee said, trying to be encouraging but wondering how much money he might have saved up. She'd never liked budgets or sensible spending.

"God, everything seems to have changed overnight. All those crazy parties and balls are suddenly a thing of the past—who can afford it? I can't believe I had you holed up in here thinking it would go on forever. I should have taken you out more—"

"Paris is still Paris, Man. There're good times ahead, I'm sure of it."

He paced behind her as she washed the dishes, then trailed upstairs to watch her dress. When he had to go to the toilet, she slipped into the darkroom to have a little time to herself. She quickly pulled out the trays and chemicals and turned on the red light. With a long stretch, she selected a developed plate at random—a portrait of Sinclair Lewis—to see how she could alter it in the printing. But already, there was a knock on the door.

"Lee? What are you doing in there? I thought we were all caught up."

"I'm just fooling around. Recropping and adding shadow. Just practicing."

"Do you need any help?"

"No, thanks."

"Well, remember to hold the plates by the edges—you don't want to smudge them with fingerprints."

"Don't worry." She shook her head, half-amused, half-annoyed at the perfectionist behind the door. "I know what to do."

"Call me if you have any questions."

When she heard his footsteps disappear, Lee looked at the plate carefully. In it, the famous novelist sat on the floor in his overcoat, staring into space, a huge screw from a wine press looming behind him. It was something Man had picked up to use in an art piece—like so many things around the flat. He'd told Lee that Sinclair Lewis was so drunk when he'd shown up for his sitting that Man thought the old wine screw would make a fitting background. Lee flipped the image to make him look right instead of left, then turned the knob to enlarge it. She stared down at his lonely face. Man had been afraid that Lewis would be furious when he saw the print, that he'd rip it to shreds; instead the writer had congratulated him on taking his favorite portrait to date. She put the paper in the developing tray, prodding and swishing it with the tongs, and smiled to herself. Man Ray was like none other.

When she emerged from the darkroom, she found him smoking his pipe in silence, staring out into the soft rain. His eyes, big and round like an orphan's, made her feel guilty for leaving him alone when he was feeling blue.

"Hey, baby," she whispered into his ear, wrapping her arms around him.

"Did you make any improvements in there?"

"Nah. You'd already found the best angle, the best light. But I enjoyed having the opportunity to look at your work so closely. The Sinclair Lewis portrait is a brilliant shot." She kissed his cheek. "Listen, I know that things are slow at the moment, but that might be a good thing. Now that you finally have some free time, you could do some painting. Maybe one of your friends could get you a show."

"I don't know." He flipped open his lighter, then snapped it shut. "I don't have any clear ideas in my head."

"You just need to spend some time at the easel. Something will come to you." She considered adding something about his "subconscious"—to let it take over, or some such rot—but just couldn't. Although Lee was drawn to many of the Surrealists' ideas—alternative visions, the absurd, wordplay—some of them, like automatic writing or hypnotic trances, seemed more akin to parlor tricks than art. "Really, Man," she continued, "it would probably make you feel better."

An hour later, he had a canvas set up in the corner of the studio. As "Ain't Misbehavin'" blared from the gramophone, the photographer took respite from black and white and filled his palette with color. Lee blew out in relief and climbed the steep stairs, delighted to have diverted him. She didn't know what to make of this new Man—an insecure ball of nerves with too much time on his hands—or how she could help him.

In the bedroom, she stumbled on one of her shoes and banged her leg on a wooden crate. Man had dragged it in from the street a week ago with the idea of making a new ready-made, but there it was, just taking up space. "God damn it!" she muttered, clutching her shin. The flat had been packed full before she'd even moved in; her things were homeless, in piles, or lost amongst his. Grumbling, she flopped on the bed and picked up *Ulysses*. Compared to the chaos of the studio, James Joyce's novel was a beacon of clarity.

"Some of the Surrealists are coming over this afternoon—"

"Wonderful! I've been wanting to meet your cronies."

"They're not just my cronies, Lee." He put down his coffee cup to pick at a patch of dried paint on his thumb, left over from the day before. "They are some of the most original think-ers in the arts today. Poets, painters, intellectuals—"

"Wonderful. Like I said." She nipped at his earlobe. "Who's coming?"

"Today it'll just be a few of us. There's André Breton, the leader of the group. He's a psychiatrist by trade and worked in a neurological ward during the war—talk about a fine intro-duction to the absurd! Then Max Ernst, the painter and phi-losopher. He's German, but we don't hold it against him. And a couple of poets. Louis Aragon—he lives in the building next door—and Benjamin Péret."

"How exciting!" Lee beamed, sure she'd have more success with this bunch than she had with Kiki. She'd always had a way with men.

"They'll love you, kid. Who wouldn't?" Patting her hand, Man glanced out into the living room. "We need to straighten the place up. Jesus, your stuff is everywhere."

She frowned. "You know there's nowhere to put it."

"Well, pile it up on the bed for now. Cram it underneath, if you have to. I'd like the group to see my new work, not all of your hats and jackets. Come on, you—get cleaning."

"Yes, massah." She took the coffee from his hand, poured out his last sips, and rinsed the cup.

"Lovely," he said drily. "So helpful."

At five o'clock, the bell rang. The room was back to the way it had been when she first saw it—filled with Man's objects, all arranged just so—with the addition of several new prints, enlarged and matted for display. Four men bustled into the room. Hovering in front of the sofa, Lee eyed them with an expectant smile. They were older than she, some ten to twenty years older, and all rather attractive, though pale and unathletic.

"Man!" they exclaimed, clapping him on the back, shaking his hand. "Christ, we haven't seen you for weeks, months! What have you been doing?"

He gestured behind him. "I'd like for you to meet my new assistant, Lee Miller."

They turned to her and began nodding their heads, laughing. "This explains it!"

"Yeah, she's a shade different from your last assistant," said

Aragon, shaking his finger at him. "Berenice wasn't half as pretty—and this one looks like she might even like men!"

"Oh, shut your mouth, Louis. Berenice Abbott was a good old girl and a fine photographer." He joined Lee by the couch and took her by the hand. "But it's true that Lee is more to me than an assistant. She is my muse."

"*Enchantée.*" Lee made the rounds, kissing everyone on the cheeks. "Can I offer you an aperitif? Campari and soda?"

While she made the drinks, Man showed the group his latest photographs. They were all nude shots of Lee, remarkable for their poses and lighting. Lee looked over at Man, listening proudly to their praise. She wanted to mention that a couple of the ideas had been hers, but decided it would seem too childish.

Drinks in hand, they made themselves comfortable. Lee sat on the arm of the sofa, leaning slightly on Man.

"Gentlemen," Breton spoke importantly, getting down to business. "I think it's time to write a second manifesto. We need to assess the degree of moral competence among our members and excommunicate those uninterested in collective action. Surrealism needs to be at the service of the revolution." He looked at each of them in turn. "We need to formalize our support of communism and the Soviet Union."

There were murmurs of assent—"hear, hear"—and raised glasses.

Lee suddenly spoke. "Sometimes I wonder, though. If the Soviet Union is so great, why is Paris filled with Russians?"

They all turned from Lee to Breton in silence. He raised an eyebrow and looked down his nose at her.

"I congratulate you, Man. What a catch this woman is. All

this"—he pointed to her with an outstretched hand, sweeping it from her head to her foot—"and beautiful, too."

Lee realized she'd been slighted as their guests began to snicker. She opened her mouth, a retort ready, when Man squeezed her hand.

"Why don't you get us some snacks?" His eyes begged her to be quiet. "Thanks, kid."

"And I could use some coffee, if you've got some," added Péret.

Flushed, she stood up and smiled at them stiffly. "Of course."

From the small kitchen, she could still hear Breton's loud voice. "Most women are so much more delightful with their mouths closed."

"Or wide open!" cried one.

She heard the guffaws and could imagine the obscene gesture. Lee bit her lip, bitterly disappointed. They obviously thought her an idiot, nothing more than a pretty face. Sometimes she regretted her halfhearted attempt at a formal education. She'd always hated rules and authority figures and, after being expelled from a half-dozen institutions, barely finished secondary school. She'd never had the discipline for theoretical lessons—her intelligence was more intuitive, more fluid—and was easily bored. Lee liked hands-on projects, much like Man Ray. He knew she was smart; he understood her. Why hadn't he stood up for her in front of his snooty friends?

She set the coffeepot on the stove, then automatically arranged crackers around a block of pâté and poured nuts and olives into bowls. Man had put a jazz record on the gramophone, but the odd word still drifted in from the salon. All talk of politics was stalled as they continued to talk about women. She was straining to catch the gist of their conversation, when Breton's voice rose above the music. "But, *mes amis*," he pronounced with authority, "the female orgasm is of no importance!" She rolled her eyes, incredulous. Jesus! At least Man didn't agree with him on *that* point. Or was he in there nodding just the same? What contradictions these men were: avant-garde yet antiquated, sternly judgmental yet boyish and silly. Lee was sure that, as soon as she walked back into the room, they would resume their stuffy talk of communism and allegiances, thinking themselves superior.

She took a full tray out to the living room, then slipped on her coat.

"Gentlemen, it's been a pleasure, but I'm afraid I have a few errands to do. If you'll excuse me."

She swept out of the room, without even looking at Man. It embarrassed her that he'd let his friend insult her right there, in their very home. She blinked back tears. It seemed his studio wasn't her home anyway. She had no presence there, no respect. Lee knew that, at her parents' house, her father would have never stood for such a thing.

Lee walked briskly up the boulevard. At le Dôme, she ordered a brandy, then quickly scanned the room for someone to talk to. The place was nearly empty except for one large table of artsy types, presided over by Kiki. Giggling with another model, she peeked up and saw Lee on her own, but didn't call her over; she puffed on a cigarette and pretended not to see her. When two girls—teenage sisters—walked in, the group scrunched together to make room at the table, and their loud chatter redoubled. Love affairs, tragedies, the latest exhibitions. Lee watched their reflection in the mirror behind the bar, telling herself how ridiculous they were. Their outrageous makeup, their thin voices and vulgar laughter. One girl with flowers in her hair sat sucking her thumb while a shirtless man in top hat and tails stroked a Siamese cat. Lee rolled her eyes.

Alone at the swanky bar, however, she felt rejection radiating from her, their laughter bouncing on her back. This was new. Usually, Lee was sought after, a coveted conversation partner at any gathering. What was wrong here? She finished her drink and walked out, her head high.

Ten minutes later, she found herself at the Montparnasse cemetery. Winding through the crowded gravestones, she decided she preferred the company of the dead to that of Man Ray's friends.

VIII

Lee stood before the mirror in the hallway, nearly ready to go out. She slipped on a black velvet hat, then the matching jacket. After cinching the belt, she pinched a lily from the vaseful Man had photographed the day before. Large and white, she set it at an angle on her lapel. She smiled at her reflection and grabbed her bag.

"I'm going to *French Vogue* today," she announced. "To see if they have any work. I know the summer collection won't be out until February, but they might have something for me to do."

"You don't want me to go with you?" Man asked. "I'd be happy to—"

"Thanks, sweetie, but I'm sure you have better things to do."

He gave her a long kiss at the door, then she was free, out in the autumn sun. Lifting her face toward the chill blue sky, she breathed out, glad to be in the street. She'd been feeling claustrophobic; they'd barely seen anyone since the Surrealists visited two weeks earlier. Between the November rains and their lack of sitters, Man's worry and watchful eyes, it was all getting under her skin. She needed time away from the studio, more independence, her own work. And though Lee longed to focus solely on photography, she'd come to realize that, during these times of skinny cows, she'd need to return to modeling.

Even though the *Vogue* offices were on the Right Bank, she decided against taking the metro and headed toward the Seine, down the long boulevard Raspail. Passing florists and fruit stands, Lee eyed the other strollers and peeked into shop windows. After coffee at a café terrace, serenaded by a street violinist, she started across the Pont Royale, the Louvre large on the other side of the river.

She paused on the bridge, watching a seagull bobbing alone on the steel-gray Seine, like the commander of a vast vessel. Rivers make cities, she thought. Especially here, where the current cut the city in half and formed islands in the middle. She leaned against the coarse stone. Upriver, she could see the clunky Notre Dame without a proper spire and the haughty dome of the Academie Française. The buildings were solid and timeless; the water flowed clumsily beside them, constantly changing.

But it wasn't just the Seine or the old stones that Lee loved about Paris. It was its energy and rhythm. The church bells and car horns, the click-clack of high heels on cobblestones, the French language itself, in which the worst insults managed to sound delightful. It was its streets, littered with smells: black tobacco, fresh bread, mop water, frying onion, the cacophony of perfumes. The Parisians, who looked at each other unabashedly with heavy-lidded eyes. There was poetry on every corner, dance on every hip. History—be it fleeting or rock-solid—was the present. Paris, now. Lee belonged here, despite her misgivings about Man Ray's friends. Who cared? She unpinned the white lily, tossed it into the languid water, and watched it amble under the bridge. Why would she be anywhere else?

She continued through the Tuileries gardens. Walking slowly, she passed uniformed nannies with well-dressed babies, and a quiet group of veterans from the Great War sunning themselves in wicker wheelchairs. Paris was much more conservative outside of Montparnasse. With her *Vogue* looks—the chic suit, the tasteful lipstick, the new pumps—Lee felt like an undercover spy; she could fit in anywhere. One of the veterans doffed his cap at her as she passed by; she winked at him like a fellow conspirator.

When she finally arrived at the offices on the Champs-Élysées, a river away from Man's cluttered, cramped studio, she felt energized and refreshed. Alive.

"I'd like to see the see the editor in chief," she told the secretary, with a self-assured smile. Even at the French offices, she was in her element at *Vogue*. "My name is Lee Miller."

After just a few minutes, she was shown into his office. A portly man rose from behind an orderly desk. "Lee Miller? Michel de Brunhoff." He switched his pipe into his left hand to shake with her. "I've heard of you. You're Condé Nast's protégée, am I right? I remember some of Edward Steichen's photos of you," he said, taking in her features, glancing over her limbs. "We'd be delighted to have you here with us. But, um, no posing for feminine products, eh?"

His eyes twinkled. In New York the year before, there'd been a scandal when one of Steichen's elegant fashion shots of Lee had been used in an advertisement for a distasteful new product, a sanitary pad called Kotex.

"Of course not," she said with a faint blush. "And if you need a photographer, I have quite a bit of experience. Steichen taught me some of his techniques back in New York, and here in Paris I've been training with Man Ray."

"Possibly, possibly," he said, relighting his pipe. "Our head photographer here is George Hoyningen-Huene. A fascinating character! His father was a Baltic nobleman—chief equerry to the tsar, if I'm not mistaken—and his mother the daughter of the American ambassador to Russia. Needless to say, they fled after the revolution"—he took another puff—"and came here. He's a moody sort—and a baron!—but an excellent photographer. We'll get you settled in as a model first. Then we can talk about photography."

"Fabulous," she said.

Lee had been confident that de Brunhoff would hire her on as a model, but was pleasantly surprised that he was open-minded enough to even consider the idea of her working on the other side of the camera. Man had needed more convincing.

"Why don't you come in tomorrow around ten? You should visit our coiffeur first—you could use some marcel waves—then be fitted for some evening dresses. Oh, Miss Miller," he added. "As far as *Vogue* is concerned, there has been no Crash. Luxury, money, and good times—that's what we sell."

The next day, Lee sat comfortably in hair clips, waiting for the hair lotion to dry, while a chatty young woman painted her nails a bright red. A tiny barrel-chested woman with stick legs poked her head into the dressing room. "*Vous êtes l'américaine?*"

"*Oui, c'est moi.*"

"I'm Jeanne. I'll be doing your makeup." Standing, she was face-to-face with a seated Lee; she stared at her with a professional's gaze. "My goodness, child, you've let your eyebrows grow wild."

"Please don't pluck them too much," Lee said, thinking of Kiki and her absurd penciled brows. "I like a more natural look."

"Natural for evening wear?" Jeanne gave the manicurist a knowing smile. "It doesn't exist. But I can try."

An hour later, with dramatic eye shadow, dark lipstick, and perfect finger waves, Lee went through the rack and chose a jeweled gown, which glittered like sapphires. Finally ready, she crossed the hall and waited at the door of *Vogue*'s studio. Unlike Man's corner chair, it was big enough to make a motion picture in.

She watched the photographer, a tall, slim man in his late twenties with a long face and a receding hairline. Elegant in shirtsleeves, he stood behind a large camera aimed at a black-haired woman in a backless dress posing on a brilliantly lit pedestal. His beautiful hands made impatient gestures: he came out to adjust her chin, toss her hair, tilt her shoulder, then twisted his fingers like an angry spider. His high forehead looked down at her in disdain. This had to be the Russian aristocrat.

"Are you ill?" he snapped at the model, moving the camera even closer. "You're supposed to be seductive, yet you stare at me like you're going to be sick. I can't take this picture." He looked up to implore the heavens.

Lee smiled to herself. She couldn't help comparing his way of working with that of Man Ray. Not only did Man keep his distance and rarely speak to sitters, this photographer's gaze was absolutely devoid of desire.

Man had once told her that, as a young artist, if a woman was modeling for his life-drawing class, he'd become too nervous and excited to work. That emotion—that longing in his large, round eyes—could still be read on his face whenever he photographed attractive women. The exasperated man before her did not look at this model as a sexual being; there was no hint of seduction, no tension. He could have been shooting photos of livestock. This could be a refreshing change.

When the photographer's gaze fell back to earth, he saw Lee in the doorway. "Come in, come in. Don't just stand there."

She strode in with an unabashed smile. "You must be the Baron Hoyningen-Huene," she said, stretching out her hand. "Delighted to meet you. I'm Lee Miller."

"Ah, the New Yorker," he said in American English, a legacy from his mother. He shook her hand while sizing her up. "You're Man Ray's lover."

"Well, to my face, I'm usually called his assistant," she said, "but yes."

"He taught me the basics of photography when I first arrived to Paris. He's a good man with a good eye. But, to my mind, he can't really compare to Edward Steichen. You worked with him, too, didn't you?" The envy in his voice was genuine, but good-natured.

"The Colonel?" she asked, deliberately using his pet name. "I modeled for him at *Vogue,* but he also showed me some darkroom techniques. 'Faking,' he calls it. Hopefully, I'll have a chance to show you one day."

"That's a date! But today you seem to be dressed for other things. Here, let's take a few shots. You," he said, pointing to the dark-haired model sulking on her pedestal. "You can go."

Hoyningen-Huene took a dozen photos of Lee in various poses: looking over her shoulder, half-reclined, perched on a classical column, looking serious, innocent, haughty or sensual, but none with smiles. Lee had never been too keen on her teeth; slightly crooked, a bit too big, they were her worst feature. When posing, she kept her mouth closed, emphasizing her full lips, perfectly shaped and painted red. And besides, she liked to exude power when modeling, not sweetness. There was no reason to smile at the camera like a tourist on holiday.

"What depth," the photographer exclaimed. "Depending on just a look, you can be a vamp or a virgin."

"A virgin? Looks can be deceiving, can't they?" She jumped down from the pedestal.

"Well, your talents are sorely needed here. Welcome to *Frogue*."

"*Frogue?*"

"That's what all us staffers call *French Vogue*. A Brit probably thought that up, wouldn't you say? Hey, and call me George."

Lee looked at her watch. "Do you fancy going out to lunch, George?" she asked him.

"If that includes a gin fizz or two, you're on."

"Ah, a man after my own heart."

After the new year, Michel de Brunhoff called Lee into his office. George Hoyningen-Huene was already there, seated comfortably with a cigarette in his hand.

"Lee, George told me about your session in the darkroom yesterday. He says you're competent, organized—and that you were even able to give him a few pointers."

"Tricks of the trade," Lee said breezily, but was delighted with the praise.

"We've decided that you'll be his new assistant." Her mouth fell open. "You'll help with the shoots and in the darkroom, but if he needs you to model, you'll do that, too. Questions?"

"So, I get to take pictures?" she asked.

"Soon enough," George said, smiling at her wide-eyed surprise.

She hugged them both. Although she was still a man's assistant, it was her first real photography job. Lee was chosen not because of looks or romance, but because they thought she would do a good job. She was on her way to becoming a professional.

That evening, Lee threw open the door to the studio and found Man in front of the easel, his brow rumpled in frustration.

"Guess what, darling?" she said, her face glowing with excitement. "They've made me a photographer at *Vogue*! I'm an assistant for George Hoyningen-Huene. Jeanne and the models were teasing me, calling me the Baron's slave. And you should hear him shouting out orders!" She put on a deep voice and began pointing in all directions. "'Wheel this camera here, raise that one there, readjust those lights, and *please* dab that model's face, she's sweating like a pig!'"

Man was unamused. He rose from his stool and grabbed his cigarettes. Pacing the track from the door to the easel, he filled his chest with smoke, then snapped his lighter shut and looked at Lee. His dark eyes glowered.

"I can't believe you took a job with another photographer without asking me first. I need you here, with me. George can find his own slave."

"Are you crazy?" She shook her head in disgust. "I'm not going to quit. It's a real job, Man. They *pay* me."

"I pay you, too! Rent, food, clothes, drinks, everything you want, I pay for. And I don't like the idea of sharing you with a fucking baron."

"Being a kept woman isn't really what I'm after, Man." She spoke slowly in an effort to keep calm. "And it's a chance for me to learn from someone else. To expand my knowledge. Don't you think that's a good thing?"

"What can you learn from him that you can't learn from me? For God's sake, I was *his* teacher, too." He rolled his eyes at the absurdity of it. "I want you here, Lee. If you need wages on top of everything else, hell, I guess I can do that, too."

"Jesus, how generous you are!" She felt like spitting in his face. "But I'm going to do what I damn well please."

She left him with his half-daubed canvas, stormed around the block, then stopped at the Bateau Ivre and had two shots of cognac in quick succession. At the beginning of their relationship, his nervous jealousy had amused her, but it had gotten old fast. She tapped the zinc bar with her fingernails. What to do with a possessive man? Up until now, whenever a relationship got troublesome, Lee had just moved on to the next one. But she knew she wasn't ready to leave Man; here in Paris, he was the person closest to her: her companion, her mentor, her lover, her guide. Lee drained the last drops from her glass. Now calm, she paid the bartender and slowly walked back to the studio.

Man greeted her at the door. "God, kid, I'm sorry. You know what a hothead I am." He pulled her in tightly and gave her a fiery kiss.

"Mmm. Sometimes it's in your favor."

He smiled back at her. "So the people at *Vogue* have finally figured what a gold mine they've got working there. I'm not surprised." Obviously relieved the row was short lived, he kissed her again, his hands all over her, taking a quick inventory to assure himself that everything was still there.

She spoke in his ear—"Do you fancy a bit of mining, then? If you dig deep enough, you might strike it rich"—and led him to the bedroom.

Lee began getting up early several times a week—tiptoeing to let Man sleep—to spend the day at *Frogue*. Unlike at the Montparnasse studio, the relationships there were simple, the mood almost always lighthearted. Lee and George shared the honesty and familiarity of siblings, the good-natured rivalry, the bickering and joking. Jeanne was like an auntie, and the models— some delightful, others insufferable—were like cousins. Michel de Brunhoff—puffing on his pipe, encouraging his fold with friendly pats and praise—played the affable father figure. And even though Lee was the Baron's assistant, he was interested in what she could teach him; George never scrutinized her movements, or gave her unneeded, repeated advice. At *Vogue*, she felt like a real photographer, not just the sorcerer's apprentice.

IX

―――――

"Great prints, doll." In the amber light, George examined the photographs Lee was hanging like a row of laundered handkerchiefs. "I especially like the one of Tatiana in the mink coat. Her hands have a life of their own."

"Thanks. I love this one of yours. Who is that model? He's gorgeous."

"Come now, Lee. I have to have *some* professional secrets."

"Fine. Keep your Adonis anonymous. Could you hand me that funnel? I'm ready to put these chemicals away."

Five minutes later, George turned on the light. Lee blinked, then squinted down at her watch, her vision still adjusting to the brightness.

"Damn, it's after eight," she said.

"That explains the hunger, but look," he said, gesturing at the clotheslines of dripping prints, "it's all done."

"I'm absolutely starving." Lee reapplied her lipstick. "Hey, let's go have dinner at that place in the Marais."

"With the fabulous *soupe de moules*? The duck? The profiteroles?" He adjusted the brim of his hat, licking his lips. "Lead the way, darling."

At the crowded bistro, they were seated next to a staid married couple who chewed their main course without exchanging a word. By the time their mussel soup arrived, however, the thin twosome had waved away the dessert menu and quietly left, to be replaced by a trio of university students. These three plopped down next to them and introduced themselves with half-drunken grins. By the end of the meal, they were all laughing together, clinking glasses and tossing cream puffs into one another's mouths.

"We're off to a party now if you'd like to go," said one of the students as he slyly dipped the tip of his friend's tie into the chocolate sauce. "Should be a good one."

"We're game," Lee said, giving George a stern look, as if daring him to be sensible and mature.

Arm in arm, they crossed the Île Saint-Louis and stumbled into the Latin Quarter. From a block away, they could already hear music and squeals drifting out of a courtyard. They passed through the iron gates. A monkeyless organ grinder was cranking his heart out while a circle of girls did the Charleston, their arms and legs flailing in every direction. Lee and George made their way into the small, ground-floor flat, the hub of the din. In the middle of the room, laughing and shouting, a group of people surrounded a vat of cheap brandy, taking turns to generously serve themselves, plunging coffee cups and jam jars so far in that they soaked their shirt cuffs. A winking boy handed Lee a dripping mug. She passed it on to George and held out her hand for another. They winced as they drank.

"Damn, it's hot in here," George said, stuffing his gloves into his hat and throwing his coat over his arm. He nodded at a couple of girls dancing in silky slips, their wool dresses in piles on the floor. "They've got the right idea."

Lee wanted to peel her dress off, too, but remembered the long row of buttons in the back. It had taken Man a good five minutes to fasten them that morning.

"The courtyard must be cooler," she said, edging toward the door.

They wandered out into the night air where the music man was grinding out a foxtrot. A pair of boys asked Lee to dance, sandwiching her between them, each one holding her tightly against him. Laughing, Lee did one turn around the courtyard with them, then cast them off, tired of their sweaty smell and obvious excitement. She was turning to George, still standing on the sidelines, to see if he wanted to dance, when one of the slip girls lunged out of the flat and vomited next to Lee's shoes. With a disgusted screech, Lee jumped back and grabbed George's arm.

"Christ, I haven't been to student party in ages," she said. "We'd better get out of here before the walls start crumbling down."

"Or the natives decide to make a ritual sacrifice." He stroked his neck lovingly in mock panic.

"Shall we go back toward l'Étoile?"

George led her through the gate and hailed a taxi. "I've got a better idea."

Lee sat back in drunken contentedness, happy to rest her feet, off on a new adventure.

"What a dump that was," George said, his words a cranky slur. "Dammit, I hate being the oldest one in the room. You'll love this next place." He gave her hand a lopsided pat.

While the cab rolled down the long boulevard from the

Bastille to the Gare du Nord, Lee smoked a cigarette and peered out the window, wondering where he was taking her. Solitary cats prowled around the trash bins as beggars and lovers vied for the empty street benches. Prostitutes stood on corners, serious and immobile, ignored by the cops in their kepis and capes. The taxi climbed the hill up to Montmartre, then stopped alongside a windowless shopfront with a closed door.

With a mischievous smile, George rang the bell; it was immediately answered by a dumpling of a little man, his cheeks spotted with rouge.

"George! How delightful! It's been ages!" he cried, ushering them in.

The large paneled room glowed dimly with low-burning gas lamps, yet everyone was dressed to the nines. As they fumbled to their table in the semidarkness, Lee glanced around—was she underdressed?—feeling strangely unsettled. The men, decked out in white tails and tuxedos, were unusually baby-faced—short and plump, for the most part—while the women were tall and homely, lavishly dressed in feathers, beads, and fringe. The waitresses, in contrast, were all bare to the waist.

"We'd like a bottle of champagne," George ordered as soon as they'd fallen into their chairs. "And bring me a good cigar, too, darling."

"How 'bout you, honey?" the waitress asked Lee suggestively. "Do *you* need a big, fat cigar?" She made a lewd gesture with her fist and let out a low cackle.

Lee's mouth dropped open and she looked up, shocked to find the big, rounded breasts in front of her were made of rubber.

She blinked. Under the face paint, Lee could see the waitress's five o'clock shadow, the ungainly Adam's apple. As the he-woman spun around to fetch the champagne, Lee turned to George.

"What is this place?" She grinned in wide-eyed wonder and peeked about, eager to take in the strangeness around them.

"It's the world upside down," he said, sweeping his hand around the room, "where the men are women and the women, men."

After guzzling down a glass of champagne, they hit the dance floor; a transvestite with a bad Louise Brooks wig immediately cut in.

"May I have this dance?" he asked, not bothering to heighten his voice.

Lee turned toward him, but he had already whisked George away, winking at Lee with a blue-caked lid. At that moment a slim young man in a velvet smoking jacket swooped Lee up.

"We can't have you out here alone, my dear."

Lee fell into a fast waltz and scanned her partner's swirling face: the short hair slicked back, the freckles dotting hairless skin, the innocent eyes, the shy smile. Was this a woman? Wildly curious, she tried to focus on him or her, thrilled by the decadence of it all. Was this even legal?

Through occasional bursts of giggles, Lee danced five more numbers, new partners cutting in every few minutes. Some held her close, while others gazed into her face. When she asked their names—her wily investigations into their private lives—they all answered with initials or nicknames: "I'm J.B." or "Call me Gutsy." And when the orchestra started in on the Charleston, a threesome in top hats lifted Lee up onto a table.

"Go, Legs, go!"

She kicked front and back, fanned her hands at the knees, and then jumped down (the table was too unsteady to risk it any longer) to vigorous applause. She took a short bow, then put her arms straight up and, with a wink, waved her fingers. Out of breath and rather dizzy, she found George at the table, smoking a cigar. He filled her glass.

"You see, Lee, here the people can hold their liquor. And you don't have to dance sandwich-style." Lowering his voice, he added, "though I'm sad to say that all my partners—these ravishing ladies here—kept sticking their tongues in my ear." He raised his glass to a passing group in blond wigs, giving them a gentlemanly smile. "At least we can agree that, here, I am the most handsome man in the room. More champagne!"

Halfway through the next bottle, however, George began nodding off. It was time to head home. With the help of the muscular blondes, Lee was able to usher him into a cab. She bid heartfelt farewells to her cross-dressed companions—waving good-bye from the car window till the end of the street—then headed back down the Butte. George was nestled in the corner of the cab, snoring lightly.

"Where we going, lady?" The taxi driver was unamused, his French hasty.

Lee tried to remember the name of her street but, drawing a complete blank, she told the driver to leave her on the boulevard Montparnasse. He dropped her off in front of la Coupole and drove off with George sleeping in the back. Lee was stumbling back to the studio when she heard a bicycle bell.

"Mademoiselle!" A young gendarme straddled his bike next

to her. "What is wrong? Do you need assistance?" His big brown eyes were wide with concern.

She leaned into him and whispered in his ear, "Officer, could you take me home?"

He coughed as she snuggled into his cape, her arms around his waist, rubbing her cheek against his. "*S'il vous plaît?*" She stretched the words out, her breath hot in his ear.

He looked around helplessly, then yielded. "All right, miss. Up you go." He gave her backside a push and helped her onto his handlebars. Lee squealed in delight as, for two blocks, they bumped over the cobblestones and nearly fell twice.

She peppered his face with kisses, then dug for her key at the bottom of her bag, pleased with herself that she hadn't lost it. Her mood quickly darkened at the key's stubbornness; it would not let her in. She was about to throw it across the courtyard, when the door swung open. The anxious young policeman faded into the night.

"Goddamn it, Lee, it's four o'clock in the morning!" Man yanked her into the apartment and sat her down on the couch. "And you're drunk!"

"I think the appropriate euphemism here is 'chipper.' Or 'merry.' 'Jolly,' perhaps." She looked up at Man and slowly processed his fierce glare. "Well, not anymore."

"Where the hell have you been?" He flipped his lighter open, then slammed it shut.

"George and I went out after work. You'll be happy to hear that I only danced with other women. I swear." She held up her hand as if taking an oath, then broke into uncontrollable giggles.

"You've been gone the whole damn day! First at *Vogue,* then off dancing. George spends more time with you than I do. We could've gone out tonight." He jabbed his chest with his finger. "You and me, here in Montparnasse. I went up to the boulevard looking for you and everybody was there. Things were really hopping."

"Everybody? You mean *your* friends. The ones that call me Madame Man Ray, as if I didn't have a name. You know, when you aren't around, they snub me." She sat up, now cross, and lit a cigarette; her giddy drunk had already turned into a dull headache. "Kiki and her set, all those *flâneurs* who have nothing better to do than sit around cafés all day. I guess they think being American makes me a rich snob or that having a job makes me boring. Christ, I don't know what they think, but I know I'd rather be myself with my own friends than be Madame Man Ray with your stuck-up bohemians."

"Aw, to hell with them." His gruff voice became soft. "*I* need you, Lee. Here, with me. You're my inspiration, in my work and in my bed."

"Speaking of bed, that's where I need to be. I'm beat." She stood up, weaving slightly. After a fun night out with George, she resented coming home to this. Man could be such a killjoy. She was fed up with having to answer to him—to anyone. Lee wanted to be young, in Paris, free. "We can talk tomorrow."

"Leeee." His voice was urgent.

She turned to him from the top of the stairs. "What?"

"I love you."

She produced a frozen smile and nodded. "We can talk to-morrow," she repeated, though she hoped they wouldn't. Love?

She had never exchanged "I love you"s with anyone except her father. Between them, two practical, unsentimental sorts, the words were rather mechanical, formulas for a pre-good-bye, said unthinkingly on the telephone or at ports and train stations. She had never uttered such a thing to a man. Far too encouraging, the words screamed of indefinite commitment. She crawled under the covers, feeling smothered.

The following day, Lee awoke with her nose plastered into the nape of Man's neck. His curly hair reeked of black tobacco, and from his moist skin came the distinct odor of whisky. Had he been drinking, too? God, she hoped so. With a wave of nausea, she slowly rolled away from him, with her eyes closed but her mouth open in a vain attempt to air it out; it tasted like she'd been licking a speakeasy floor. Man's hand swung over to find her leg, patting out a clumsy greeting.

"Are you awake?" he asked.

"No." She groaned at his naked back. "I feel like shit."

He rolled over to face her. "You don't look so good either."

"Could you get me a glass of water? Please?" she begged.

Man got out of bed. "I suppose you'd like some coffee, too. And breakfast?"

"Maybe after a while." She smacked her dry lips.

"It's raining," he announced from the window, then went down to the kitchen. He came back a few minutes later with a highball glass full of water. "Here, kid."

She sat up creakily and drank in tiny sips like an invalid child; he gently stroked her back. With a sheepish smile, she handed him back the glass and sank back under the covers.

"Thanks for taking such good care of me."

"My pleasure, baby. I care about you. That's why I worry."

She nodded nervously, afraid he was going to launch into an earnest discussion about love. His desires and fantasies, their future together. As for herself, she wasn't exactly sure how she felt about him. It was a cocktail of fondness, admiration, camaraderie, and exasperation, in varying measures and unevenly shaken. Man opened his mouth, hesitated, then snapped it shut like his lighter top. He kissed her forehead and stood up.

"I'm going to paint awhile. Call me if you need anything."

He clomped down the stairs, and she closed her eyes, relieved to have sidestepped the love talk, glad for some time alone. Lee needed to think. Man was not an easy person to be with. Along with all his positive qualities—he was brilliant, playful, generous, loving—there were his unpredictable temper and oppressive expectations to put up with. And to complicate matters, they shared a profession (and, face it, his tutelage and contacts were still important to her) and a flat. A flat where her things were *de trop*. Was it time to find her own place? Living together was suffocating them—or her, at any rate. Wouldn't they be happier together with separate studios? Or would they drift apart? She put the pillow over her head to drown out her thoughts. With this hangover, making decisions was the last thing she wanted to do.

X

———

"Her hair. You really need to highlight her hair," Lee said. She stood next to Man, behind the camera; Jacqueline, Man's favorite model next to Lee, was sitting on the posing chair, holding a black drape over her breasts. "Women have been bobbing their hair for twenty years now. But take a look at this." She went over and picked up Jacqueline's jungle of dark, unruly hair, exaggerating its bulk. "It has a life of its own—it makes hair seem like something new. As pretty as her face is, this hair should be the focus."

Man nodded. "You're right. Let's make a long-haired woman into a novelty. Can we do something to make it even bigger?" His hands gestured wildly around his head.

"I'll brush it upside down." Delighted, she began bounding up the stairs to fetch her hairbrush, but stopped with a jerk at the tungsten light. She skittered it a foot to the right. "Let's try lighting her face from the side. Or backlighting? What do you think?"

When the photo session was over, they went into the dark-room, anxious to see how the shots had come out.

"Oh, I forgot to tell you," Man said, dipping the plates into the basin. "I got a call this morning from the Sorbonne. They need some photos made before the end of term. I'd like you to take the assignment." He'd been sending her out on jobs: less prestigious projects, ones that didn't interest him or those with a smaller budget. Work for clients who wanted Man Ray, but would accept the work of Madame. Lee suspected it was his way of keeping a watchful eye on her, but she didn't mind. It was an opportunity to learn new things and hone her reputation as a photographer. "It's for the medical school. Anatomy classes, operations. I hope you can handle it."

"Sounds interesting." The macabre had always tickled Lee. "Are you sure you don't want to do it yourself?"

"I've got plenty to do without shooting blood and guts," he said gruffly, then dropped his voice to an apologetic whisper. "Truth is, I'd probably faint."

Lee kissed his cheek. The darkroom always made them less inhibited, more honest.

"There's something I need to tell you, too." Nervous, she twirled a tong in the tray, making a ripple in the chemicals. "I've been mooching off you way too long. I've seen a place near the Place Vendôme and—"

"What are you saying?" His body froze. "Are you moving out?"

"We never meant this to be permanent—"

For weeks now, Lee had been looking for TO RENT signs on her way to *Vogue* and examining her friends' available rooms; his studio had always been small for the two of them, and lately it seemed to be shrinking. She needed somewhere she could do her own work, entertain her friends, smolder after an argument, or just sit in silence.

"I know, I know." Surprise was quickly turning to anger. "But the Place Vendôme? Are you crazy? That's on the other side of the river! Since when have you been looking at flats? You could have said something."

"Look, we're stepping on each other's toes here. This new place is nice and not too—"

"Stop. I know living together in this shoebox was supposed to be a short-term thing, but before you go making up your mind, give me a couple of days to ask around. I'm sure we can find you something here in Montparnasse."

"God, Man, you act like the rest of Paris doesn't exist." She glared at him.

"I'm just thinking of you, Lee," he said, softening his tone. "You want to live near the studio, don't you? So we can work together. Like today."

They'd been collaborating more and more. And not just on outside assignments, but on his creative projects, too. Even though she had often helped set up shots when posing, she especially enjoyed working with him with other models. To see what he was seeing, to be able to alter the image before it was taken.

"All right, then. I'll put the Place Vendôme on hold. See what you can do."

Over the next few days, he made inquiries with all-knowing barmen and gossipy concierges; rejecting anything too far away, he inspected a handful of apartments.

"Lee?" He walked into the bedroom; she was reading a magazine with her back to the door. "Hey, baby, you want to see your new place?"

"You've made a decision? Without me?" She turned to him, piqued. "I can't believe it."

"Just come with me," he said, taking her hand. "You're going to love it."

She put on her shoes, shaking her head in frustration. He was much more controlling than her father had ever been. Even as a small girl, he'd let her take decisions, make mistakes, do as she pleased.

They walked down the boulevard Raspail in silence, then turned down a side street; the ivied wall of the old cemetery ran its entire length. Since the disappointing Surrealist tea party, Lee had gone there exploring several times and had even left a lipsticked kiss on the tombstone of her favorite poet, Charles Baudelaire, the syphilitic opium addict who wrote of sex and death. She liked the quiet here, just a home-run hit from the busy, bar-filled center of Montparnasse. Opposite the graveyard, she noticed for the first time the row of artists' studios.

"This is it," said Man.

He stopped at the entrance of a white building with large windows cut in the Art Deco style. The small courtyard babbled with the song of the tiled fountain in the center. Inside, a tiny elevator was tucked into the stairwell.

Man led her into the elevator, yanked the accordion brass door closed, and pushed 2. She laughed as it rose with a jerk, then kissed Man. "You lucky bastard," she said. "This may do."

He handed her the key. She unlocked the door and swung it wide open. Light streamed into the apartment, more luxurious and larger than Man's place. Lee examined every corner, then turned to kiss him again.

"It's wonderful!" she cried. "The lines, the windows, the views. Look at the boneyard down there! It's like a miniature city filled with marble houses. And look over here!" She pointed to a closet next to the bath. "It's a perfect place to put a darkroom."

"You can still use mine, Lee." His mouth twitched. "I was thinking that we could work at my place and come here to sleep."

"Sure." She nodded. Lee wanted to set up her own studio, to have her own clientele, to be in business for herself, but she didn't want to argue. Not today. She was delighted with this place, happy he'd found it. "I'll still set up a work space here. For rainy days when I don't want to get out of my pajamas."

She spent the next week decorating. On one wall, she hung flea-market gramophone records on top of bright fabric, creating a chic wallpaper collage. On another wall, she put up silver paper to reflect the light. Pleased with its swanky look, she nonetheless kept one corner bare, reserving it for future sitters. Man brought over some of his handmade lamps, whose shades unwound in long spirals, and a Cocteau tapestry to hang behind the bed. When it was finally done, he went out for champagne.

Alone, Lee reinspected each room. With contented sighs, she smoothed the blanket on the bed, reorganized her lipsticks and powders, peeked into the half-empty cupboards, and straightened her hatboxes and shoes. How thrilling to have her own place—in Paris! Here she was neither accessory nor assistant. In this studio, she was queen.

They toasted the new apartment, again and again. When the bottle was empty, she led Man over to the bed and removed his tie. Staring him in the eye, she threw it over her shoulder, wetting her lips with her tongue. Then she began unbuttoning his shirt. She was going to take this slow, make it last. For the last month or so, she'd been so preoccupied and confused—about their relationship, the move, work—that her lovemaking had become quick and mechanical. Not tonight. Her newfound independence made her feel even closer to him, generous and happy.

Lee stood smiling in front of Man's studio door, her portfolio under her arm. She was trying to decide whether to ring or use her key, wondering which would surprise him more. She'd been in her own place for two weeks now and, although they still saw each other every day, they were enjoying each other more than ever. It was like starting all over again.

Having her own space and a private darkroom had also boosted her creative energy and made her more experimental. Cityscapes or pretty postcard pictures didn't interest her; Lee looked for unusual images, bizarre contrasts. Quietly taking everything in, she meandered around Paris neighborhoods with her camera, a dreamscape naturalist looking for unrecorded specimens; using her viewfinder as a microscope, she framed the shots to make new discoveries. A blob of tar seemingly crawling toward a man's well-shod feet; a mysterious walkway shrinking into a tunnel. She loved playing with light, form, and technique, making her own mistakes, choices, and decisions. When she was pleased with an image, however, she would run to Man's studio to show him, still keen on her mentor's praise.

She turned the key and opened the door, calling, "Mr. Man Raaaay! Delivery!"

He poked his head out of the kitchen, trying not to smile. "Whatcha got, bub?"

"Fresh bearded clam! The best of the season."

"Give me all you got." He pulled her toward him and kissed her. "Hey, what've you really got here?" He slid the portfolio out from under her arm. "New pictures?"

"Just one."

Snuggled together on the sofa, he opened the portfolio with playful ceremony. But when he looked down at the print, his mouth fell open. "Wow." In it, a woman's hand appeared to explode as it touched a doorknob. "Let me get my glasses." He examined the photo carefully. "I see. That flash is caused by all the little scratches on the glass door. The lighting is just right." He nodded at her. "I'm impressed, kid. It's a fabulous shot of a Surrealist image. You've done your old man proud."

"Thanks, honey," said Lee, bubbling with self-satisfaction. "I took a whole roll of the windows at the *parfumerie* Guerlain. The Art Nouveau glasswork, the reflections of the street lamps and clouds on the perfume bottles. It was all shit. It wasn't until a woman was leaving the shop that I saw the hand explode. She was pleased to pose." Lee grinned at the shot. "Lucky for me she was wearing that bell-shaped sleeve. Makes it look like a witch's hand. Like she's casting a spell and sending out sparks."

The doorbell buzzed; Lee looked at Man.

"That's Breton." He put the photo on the table and stood up. "I'm taking his portrait this morning. He wants a formal shot for the back cover of his new book."

Lee lit a cigarette as Man disappeared into the hall. She was no longer intimidated by André Breton or the other Surrealists. After meeting them another time or two, she found them pleasant enough—and some quite charming, attentive, or flirtatious—but had long realized that none of them were interested in her opinions. To them, she was not one of their fellows, but Man Ray's muse: his inspiration, his well from which to draw creativity, *his*. And these men generally preferred their muses to be quiet and submissive, not equals with whom to discuss their projects or exchange ideas. Lee was always intrigued by the new work they brought round the studio, the mysterious canvases, quirky poems, or funny drawings, but when they came by to see Man, to make plans, play chess, debate, or get their pictures made, after a half-hour or so—the time for a drink or a bit of playful banter—Lee usually left.

"Oh, hello, Lee," said Breton as Man led him inside. He was dressed in a conventional double-breasted suit with a tie that matched his pocket handkerchief; as always, his hair was slicked back, an immobile military helmet, constantly ready for battle.

"André." They exchanged halfhearted kisses. "Can I get you anything?" she asked, still the lady of the house.

"A glass of water, thanks."

When she came back from the kitchen, Breton was holding her new picture.

"Bravo, Man! This is brilliant! It's the most interesting shot you've taken this year."

She handed him the glass and retrieved the photo. "Actually, it's mine." She popped it into her portfolio with a sweeping gesture. "All this, and beautiful, too."

Lee kissed Man good-bye and walked out the door, relishing the moment. She had left André Breton speechless.

XI

Taking a deep breath, Lee tried to harden herself against the rancid pickling odor of formaldehyde, which crept onto her tongue and into her hair. As for the corpses, although they were gruesome—waxy, bloated, yellowed—she couldn't turn away from them. It was her first day on assignment at the Sorbonne medical school.

She moved around the room to find the best angles of the young men in white robes skinning bodies to get to the discolored layers below. Over human remains, a few of the students tried to catch her eye, winking at her or whispering offers: cigarettes, drinks, outings. She wasn't tempted by their rosy cheeks or boyish grins. They seemed impossibly young to her—far too young to be cutting cadavers—though she had just turned twenty-three.

The next week, a doctor reluctantly asked her if she could take photos inside the university's operating theater—"Young lady, I'm afraid you may not be able to stomach it"—which only piqued her morbid curiosity. The first patient was wheeled into the center of the well-lit room. A full house of students gazed down from the galleries as a surgeon appeared and gave his audience a slight bow.

"Today we will be performing an appendectomy," he said, with the projection and timbre of a Shakespearean actor. "The patient is a sixteen-year-old girl."

From the side of the room, Lee took pictures: nurses handing over steel instruments, the intensity of the masked faces hunched over the girl, the tongs finally capturing the small, ragged organ and brandishing it to the crowd. Lee tried to make out the students' expressions in the relative darkness of the gallery. Had some of them fallen asleep?

Engrossed, she documented the removal of various body parts that week, playing with the lighting and groupings of medical personnel. She liked the quiet intensity of the operations, their urgency and success, but was fascinated by the castaway parts—the hairy, detached limbs or graying organs—left on zinc trays, now useless and unwanted. Despite the blood, odors, and horror, from her place behind the camera, she managed to put herself at a distance and concentrate on picture-taking.

On her last day, as the students were pouring out of the galleries, Lee hesitated at the door. She looked back at the day's remains lying motionless on the metal tray, and had an idea for an interesting photo shoot: a Surrealist meditation on beauty and desire. Putting on a formal expression and a professional tone of voice, she approached the surgeon who had just performed a radical mastectomy.

"Excuse me, sir?"

He looked up at her, almost startled, removed his mask, and gave her a seductive smile. During the operation he'd been too focused to notice the woman taking pictures.

"Yes, *mademoiselle*? How may I be of service?"

"Are those leavings to be discarded?" she asked, pointing at the orphaned breasts. "Might I take one?"

"Of course," he said, not bothering to ask why. "Here, let me wrap it up for you."

He absently picked up his mask and tucked one malignant breast inside. Still smiling, he handed the damp package to her, like a butcher at the market. She thanked him with a pat on the shoulder, then turned and left, the surgeon's mask heavy and squishy in her hand. Keeping her bundle at arm's length, she walked through the twisted streets of the Latin Quarter, heading toward the Right Bank. She had a modeling session at *Vogue* in an hour, but thought she'd have time to take some photos first. The mask soon began to leak, so she stopped at a restaurant to collect the necessary props.

Lee motioned to the first waiter she saw, who was wiping glasses by the side bar. He immediately forgot the wineglass, threw his towel jauntily over his shoulder, and hustled to the door.

"May I borrow a place setting?" Lee asked in an intimate whisper. "I could bring it back to you this afternoon. Just a plate, knife, fork, spoon, napkin. That's right." She nodded as she watched him collect the things from a table already set for lunch. "Oh, and could I have the salt and pepper shakers, too? Wonderful."

The waiter's moustache fluttered as his hand grazed hers. "Here you are, *mademoiselle*. Anything else?"

"No, but thank you," she said, her words exuding warmth, gratitude, and a slight hint of siren song. She slipped the condiments and cutlery into her bag, put the surgeon's mask on the plate, then covered it with the napkin. "I'll be back later to return these things."

"I'll be waiting," the waiter said, waving from the door.

At the river, she hailed a cab and, once inside, held on tight to the dinner plate. As they sped along, she was reminded of the grisly paintings of the saints she'd seen in cathedrals and at the Louvre: Francis of Assisi, stigmata bleeding onto the skull in his hand; Saint Lucy carrying her woeful eyes on silver dish; John the Baptist's head, at rest, on a platter; and the one that had captured her attention most of all, Saint Agatha, whose torturers had cut off her breasts. In paintings, she carried them before her on a plate, looking much more like wobbly custards or cherry-topped cakes than what Lee had here. Looking down at the napkin, she regretted not requesting the pair.

She struggled with the door at *Frogue*, anxious not to spill, then quickly made her way to the photography studio. On a side table, she laid out the napkin, pleased with its home-style checkered pattern. After carefully removing the breast from the bloodstained mask, she arranged it on the plate. She flattened the thick skin, which was already hardening, and tried to highlight the nipple, inverted from the cancer and no longer very recognizable.

Looking down at it—a human slice, a gelatinous mass—she wondered at how, when attached to a woman, this object could make a man red-hot. Man Ray had cropped photos of her to emphasize her breasts, decapitating her, making her a torso. What would he make of this bodiless breast? Would it entice him? She dragged over a light and cast its bright glare on the plate's center. An operating table without a patient. Placing the cutlery around the plate, she decided on the French fashion, with the dessert spoon laid across the top of the plate. She was staring down at that spoon—an unlikely instrument to tackle this feast—when George walked in.

"What is that?" he asked. Reluctant to come closer, he pointed at the table, looking very suspicious. "Is it food? Something you made?"

She smiled at the idea. Lee was *not* a very good cook and generally preferred restaurants and bistros to the kitchen. In fact, the last time she had tried to roast a chicken for Man, she got distracted and burned it. That skinny black bird looked even scarier than what she had here.

"It's a still life," she said, "though really, the French term is much more appropriate: *une nature morte*. Come, look at it," she said as she pulled her camera out of her bag. "See if you can tell what it is."

"Is that blood?" he asked, his nose wrinkling. "Is it a dead animal?"

"No, George," she said, her eyes sparkling. "It's a woman's breast."

"Lee, you are disgusting!" He flew out of the room.

She had taken two shots when Michel de Brunhoff crept up behind her. "What's the matter with George?" he asked, then looked down at the table. "And what the hell is that?"

Lee turned around, blocking the place setting with her body, trying to come up with a plausible story.

"Oh, hello there, Michel. Yes, well, I've been doing a stint at the Sorbonne, taking medical photographs. One of the surgeons asked me if I could get a good close-up of this severed breast—"

"With a knife and fork?" he cried. "Who do you take me for? Get that thing out of here at once."

He stood sternly by as she picked it up with her thumb and forefinger, tucked it back into the dirty mask, and went to chuck it into the bin.

"Out!" de Brunhoff shouted, pointing dramatically to the door.

In the street, she hesitated; it seemed outrageously disrespectful to just toss out a human body part. This breast, which had hung so close to a heart, could have lured lovers or fed a child. She considered burying it next to a tree, below the reach of dogs, but she hadn't any tools. She looked down at her manicured nails, then back at the studio door where Michel was waiting. With no ceremony, she let it drop from her hand; it fell into the gutter among leaves and wisps of paper. She slumped back to the studio.

"George and Tatiana are waiting for you. It's swimwear today. But afterward, I want to see you in my office. We need to talk," Michel said, then swept out.

Lee walked into the dressing room and found Tatiana Iacovleva looking at bathing costumes. Tall and blond like Lee, Tata was a Russian émigré, the daughter of St. Petersburg intellectuals; with the bearing of a war goddess, she was brazen, haughty, and intent on marrying into the nobility. Lee thought she was a riot.

"George is fuming. He says you were taking pictures of a bloody breast. A real one." Tata's accent in French was deliberate, filled with Slavic swishes and trills and with occasional grammatical snags; her eyes were laughing. "I'm not surprised it upset him. It's probably the first one he's seen since he was baby."

Lee looked at her in confusion and then nodded knowingly. "Right. He's not too keen on lady bits," she said, marveling that she had never realized it before. That outing in Montmartre should have at least given her a clue.

After their modeling session—a madcap couple of hours, where George had them posing with faux pool ladders and pretending to dive off of wooden crates—they were all in a good mood, now able to laugh off their earlier clash.

"You two up for a drink?" George asked as they made their way back to the dressing rooms.

"Not me," Lee said. "Michel wants to talk to me. I think he's pretty upset about my anatomical photo session today. I hope I'm not fired."

"Well, you probably should be," he said, with a harsh expression that immediately melted into a chuckle. "But I doubt it. You know, before his career at the magazine, he used to be an actor. He's an incredible mime." George went into a two-second Tramp impersonation, twitching an invisible mustache while swinging an imaginary cane. "I wouldn't worry too much, Lee. He's an open-minded man."

"Good luck," said Tata thickly, patting her arm with a serious smile.

She knocked on de Brunhoff's office door.

"Ah, Lee," he began, pulling the pipe from his mouth, then using it as a pointer. "Sit down."

"Michel, listen, I'm sorry about bringing that, uh, organ

into the studio today. I was doing a little experiment." She raised her eyebrows uncertainly. "Maybe I should have asked you first?"

"What I want to say to you is this: If you are capable of taking photos of such things—surgeries at the Sorbonne and so forth—then I've been underestimating you here. I believe you're ready to take on your own assignments. You seem to have an interest in the still life. Show me what you can do with the new line of Chanel fragrances. You'll start tomorrow."

Lee jumped out of her chair, excited and relieved both. "Oh, Michel, thank you! I'll do something original, something new. You won't be disappointed."

"Uh, Lee—nothing *too* original, please."

"Don't worry, chief." She smiled. "I can do this."

XII

As Lee puttered around Man's studio, choosing masks and chessboards to set off the perfume bottles, she received a telegram. She used her index finger as a dull letter opener, then scanned the short note. Tanja Ramm was returning to Europe; she was about to board the SS *Paris* and would be arriving the following week. Lee beamed down at the paper.

"Man!" she called. She popped into the bathroom where he was half-soaped, half-shaven. "Tanja is coming to visit. She'll be here next Thursday."

"Tanja?"

"My oldest pal." She couldn't stop smiling. "We were together in Florence before I came to Paris. We met at the Art Students League back in 'twenty-six."

"Of course," he said with a nod. "It'll be great to meet her. You know, it always seems funny to me that we both took classes at the same place. Too bad we didn't meet back then."

"You cheeky monkey. When you were at the League, I was way too young for you." She pinched his creamy cheek. "I still hadn't been kicked out of all the schools in Poughkeepsie."

"What a bad, bad girl." He pinched her back.

"Those prudes would expel you for anything. Swearing, smoking, pranks—"

With a dab of shaving cream, he gave her a thin moustache and goatee, like Marcel Duchamp's Mona Lisa. "And Tanja?" he asked. "Is she a painter now?"

"No. She stayed at it longer than I did, but she makes her living as a model, too."

"Well, then, maybe she can model for me." His thin lips curled into a suggestive smile. "The two of you could pose together. Double nudes. Maybe some kissing? How would you feel about that?"

"Actually, Tanja and I have already done a shoot like that. A few years ago, my father took a whole series of us together on the sleeping porch."

The razor in Man's hand froze on his outstretched upper lip. His eyes found Lee's in the mirror.

"What?" said Lee, staring back at him. "My father's taken pictures of me since I can remember."

Man's brow was lined in confusion, poorly disguised aversion. "In the nude?"

Frowning, Lee toweled off the lines of shaving cream from her face. There was no one she loved or trusted as much as her father, and she didn't like Man's expression. As if Theodore Miller were capable of anything indecent or inhumane. She'd known a man like that—in fact, he'd had a Brooklyn accent similar to Man Ray's—but her father, though generous and doting, was a man of dignity, beyond reproach.

"They're art. He's done nude studies of my mother as well. He takes them in stereoscope so they can be seen through a viewer. It gives them a three-dimensional effect, you know." She gave him a defiant look. "Funny that you of all people should be shocked by nudity. It's art," she repeated firmly.

"Of course, Lee," Man said, fanning his hands out in surrender. "It's all about the art. I'm just surprised he used his own daughter as a model."

"I started posing for his studies when I was nineteen. My father's always had a progressive attitude toward nudism." Lee paused a moment, remembering, and pursed her lips. "Although, I'll admit it, in the beginning it felt a bit weird."

Recently home from her first trip to Paris, she'd had a bad case of the blue jitters—that restless, edgy sadness that overtook her at times—made much worse by the flare-up of a childhood illness. One day, after the painful treatment, her father had proposed a photo shoot; Lee supposed he'd wanted to make her feel better by giving her special attention.

For their first session, Theodore had taken her to a quiet area in the woods. She undressed awkwardly, her heart beating wildly, a lump in her throat. He spoke to her gently, asking her to sit this way, to lean back, to look at him; she complied, but never quite relaxed. Later, after he'd developed that first batch of photographs, she sat in the wingback chair in his study, looking at them in the stereoscopic viewer. Like the other images she'd seen in the device—the Taj Mahal, Mount Fuji, the Roman Coliseum—the body jumped out at her. In the first one, it covered its face with its hands; in another, it exposed itself, looking away; in yet another, it stretched out, the eyes vacant. Lee'd hardly recognized that pretty young girl; it seemed a different person. With time, however, she got used to posing for her father, to his requests, to his gaze. It was harmless. In fact, he was trying to help her.

"I think he was trying to make me feel comfortable with my body."

He looked her up and down. "Why in God's name wouldn't you?"

"Indeed." She flashed her tits at him, then, with tarty wink, left him to finish shaving. She was done justifying her father's art.

On the sofa, she reread Tanja's telegram and immediately felt better. Lee had so few close female friends that their relationship had always seemed special, unique. She propped the telegram on the dresser next to the photo of the exploding hand. She looked forward to sharing her Parisian life with her old friend.

That evening, Lee decided to make headway on the series that she and Man had taken the day before. When working together, he usually manned the camera; then, in the darkroom, she coaxed out the best possible shot. These were nudes of the singer Suzy Solidor, an attractive blonde who owned a popular nightclub. Lee had a dozen plates nearly developed when a rat scurried across her foot.

"Fuck!" she shouted with a shudder. She kicked her feet and quickly turned on the light. With a jolt at the sudden brightness, she glanced at the negatives and turned it off again in a panic. Had the exposure ruined them? "Fuck, fuck, fuck, fuck," she mumbled, trying to decide what to do.

Always an advocate for denial, she quickly rinsed them, then plunged them back into the developer. Wringing her hands, waiting for images to appear, she finally called Man.

He slipped into the darkroom, "What's the matter? What's happened?"

"I turned on the lights by mistake," she said with a groan.

"Holy hell, Lee, what were you thinking?"

She felt the heat from his angry face in the dark, the tilt of his eyebrows, the flash in his eyes.

"A rat nearly bit me! What a flea hole this is."

"Christ, don't start blaming your mistakes on the studio! We can't redo these. Suzy's left town."

"I've put them back into the developer—as if nothing happened."

Still ranting, he plucked out a plate from the holder, his fingers delicately pressed against the sharp edges of the irreplaceable glass. As they stared at the wet, reflective surface, deciphering it, he went quiet; Lee breathed out in relief. An image was there, but it was reversed: some of the black areas were now white. Even more remarkably, a fine silver line had appeared around the singer's body, as if a talented draftsman had traced her outline.

"God," Lee whispered finally. "It's lovely."

"You're damn lucky, you know that?" Man pulled her close and kissed her hard.

"You seem pretty lucky yourself." Exuberant, she unbuckled his belt, sliding a hand into his pants. "That woman you're with! What spirit, what talent! In fact, I think she's just made a great new photographic discovery."

"Yeah, dumb luck," he mumbled, grasping the sink. He closed his eyes as her lips drifted down his torso, the discovery on hold.

Later that evening, Man went back to Suzy Solidor's salvaged plates and, for days after, continued experimenting with the process. For better or worse, shadows were lost, images melted, grays predominated. When he had finally learned to control the new technique, he came out of the darkroom and poured them two whiskies.

"Solarization," he said to Lee, clinking glasses. "That's what I'm calling it, kid. Solll-arization," he drawled, then gave her a smug nod. "It'll be a Man Ray trademark."

She took a sip, observing his self-satisfaction with amusement. "You know what?" She slowly licked the whisky off her lips, then smiled. "I do believe it'll be a Lee Miller trademark, too."

Tanja arrived with three enormous steamer trunks, prepared for a long stay. Man gallantly gave up his side of Lee's bed and returned to his studio, but came round every day to visit. Lee took a week off work to show Tanja around town. Although she'd done the Grand Tour on her last trip—Italy, Switzerland, and Germany—she'd missed out on Paris. Lee smiled as her friend gawked at everything: an artful street mime performing with poodles; window displays of dazzling pastries; a chic lady with a jade cigarette holder—her dress unbuttoned to expose the legal limit of cleavage—being sketched by an unwashed artist squatting atop his chair; drunken men laughing riotously inside a *pissoir*; hawkers selling everything from sprigs of lavender to a good time.

"I love it! It makes Florence seem like something out of the Middle Ages."

"You mean the Renaissance," Lee corrected.

"And it's a far cry from all those double dates we used to go on in New York," Tanja continued happily. "The polo matches, sailing in the Hamptons, your brother's flyboy friends taking us up in their two-seaters—or even the *Vogue* parties at Condé Nast's place. This is it! The real thing."

It was fun to see it all through Tanja's eyes, to feel like Paris was new.

They went out, arm in arm, and flirted with students and businessmen, danced and drank with pianists and sculptors, and were swept off to parties by international aristocrats. From time to time, Lee would disappear with a man for an hour or so, but at the end of the night, she would return to her studio, a five-minute walk from Man Ray's.

"Where did you go off to?" Tanja asked Lee one night. Still awake, she was reading in bed. "I couldn't find you, so I left."

"I went back to Vincent's place." Lee, tipsy and tottering, kicked off her high heels and dumped her coat on the floor. "I was just testing that theory. You know, that men with big noses have big . . . appendages."

"My God, Lee, you're joking. I thought you were serious about Man—whose nose, by the way, should be big enough to verify any theories." Tanja, trying to be severe, bit back a smile. "You've never been with one man for so long. I thought you two would get married."

"Marry him?" Lee dissolved into giggles. "As in a big white wedding followed by lots of babies? Come on, now."

"But aren't you happy together?"

"I enjoy his company. He's interesting, sharp, very well connected—he knows absolutely everybody—and I love working with him. But we're very different. And sometimes he drives me crazy." Lee sat down on the edge of the bed and lit a cigarette. "Really, though, I'm faithful to him in my fashion."

"Does he know you see other men?"

"We don't discuss it, but I assume so."

"Doesn't he say anything?"

"In *theory,* none of the Surrealists believe in *fidelity* or *monogamy.* Those ideas are *antiquated* and *bourgeois.*" With a scholarly finger raised, Lee emphasized the words like a Harvard lecturer, then quickly slouched down and looked over at Tanja. "You know, Man and his friends want freedom from commitment, but I'm not sure they want it for their women. Man's awfully jealous."

"Does he sleep with other people, too?"

"I doubt it, but I wish he would. Then he might stop obsessing so much over me—where I go, who I'm with, what I do, how I look." She blew a smoke ring, then watched it disappear. "Some of his cronies have several lovers. Others let the men they admire sleep with their wives, offering them up as some kind of tribute."

Tanja's hand flew up to her mouth. "Man doesn't pass you around, too, does he, Lee?"

"Now you're the one who's joking. Man wouldn't share me with anyone. He'll barely let another photographer take my picture."

XIII

———

"Do you think this miserable little drizzle will stop before the opening?"

Tanja and Lee, still in their bathrobes, looked out on the slick, wet tombs in the cemetery below. There'd been erratic showers every day since March began, and they were fed up with it.

"I hope so," Lee said, with an annoyed sigh. "I'd like to wear my open-toed shoes."

"That reminds me, what exactly does one wear to a Surrealist art exhibition in Paris?" Tanja lit a cigarette and started rifling through a trunk. "Any ideas?"

"I usually wear something simple. I like to leave extravagance to the plain girls. With their jellyfish hats and necklaces made of fingers, they're sure to get plenty of attention. Face it, sweetie, we don't need props."

They decided to wear contrasting colors, fair Lee in black, dark Tanja in white. Man came round to pick them up at eight.

"You two look lovely," he said. He took off his red scarf and wrapped it around Tanja's head, letting it drift over one shoulder, then plopped his fedora on Lee. "Now even better."

"Won't your head be cold?" she asked, admiring the angle of the hat in the mirror.

"Nah, it's stopped raining."

Man hailed a taxi on the boulevard Raspail and the trio slid in. *"On va à la Galerie Goëmans dans la rue de Seine,"* he said to the cabbie, then nestled between them. "This should be a great first show for you, Tanja. My pal Louis Aragon helped organize it. It's all collage—it's the first show of its kind, I think—with Dadaists, Surrealists, and Cubists. Really, everyone's in this show. Picasso, Duchamp, Dalí, Picabia, Magritte—"

"Man's showing two pieces," Lee said proudly. She gave him a kiss, leaving the mark of her lips on his cheek. She loved going to art events with him, both to watch people fawn over him and to talk with him about the pictures. They reminded her of the things she loved most about him—his cleverness, his creativity, his importance in the art world—and allowed her to completely forget her intermittent urges to be on her own.

Man nodded, pleased. "It'll be an interesting show."

The cab pulled up in front of a colorful crowd, which had already spilled out of the small gallery and onto the street. Heads turned as they got out.

"Regardez! C'est Man Ray!"

He was immediately swept away by admirers and fellow artists. Lee smiled at Tanja. "Everybody loves him."

The two women made their way through the mob of well-wishers and acquaintances, greeted by kisses, compliments, and inquiries about Man, and squeezed into the gallery door. Once inside, a man in a silver top hat handed each of them a glass of wine.

"À votre santé, mes belles filles."

Lee lifted her glass to him. *"Tchin-tchin!"*

Tossed around by the spirited crowd, unable to see the pictures, they finally came to a stop in a corner of the room. Lee lit two cigarettes and handed one to Tanja.

"Let's catch our breath. Here we have a good view."

"Who's that short man in the middle of everything?"

"The man in the brown suit?" Lee asked. "That's Pablo Picasso."

"No! With that terrible comb-over?" She stifled a giggle. "He's tiny."

Lee nodded. "But when you're with him, he somehow grows tall and powerful. It's the strangest thing. I've actually wondered if he's a hypnotist."

"And that furtive-looking fellow?"

"The skinny one with the thin mustache? That's Salvador Dalí, the Spanish painter. I've only met him once, but he seemed a complete neurotic. Hey, let's try to edge over to the canapés. I'm starving."

Lee ate three vol-au-vents in quick succession, and as she was pouring herself another glass of wine, Man joined them.

"What do you think?" He was beaming.

"It's a great success, darling. What a turnout!"

"I wish I'd brought my camera. It'd be great to have a shot of everyone here. Do you like the show? Picasso told me that he made that guitar with one of his old shirts. Which is your favorite?" Before she could say anything, a man in a monocle tapped him on the shoulder and led him away.

"Let's elbow our way to the pictures. I'm dying to see them," Lee said, "even if we have to start a brawl."

The first canvas they saw was by Picabia. Here, a string

made a curved line ending in a party invitation. At the top he'd painted the words *Chapeau de Paille?*

"What does that mean?" asked Tanja.

"A straw hat?" Lee exaggerated the inflection with wide, uncertain eyes, then giggled.

"I don't get it."

"It questions what you see," Lee said. "What's there and what isn't."

"If you say so. But I wonder what our old art instructors would say about it."

"I don't know about you, but when I think back on it now, I can hardly believe I ever went to the Art Students League. I mean, they claimed to be the most progressive art school in the country, but it was all so traditional. These things were unimaginable." She gestured to the various abstract collages in front of them. "Remember the classes we took? Life drawing, antique drawing, constructive figure drawing . . ." She recited the list of classes like a death toll. "It was all so tedious."

They stopped in front of Picasso's *Guitar*: a rectangular rag with a hole torn out, two strings stretching over it.

"Jesus, Lee. I don't know about this." Tanja's mouth bunched to the side. "I mean, I've seen copies of Picasso's early work. It was wonderful! When he was a kid—and I'm sure he took those same tedious classes we did at some point in his life—he could have a painted a perfect guitar standing on his head."

"Who cares about a realistic representation of a guitar? This is the essence of a guitar. A guitar at its most primitive state.

And if this is his shirt,"—she leaned in to inspect it—"he's put a bit of himself in it. His Spanishness, his song. I love it," she decided. "Let's get some more wine and make a toast to it."

"Maybe you'd be happy with just the essence of some wine? I think there's a wine stain on Picasso's shirt there."

She gave Tanja a condescending smile—"Such a card!"— but remembered having similar conversations with Man when she'd just arrived to Paris. Although she had immediately loved many of the paintings she saw—the mysterious visions of Magritte, say, or de Chirico—he had helped her understand the hidden beauty in some of the more difficult pieces, their challenge to think in a different way.

They weaved their way back to the refreshments, past women in outlandish makeup and collage dresses and men with strange accoutrements: homemade hats, a nose tie pin, a live iguana. When their glasses were refilled, Lee turned back to her friend.

"It was actually the art history class that made me want to quit painting. Studying Michelangelo, Durer, Delacroix, Goya—it seemed that all the possible paintings had already been painted. I thought, what could I possibly do that was new? Then I came here and saw what Man and his friends were doing. Turning art upside down and on its head." She took a long sip. "And I think it's more than just interesting, funny, or what have you. It's necessary."

Tanja nodded. "That, I understand. To necessary art!"

They raised their glasses and everyone around them chimed in. "Hear, hear!"

"So, do you think you'll keep up with photography?" Tanja asked quietly. She had seen Lee enthusiastic about a variety of things over the years, from screenwriting to modern dance.

"Absolutely! It's mechanical, chemical, magical, wonderful." Lee gave her a tipsy smile. "I can't imagine why I'd stop."

At the end of the evening, they were outside the gallery with Man and a dozen newly close friends: artists, poets, and the last to leave. While laughing and drunkenly singing the essence of a song, Lee stepped into a rain puddle under the street lamp. In her wet shoes, she skipped and danced, making a design with her tracks on the sidewalk. Then, with her open-toe, she topped it off with a light splash. Man Ray gave her a hug.

"That's the finest collage I've seen all night," he declared.

XIV

———

"I've got a great idea. I hope I can make it work," Lee told Tanja one morning, radiating nervous excitement as she adjusted the lights and tripod. "Look, stand behind the table and put your chin on that big book."

Lee watched as Tanja bent forward and obligingly rested her head on the book. George was also using Tanja as a model for *Vogue,* but he liked to deck her in youthful fashions to emphasize her fresh-faced good looks. Man preferred to shoot her with Lee, exaggerating their intimacy: holding each other spoon-style, double portraits, photos of near-kisses. When Lee worked with Tanja, she tried out experimental shots with her old friend, using her as an accomplice.

"No, crouch down—I don't want to see anything but your head. That's right." Lee put a large bell jar in front of the book, then checked the image through the viewfinder. "Fantastic! It looks like your head's inside the jar."

"Oh, lovely."

"Close your eyes. Right, now open your mouth a bit. Like you're having trouble breathing in there." Lee snapped several pictures. "You look like a laboratory specimen. Or like something out of *Metropolis.*"

"Can I get up now? My knees are killing me."

"Just one more. Hold it." Lee looked through the camera with a smile. "These are going to be great."

That afternoon, Lee ran through the rain to Man's studio; she wanted to use his darkroom, which was better equipped. She was still shaking her umbrella when Man handed her a new photo of his own.

"Have a look at this one." He gave her a cocky grin. "I just printed it this morning."

In it, Lee's head was thrown so far back, all that could be seen of it was the tip of her chin, transforming her long neck into something else entirely.

"It's amazing, Man." She held the photo at arm's reach and squinted her eyes. "It becomes a big prick right before your eyes."

"You *would* see that, Lee." He laughed. "Hell, I guess anyone would. I call it *Anatomies*. Most of the other ones weren't as good."

"Do you mind if I use your darkroom? I took some interesting shots of Tanja today."

"Marcel's coming over for a game of chess anyway." He motioned toward the table, where the board was already set up. "Not that I have a prayer of winning, but he always teaches me some new move."

As she was mixing the vinegary chemicals, Duchamp rang at the door. Murmurs came from the living room and Man put on a record. Lee stretched. Alone in the darkroom, the space seemed almost roomy. Gathering the trays, she noticed that Man had thrown a plate away. It was a three-quarter profile of

Lee, but turned away from the camera. It must have been taken the same day as the neck-prick. She washed it off and inspected it; Man had obviously found the negative flawed. She'd work on this one, too. The rain beat a pleasant, erratic rhythm on the outside pane of the boarded window; in the soothing darkness, she lost all track of time. It was night when she emerged. She found Man on the sofa, by himself, smoking a pipe and reading.

"I was beginning to wonder about you. I thought maybe the chemicals had done you in."

"You look really worried, too." She was holding two prints, pleased with herself. "So, do you want to see the latest Lee Miller sensations?"

He looked at the back of the photos, with the bland smile of a father waiting to see his child's finger-painting. Along with the photo of Tanja, she'd made a fine print of the plate he had chucked in the bin. Cropping the image, she'd changed it entirely: the neck looked elastic, the facial features too small. With an excited grin, she turned it around first, saving the bell jar shot for last.

"What the fuck!" he spit out, jumping up. "That's not your work! I took that shot."

"You threw it away." Lee frowned, surprised at his reaction.

"That doesn't make it yours, you crook."

"What?" She stared at his reddening face, his clenched fists; it was like looking at a stranger. "Man, you obviously didn't like it. Either that, or you couldn't be bothered to fix it. I've spent hours working on this print, reframing it, bringing out the shadows, enhancing the tones." Her voice was rising to fever pitch. "And now it belongs to me."

"You can*not* lay claim to my work, Lee Miller. Jesus, what a greedy little assistant you've become. I've given you everything, but it's never enough." She could feel his hot breath on her face; his dark eyes looked poisonous. "You'll be after my brain soon, you little bitch."

"Christ, you're an egomaniac. Take your fucking work!" She threw the prints at him; both images fluttered to the ground. "Show your friends your swell new photo. But we both know it would still be in the garbage if it weren't for me."

Lee grabbed her coat and marched out. Shaking her head, her jaw tense, she tore up the boulevard, passing Man's favorite cafés. She did not want to be surrounded by a rowdy gathering of his friends, Kiki or anyone else. She finally decided on la Rotonde—he'd said only poseurs went there these days—and ordered a whisky sour at the bar. Pulling on a cigarette, she glanced around the dining room; off-hours on a Tuesday, only a few couples were scattered around the large interior. Lee breathed out, relieved, and fished the lemon wedge out of her drink. She bit down and sucked the liquor out of it, still shaking her head. Who *was* that man back there? She couldn't understand how that photo could have stirred up such rage and resentment. She thought Man would be pleased to see the image recuperated, that he would admire her painstaking work. What an idiot he was! She dabbed tears from her eyes with her cocktail napkin, hurt and disappointed, then quickly finished her drink.

"*Une autre, s'il vous plaît,*" she said to the bartender, tapping her empty glass.

As he whisked together the bourbon, lemon juice, and

sugar, Lee looked him over. Unlike most of the men who ran the bars in Montparnasse, he was not a discreet-looking older gent, balding and well-padded; this man was young, about her age, and strikingly handsome. She wondered if the phony artists who frequented the place asked him to model. She rolled her eyes, sick of the idea of posing.

He handed her his cherry-topped creation and she raised it in a small toast. "To la Rotonde! Where bartenders need not be portly and old to fix a good drink."

With a slight cock of his head, the bartender gestured down the counter. There stood a classic Parisian barman, overly wide, formal, and mustachioed, talking to the other solitary customer at the end of the bar.

"I'm just the assistant," he said in a mock whisper, leaning over the bar.

"Yeah, I know what that's like."

"In fact, it's so dead tonight that I'm about to get off. Would you mind if I joined you for one of those?"

"Better yet two. Or three."

After another hour at the bar, they teetered back to his place next to the Montparnasse station, climbed four creaky flights, and collapsed onto his narrow bed. A night train whistled, then chugged off, making the room tremble. He didn't bother with the light; a street lamp cast a dull glow on the opposite corner of the room. She put her cold hands up into his shirt and rubbed his smooth skin, so much tauter than Man's. He smiled as he unbuttoned her dress, his teeth a shiny white, then brought her into his arms. She wriggled up to his mouth—he was long and tall—and gently bit his lip.

"You're so beautiful," he whispered in her ear. "So, so beautiful."

She stopped his mouth with a kiss; his youthful body pleased her, but his words were unbearably boring. Under a half-dozen thin blankets, they tossed and rolled; he struggled to hide his lack of finesse behind energy and bravado. She tried to slow him down, to guide him, but it was soon over. Afterward, entangled and no longer cold, they lay unnaturally still in the dimness of the room. She looked into his handsome face—his hair now fell into sleepy eyes, his mouth spread out in a silly grin—and sighed. No matter how promising they seemed at the outset—good looks, wit, talent—one-off, nameless sex partners were often unsatisfying and, in the dark, remarkably similar. It was time to go. She kicked off the covers, ready to abandon the well-knit arms of youth for the experienced ones of middle age. Surely Man's tantrum was over and he was ready to make up.

Twenty minutes later, when Lee unlocked his studio door, she saw the photo she'd printed tacked up on the wall in front of her. She gasped aloud. Man Ray had slashed her neck with a razor. Red ink ran like blood from the image of her long, white throat.

XV

At breakfast, Man let himself in with his key. Tanja was in the bath and Lee was having toast when she heard the lock turn. She looked up at him and said nothing.

"I'm sorry about last night." His rough voice made a play at tenderness; his angular face was hangdog and sad. "When you didn't come back, I just got madder and madder. I was worried about you."

"Worried like Jack the Ripper," she said with a snort. "I don't like seeing my throat slit, Man."

He came to the table and stood behind her, massaging her shoulders, running his fingers through her hair. "I don't know what came over me yesterday." He bent down and grazed her neck with his lips. "I could never hurt you, Lee. You know that."

She believed him—although he had a temper, he wasn't a violent man—but was still nettled about his vicious words and the murdered portrait, the bloody warning about his work. She was tempted to ask if he might still reconsider forfeiting ownership of the photo she'd redone, then sighed. It was too early in the morning for a theoretical discussion—Did pushing the button make him the artist?—or worse, another nasty row.

Still behind her, talking into her neck, he continued. "Maybe it had something to do with your other photo. Lee, that bell jar shot is amazing. Your best work yet." He cleared his throat gruffly. "It was so damn clever, so accomplished; well, it almost made me jealous."

She turned around to look him in the face. He looked honest and apologetic. Humbled. It was the greatest compliment he'd ever given her. She bit her lip, moved. Lee stood up and brought Man into a tight embrace; his body went slack with relief.

Tanja came out of the bathroom bundled in a large robe, a turban teetering on her head. "Good morning." She waved at the two of them, unaware of the trouble of the night before. "Is there any coffee left?" she asked, poking her nose in the pot.

The three of them took their usual places around the small table, crowded, as ever, with coffee bowls, marmalade spoons, crusts, and fruit peels. Surrounded by ordinary things, the high emotions from the night before quickly fell away.

"I met someone I really like yesterday," Tanja began shyly, glancing at both of them. "An American named Henry. Just my luck, though. In a week he's off to Syria, on an archaeological dig."

Lee did not mention her own encounter, but teased her friend instead. "You'd better watch out for that one. Archeologists are usually mummy's boys."

Man joined Tanja to boo and hiss, then patted her on the back. "That's great."

"Of course it is," said Lee. "You can have an unforgettable week here in Paris, then, for the next few months, receive love letters from exotic places. What could be better?"

"We're having lunch together today," Tanja said. "And dinner."

"In other words, I won't be seeing you for a while. I would like to meet him sometime. See if he's worthy."

Tanja smiled stupidly, then hid her face in her coffee cup, pretending she had a sip left.

"I've got a bit of news," said Man, offering cigarettes around the table.

"Don't tell me you've met someone, too?" Lee asked.

Man chuckled, clearly delighted at the hint of jealousy. "Nooo." He slowly made the round with his lighter, before continuing. "Countess Anna-Letizia Pecci-Blunt—she's the niece of Pope Leo XIII, but don't hold it against her—is having a costume ball at her house here in town. She's calling it le Bal Blanc; everything has to be white, from the décor to the guests' outfits. She wants me to create some sort of attraction." Man looked directly at her, then flicked his eyes away. "I thought maybe you'd like to help, Lee."

"So now you're Prince Charming?" She cocked an eyebrow, then clapped him on the back. "Hell yes, take me to the ball."

All morning, side by side on the small sofa, they discussed the logistics of such an event.

"When is it, exactly?" asked Lee, pencil in hand. She had her pretty leather appointment book on her knee. Bought for sittings, it was still primarily filled with social events.

"Mid-May. The seventeenth, I believe."

"My father will be here the following Saturday." She smiled at the page.

"I'd forgotten all about that," Man murmured. He lit a cigarette.

"It's just a week. He'll be staying at that hotel near the Observatoire." Lee snickered at his boyish fidgeting. "What, are you worried he won't approve of you? That he'll think you're too old and ugly for his little princess?"

Man shot her a look of panic, which made her burst out laughing.

"I'm sure he'll love you. You actually have a lot in common." She gave him a quick kiss. "Now, tell me, where is this ball again?"

"At their place, the Hôtel de Cassini," he said, moving quickly back to comfortable ground, his own turf. "It's not far from here, off the rue de Babylone. But if you walk past, all you see is a dismal gray wall. I guess they don't want us plebeians pocketing a nice view of their palace free of charge."

"That must be it."

The son of working-class immigrants, Man's entrée into French high society had come as a professional, their photographer. Lee knew that, now, even though he was famous and well-respected, he felt ill at ease around nobles—those moneyed eccentrics who enjoyed mixing with the avant-garde—and tried never to sound unduly impressed by them.

"It'll be held outside, in the gardens," he continued. "They're constructing a stage for the band and a dance floor over the swimming pool. Since everything is going to be white, my idea is to use the scene—the people themselves—as a screen. I'm going to project movies on them from upstairs."

"That's brilliant." Lee clapped her hands. "Talk about a traveling picture show. What movies are you going to use?"

"Well, I thought I'd use my own." He couldn't hide the pride in his voice. "You've never seen them, have you? I'd like to start off with *l'Étoile de mer*—"

"The starfish?" Her face went pale, her mouth, dry.

Man didn't notice. "That's right. It's based on a poem by my friend Robert Desnos. In the film, he and Kiki play a couple who find a starfish in a jar, trapped like a disembodied hand——"

He kept talking, but Lee wasn't listening. Upon hearing the word "starfish," in her mind, she was seven years old and back in Brooklyn, New York.

Her mother had fallen ill and decided Lee—or Elizabeth, as she was called then—would be better off staying with family friends, the Nilssons, until she recuperated. In the city, little Elizabeth felt like she was on holiday: the affectionate couple took her to Coney Island, bought her doughnuts, gave her crumbs for park pigeons, and let her loose in Abraham & Straus's toy department. Mr. and Mrs. Nilsson and her brother, "Uncle Bob," were so attentive—more so, even, than her own mother—that she wasn't homesick at all.

Early one morning, the young couple had gone to Manhattan on business, leaving her in the care of Uncle Bob, who lived upstairs. When Elizabeth woke up, he was watching her from the rocking chair in the corner of her room.

"Good morning, sleepyhead." He picked her up out of her cot and balanced her on his hip. "Let's have some fun today." He carried the little girl up to his rooms. "I'm going to show you my treasures. You know, I've been a sailor most of my life and, like Sinbad, I've sailed the seven seas."

Already wide awake, Elizabeth smiled in excitement, eager to hear his adventures. In his apartment, he plopped her down on his unmade bed, the tussled blankets of a restless sleeper. He pulled a wooden box out from under it and sat down next to her. Jiggling his eyebrows, he cracked it open just an inch and peeked inside.

"I want to see," Elizabeth cried.

"Of course you do," he said, taking the lid off. He first picked up a silver medallion on a long chain and handed it to her. "Can you read?"

"Yes," she said with an arrogant toss of her hair. She squinted down at the pendant and slowly made out, "Saint Christopher protect us."

"Good for you. Ol' Saint Chris is the patron saint of travelers. Good luck for sailors."

Next he brought out a sand dollar and a smudgy tuppence coin. "Put out your hands," he said, then placed one in each of her open palms. "Now, which one do you think is worth more?"

"Can you really use this one as money?" she asked, pointing to the sand dollar with her chin, her hands still outstretched.

"No, but you should," he said, taking them back and putting them aside.

Then he produced a dried starfish. Its slim, craggy legs were poetically askew; it looked like an underwater dancer who, once in the sun, had stopped midstep.

"Have you ever pretended to be a starfish?" he asked. "See if you can stretch yourself into a star."

She lay back on the bed, put her arms out straight and opened her legs as wide as she could.

"Very good." He laughed, tickling her belly. "Except starfish don't wear nightgowns."

He reached over and yanked the loose cotton nightshirt

over her head. Elizabeth, suddenly nervous, covered herself with one of the blankets.

"I'm going to play starfish, too," he said. Staring down at her with a playful smile, he unbuttoned his shirt, then took off his trousers. Elizabeth had seen her brothers naked—swimming in the creek or getting out of their baths—but Uncle Bob's body, muscular and hairy, frightened her. When he slid off his underwear, his sex was standing straight out.

He grabbed the blankets away and hovered over her. "Come on, sweetie. Remember what the starfish looks like. It keeps its legs opened wide."

"No," she whispered.

She didn't understand what he wanted, but knew to be afraid. This was no longer fun, this wasn't a game. She tried to curl into a ball, to disappear, but he forced her down and spread her legs apart. "Make a star," he grunted, rubbing himself up and down her small frame. She was already sobbing when he pushed himself inside her. Elizabeth screamed; he immediately came. As he plopped down, spent, Mrs. Nilsson burst in the room. She screamed, too.

Lee almost never thought back on that day; so long ago, it seemed almost impossible, a nightmare in which Saint Christopher broke a delicate starfish in two. Afterward, in a furor of guilt, anger, and confusion, Mrs. Nilsson packed her bags—the new teddy bear from the department store somehow forgotten—and returned Elizabeth, freshly bathed but still dribbling blood, to Poughkeepsie on the afternoon train. When her parents came to the station to fetch her, they were oddly quiet and kept a respectful distance. But even that was hazy now. What

was far more real to Lee—the memories that scarred deep—
was the treatment she then endured for gonorrhea.

Because of the horrible shame—a small child with a sailor's
disease—Elizabeth's mother, Florence, refused to take her to
the doctor, but treated her at home. Several times a week for
the next year, her mother, a former nurse, administered the
cure. In the immaculate white bathroom, Florence would bring
out the odious instruments—the glass catheter, the douche
can, the black rubber tubing—and, pursing her lips, jab her
daughter between the legs, sending burning chemicals into her
undeveloped womb. Then she prodded her cervix with cotton
swabs to remove any lingering pus. Elizabeth howled and cried,
but her frowning mother remained clinical, bent on completing
the task. When it was finished, Florence did not hug or console
her daughter. As the little girl limped out of the bathroom to
the wide-eyed stares of her brothers, her mother, in thick rubber gloves, began scrubbing wherever Elizabeth had touched
with dichloride of mercury. The seven-year-old understood
that her body was filthy. Even her touch was infectious.

Later on that year, when the physical cure was complete,
Lee's parents sent her to a Freudian psychiatrist. He made sure
little Elizabeth understood that love and sex were two entirely
separate things, a lesson she learned well. Since adolescence,
random sexual encounters had satisfied a yearning inside her:
to enjoy lust with no strings, to wield her power and beauty, to
feel her lover's burning vulnerability, to be someone else.

"Lee?" Man asked, tapping her on the knee. "Well, what do
you think?"

With his touch, her reverie broke. She got up to get a glass of water. "I don't know, Man," she said from the sink. "That film sounds sort of dark to me."

He came up from behind and put his arms around her. She fell into him, on the verge of tears. "You silly goose," he whispered in her ear. "It's because Kiki's in the film, isn't it?"

She swallowed hard. "I guess that's it."

"Well, that puts me in a pickle, sweetheart. She's in all my best work." He paused for a moment. "Hey, I've got an idea. A few years ago, I found some hand-tinted film at the flea market. What do you think of that? Projecting color film on the all-white guests?"

"That sounds perfect." Breathing out, she squeezed him tight, relieved no starfish would be projected onto her body. "Let's have a whisky to celebrate."

She forced a bright smile and began to pour.

XVI

———

The day before the ball, Man and Lee went to the mansion to do a test run. They packed the camera equipment into Man's Voisin and drove to the rue de Babylone. At the mansion, he parked his car alongside the thick outer wall.

"I wonder if we should ring at the servant's entrance?" Man mumbled.

Since the count and countess were out, the butler showed them to the second-story room with the best view of the gardens. The white walls were covered in gold relief; rococo patterns thundered from the dome ceiling to the marqueterie floor. The furniture—prissy red armchairs and settees, spindly legged tables, large mirrors with elaborate gold frames—seemed to fight the walls for attention. Lee breathed in. She'd been in elegant old Parisian apartments, with woodworked walls and gold swirls, but this was over the top. Obviously, this mind-numbing décor had given rise to the idea of a pure white party. She joined Man at the French windows and, taking his hand, looked out on the large green lawn. The stage and dance floor were finished.

"Monsieur, madame." The butler quietly approached them on the balcony. "I believe the countess plans to hang muslin curtains through those trees"—he pointed—"and white lanterns will be lighting the gardens."

Man stared at the butler uncomfortably, unsure whether he should tip him; Lee, who had grown up in a house with servants, gave the man in white gloves a regal nod.

"I'm sure it'll be marvelous. We'll set up here. *Merci*," she said, a clear dismissal.

Man, thankful to be left to his own devices, put the 35-millimeter projector together, then pulled out the reels. He opened the tin lid and held the film up to the light.

"Imagine painting a moving picture, one still at a time." He gave out a low whistle. "Not something I'd ever do. You know, this is a Georges Méliès film—and there it was, wasting away at the flea market." She looked at him blankly. "I guess you're too young to remember *Le Voyage dans la lune?*"

"Doesn't ring a bell, but then I don't know many French films. But, you know, when I was a teenager, I dreamed of going to Hollywood to be in the movies. I even practiced signing my autograph—Betty Miller—for all my fans." She laughed at her younger self.

He handed Lee an old sheet. "All right, Betty, let's see what you've got. Go into the garden and wave this around. Through the trees, on the dance floor, by the stairs. I want to see what the effect will be."

Lee raced down the stairs—startling a pair of chambermaids—and came out on the finely cut lawn. She waved up at Man, then, from the projector, saw the piercing white dot. Throwing the sheet up to the wind, she jumped around, trying to catch the colored light like butterflies in a net. She liked having the enormous garden to herself, the only one invited. On the long dance floor, she kicked off her shoes, then twirled and leaped, limbs loose, pretending she was Isadora Duncan. She could see faint traces of pink, yellow, and blue on the white platform, on the sheet, on her bare arms. With the single sheet, she was mistress of the entire lawn.

The afternoon of the ball, Lee waited downstairs in the studio, trying to guess what Man's costume would be.

"A toga?" she called up. "An angel with big feathery wings? An egg?" She smiled to herself imagining a naked Man Ray, dark and hairy, wearing half a broken eggshell.

Finally, with a satisfied grin, he charged down the stairs in shorts, a polo shirt, and a cardigan.

"Tennis whites!" She gave him a big hug. "How swell! You look like a little boy."

"I don't remember the last time I actually played," he said, flicking a racquet to and fro. "But it's perfect for an aristocrat's ball."

"You wouldn't want anyone to think you were groveling to the ruling class, would you, Man?"

"Conquer them with nonchalance and bare legs, I say."

"So do I get a tennis outfit, too?"

"Come upstairs and I'll show you," he said. He ran up, somehow invigorated by his sports clothes, and she followed. On the bed lay a chic white tennis skirt with a halter top to match. "Madeleine Vionnet designed it. She's happy for you to wear it tonight; she says she can't get better advertising than a coat hanger like you."

Lee had modeled some of Vionnet's flattering designs for *Vogue*—exquisitely draped, natural, and timeless—and loved them. She immediately put it on: the short skirt, the ankle socks and flat shoes, the top. Man tied the halter in double knots so no wise guy could undo it. She added some lipstick, then turned to him and curtsied.

He whistled. "You'll be the belle of the ball."

"Or at least the belle of the projection room."

That evening, Man Ray slowly turned his long car into the mansion's narrow street, stopped at the gate, and rang. A couple of menservants, dressed all in white, were soon at the door; one carried the photography equipment into the house, while the other parked the car down the road. Lee and Man walked into the spectacular garden. Long, thin curtains blew through the trees, while hundreds of lanterns bobbed on the branches like houses for fairy folk.

The servants were buzzing over last-minute preparations. The champagne fountain was being arranged in one corner, while the white-clad orchestra was settling in onstage. Lee and Man followed the valet upstairs to the Louis XIV projection room, checked everything, then went to the bar for a drink.

As the guests began to arrive, Lee strolled around the garden to see if she knew anyone. There was the pianist Arthur Rubinstein, posing as an oriental prince, and Jean Cocteau, whom she recognized despite a powdered wig and plaster mask, because of his long, skinny legs. Amused, she noticed that the countess had elevated her rank and become an empress.

Back inside the mansion, she found Man on the upstairs balcony. When a handful of couples began dancing on the white platform, he switched on the projector. Vibrantly colored figures and faces, distorted by distance and movement, suddenly came to life on the guests. The dancers gasped, stopped, and tried to grab the images, to straighten them out on their clothes. People crowded onto the dance floor, whirling a waltz, laughing in delight as they saw their partner's face turn green, then orange, an oblong mermaid flit on a shoulder, yellow skeletons land on a large behind.

"It's stunning!" Lee cried, looking down from the balcony, arm in arm with Man. Her feet tapped to the music as she watched the happy crowd below. After another minute, she blurted out, "Oh, Man, you wouldn't mind if I went down for a little bit? To see the effect up close?"

"Of course not," Man said. "I can't go with you, though. When this film is over, I'm putting on another one. Then I guess I'll repeat the Méliès. They do seem to like it." He looked down on the crowd, pleased with their reaction.

"See you in a minute," Lee called from the door, then disappeared.

In the dark garden, waltz turned to jazz. She walked toward the white dance floor with her hands in the air, trying to touch the movie-colors like a child reaching for a rainbow. Suddenly, one hand was plucked down. It was the baron, George Hoyningen-Huene, dressed as a sheik.

"Lee, darling," he said, twirling her around once. "You look fabulous—and you won't get too hot on that packed dance floor." He cocked his head in that direction. "Shall we?"

After dancing with George, Lee went from one partner to the next, doing the foxtrot, the Charleston, the tango. As she started the Lindy Hop, the film changed, from colored fantasy to black-and-white script. Everyone on the dance floor tried to read each other's bodies, to find a full word. The man dancing beside her lunged at a shape on her arm: "Got 'u'!" he cried in English, delighted with his wit. Lee looked up at the balcony to wave at Man, but could only see the flickering light from the projector. After a few more numbers, she wound back through the garden and up the wide staircase, to see how he was doing.

"You having fun?" Clearly annoyed, his lips jerked into a terse smile. "You do realize, Lee, that you are not a guest. You're my assistant. That's the only reason you're here."

"I know, darling." Taking his hand, she pretended not to notice his dark mood and opted for flattery. "What a success! Everyone just *loves* your idea. It's dangerous out there, though," she said, changing to a semi-serious tone. "Lots of toe-steppers. I guess the lights distract them. I wish *you* could dance with me. You're a much better dancer than those stodgy ole aristocrats."

He slid his arm around her and gave her a kiss, cut short as the Méliès film clicked to an end. "I'm turning off the projector. The novelty's worn off, anyway. I'm going to start taking photos now. Could you carry the tripod for me?"

As soon as Man had the camera ready for portraits in the downstairs hall, a line of guests appeared, ready to be captured in tall hats and long pearls, feathers and thick makeup, as Greek statues, sailors, royalty, or buccaneers—but white, all white. Lee was setting up the tripod when the count, dressed as Voltaire, asked her to dance. She looked apologetically at Man; he couldn't rightly refuse his employer. He nodded peevishly at her, swatting the air with his hand.

"Don't be long," he muttered to her back.

The platform, without the swimming lights and colors, was not so crowded. On their first turn around the floor, the count whispered in her ear, "Please tell me you're a Yankees fan."

"Excuse me?" she faltered; had she misunderstood him?

"The Yankees! Babe Ruth, Lou Gehrig, Bob Meusel . . . Murderer's Row? Say, aren't you a New Yorker?"

"Yes, I'm from New York." She looked up at Voltaire, confused. "You like baseball?"

"Of course I do! I'm from Manhattan."

The American count spoke eagerly of home, but was interrupted when, during the next dance, a Russian prince cut in. After them, a French marquis followed an English earl. "Noblesse oblige," he said with a grin. Lee delighted in the attention, flirting and dancing—fast numbers on the platform, slow ones in the shadow of the trees—and remembered Man only vaguely. Finally, hot and thirsty, she went to the bar for more champagne and saw him there, alone, drinking a whisky.

"Rubbing shoulders with high society, I see." His voice slurred slightly, his eyes were angry slits.

"Everyone's so nice." She put her arm around him. "They just wouldn't let me leave the dance floor." She looked around. "Are you finished with the photos?"

"Ran outta plates." He took another long sip. "An hour ago."

She could feel heat rising off him; if they weren't in a palace, he'd be yelling and cursing.

"Do you want to get some food? They're setting up a buffet outside."

"I've had it with this place." He'd been working; his shift was over. "Let's go."

"You're sure?" Lee asked, disappointed.

She opened her mouth again to protest—she could have stayed till dawn—but clamped it shut when he glared at her, his eyes reflecting white. Lee wasn't afraid of him, but didn't want a fight, not there. She could imagine what that would look like: two low-born, drunken servants loudly bickering in the royal chambers, horrifying the bluebloods. "All right," she mumbled, and bolted down her champagne, dreading his jealous accusations and desperate expressions of love.

Back at his place, there was no argument. In silence, in bed, he loved her violently—strangling, bashing, grappling, pounding—as if trying to prove that her body was his, that he could do what he pleased with it. No nobleman, no party guest had access to her now. With no enjoyment, she stared at the naked ceiling; she couldn't bear to see the urgency in his eyes, the sweat dripping off his hair, the lipless mouth, grunting like an ape. She let him work out his anger, knowing it would be over soon. Long after he'd drifted off to sleep, Lee lay awake, his hot body still pressed next to hers, trying to decide if it was worth it.

When she woke up the next morning, his side of the bed was cold. She called out; no one answered. She found the downstairs empty, but saw he'd been making prints. A new batch lay scattered on the coffee table. There was a cropped enlargement of her lips, grainy but full and sensual. Underneath were her fingers, barely touching her mouth, holding back a secret. Last was her solitary eye staring back at her from the table, all-seeing, accusing, a witness. He had chopped her to bits.

XVII

Theodore Miller's train was due in from Stockholm at noon; after a business trip to Sweden, he'd been keen to tack on a visit to see his only daughter. Lee bustled Man into the car an hour early. "We can't be late," she kept repeating. Man dodged trolley cars and automobiles, street sweepers and school children—nearly hitting a chubby man who'd lost his hat in a roundabout—over the Seine to the Right Bank, past the busy hub of Les Halles, to the Gare du Nord. They arrived with thirty minutes to spare and went to wait under the glass-and-iron latticework. Pacing the platform nervously, Man fumbled with his cigarette holder, then his lighter. Lee took it from his hand and lit both their cigarettes.

"Christ, Man, you act like he's bringing his shotgun with him. 'Make an honest woman of my daughter or else!'" She said in a hillbilly voice, raising her fist. "Really, my father's not like that at all."

"I guess I don't know what to expect. All I really know about your dad is that he's an engineer who likes photography." He took a sidelong glance at her, undoubtedly thinking of her father-daughter photo sessions. "You never talk about your family. Or your childhood."

Lee raised an eyebrow. Man was hardly forthcoming about his life before Paris. In the year they'd been together, he'd only let slip a few details: his father was a tailor, he had a couple of sisters, his full name was Emmanuel, he'd been married. During the course of their relationship, she was sure she'd revealed more about her former life—always convinced, however, that some things were better left unsaid.

"All right, then," Lee said with a decisive nod. "I'll begin at the beginning. My parents met at the hospital. My father had typhoid, my mother was a nurse. They married and had three children: first John, then me, then Erik. We all lived together on a huge farm called Cedar Hill. Now, doesn't that paint you a charming picture?"

"Sounds absolutely idyllic."

"Ah, but wait." Lee held up her hand with the melodrama of a silent-picture star. "My parents are progressive sorts—modern-day eccentrics, if you will—that have shocked the town of Poughkeepsie with their outlandish ideas. Birth control, atheism, colonic irrigations, electric blankets . . . Why, the gentle townsfolk didn't know what to think when my dad brought long, flat runners back from Sweden and began gliding over the snow with them."

She chuckled with Man over these more endearing aspects of their quirky domestic life, but didn't mention the darker ones. For years, she'd overheard her parents' arguments, most having to do with her father's many affairs. Elizabeth, who had never been close to her mother—a dowdy, stern, envious woman—had understood her father's desires to have liaisons, to be with women who were warmer or more fun. Then, when she was seventeen, her mother had a nervous breakdown. Theodore, ever practical, tried to solve the problem by giving his wife a new Ford. The next morning, after making breakfast for the family, she locked herself in her new car and turned on the engine, breathing in fumes and waiting to die. Theodore broke down the garage door and pulled her into the open air in time to save her, but that turn of events had given Elizabeth pause. It was perhaps the first time in her young life that she'd realized that other people had strong feelings, that other people suffered. It didn't, however, improve her relationship with her mother.

"What about your brothers?"

"Well," Lee began, finding her carefree voice again. "John's my mother's little darling. When he was little, she dressed him in lace gowns and bonnets and let his hair grow long. And now, as a grown man, he's mad about flying machines and has become an aviator—hell, he even knows Lindbergh!—but he still likes dressing in women's clothes."

Man nearly choked on a puff of smoke. "I guess you two have that in common."

"Oh, he probably has nicer things than I do," Lee said. "And then there's Erik, my little brother. He once told me that he was glad that each of our parents had picked a favorite before he was born. They left him alone."

"So that makes you your father's favorite."

"That's right." She nodded. In fact, from the time she was born, her moods, desires, and tantrums had dominated the family home; when Florence lost patience with her, Theodore took his daughter's side. After her harrowing experience in

Brooklyn, while her mother probed and scrubbed, her father spoiled her, trying to give her back her confidence, her sense of entitlement. "But he's my favorite, too. He's always stood behind me, no matter what."

Man took hold of her waist and pressed himself against her backside. "I'll stand behind you," he whispered in her ear.

"Very funny," she said, unraveling his hands and stepping away. Would Man be jealous of her father, too? A train sputtered into the station, whistling through steam; Lee looked at her watch and her face lit up. It was time. "This must be it."

They watched the people sail past them, tall women with trunk-laden porters struggling behind them, aging blond men speaking German or Dutch, bewildered English families spending their first summer on the Continent. Lee scanned the crowd for her father with an eager smile. She finally found him down the platform—a slim, balding man, with round glasses and a high collar—and began to wave.

"That's him!"

"The one who looks like a strict schoolmaster?" asked Man, his jaw clenching.

"What were you expecting? A bohemian businessman? A foppish engineer?"

When Theodore caught his daughter's eye, his thin lips broke into a grin. He rushed through the crowd and wrapped her in his arms. "Princess!" She breathed in his scent, Ivory soap and hair oil, and felt like a little girl.

"And this must be Man Ray." Theodore kept one arm around his daughter but held out the other to her lover; he stood opposite them, far shorter and darker than the Millers, and managed a fidgety smile. While they shook hands, Lee watched her father inspect Man's face with his piercing blue eyes. "I'm an admirer of your work."

"Lee tells me you're a photographer as well," Man said. "You're welcome to use my darkroom while you're here, sir."

"It would be an honor." Theodore nodded, approval already registering on his face.

"Let's get you settled in at the hotel and then have some lunch at Man's studio," said Lee. "Tanja will join us later. She's modeling at *Vogue* today."

Theodore smiled. "Sounds perfect."

At the studio, while Lee made coffee and sandwiches, her father browsed the artwork on the walls, the objects carefully arranged on the tables. She heard him complimenting Man on the quality of the prints (and the models) and express special interest in the rayograms. Man was explaining how they were made—the tension of meeting Theodore had rolled off his shoulders back at the station—when Lee came in with a tray.

"You know, Elizabeth, I think your friend here would have made a brilliant engineer. Everywhere I look," he began, gesturing at Man's bricolage: the chess set he'd made from wood scraps, the makeshift minuscule cities towering on side tables, the wires, celluloid, and tools in his rayograms, "I see the work of a mechanical mind."

"That is high praise indeed, coming from you." Lee smiled at her father and gave Man's hand a squeeze. She broke off the end of her baguette, then asked, "So, tell me. How're things in P'ok?"

Theodore chuckled at his daughter. "Ol' Poughkeepsie

hasn't changed much. Of course, the Crash took some people by surprise. There's a soup kitchen downtown now, lots of men out of work. But our plant hasn't been affected. Everything's fine there." He wiped his hands on a napkin and pulled a thin envelope out of his breast pocket. "I haven't taken many photos since you've been away. Elizabeth here has always been my favorite subject," he said to Man, who nodded in agreement, "but I've taken a few."

Lee and Man huddled together to look at the snapshots. The first ones were of the farm—the large two-story house, the pond, the pastures. "I thought you'd like to see some pictures of home." He turned to Man. "We've got about a hundred and seventy-five acres of mixed terrain. Fields, woods, a fine stream. You should have seen our little tomboy Li-Li, climbing trees, fishing, skating on the pond, sledding. We could barely keep her in the house!"

Lee smiled down at the pictures. She'd loved growing up on the farm. That is, until she'd hit puberty, when country life suddenly became excruciatingly boring, and she'd yearned for new distractions and urban entertainments.

There was a shot of her brothers—good-looking, dark-haired young men—posing in front of an aircraft. "Erik is helping John fix that plane. It was wrecked in a flying circus." In the next, her father kneeled beside a dead stag. "Erik took that one. Hunting season was excellent this year." He sighed in satisfaction, then turned to the last one. "And here's your mother. She's well as ever," he said with a trace of indifference.

Emotionless, Lee gazed at the woman in the photo, her wide, doughy face, her double chin, her cold smile. She nodded—"Glad to hear it"—then looked up at her father. He gave her a doting look. All the things her father loved about her drove her mother to distraction. Florence had always wanted her to be ladylike, demure, someone else. She looked back at the family photos. Lee looked like none of them, not her parents or her brothers. She had no idea what strange alchemy had created her looks.

Theodore put the photos back in the envelope—"These are for you, princess"—then began to ask questions about Paris life, Man's jazz records, the pieces around the room. Lee watched the two men—her father and her lover—caught up in animated conversation. She was pleased to see them getting along so well, but couldn't help but feel a bit left out. She wasn't used to sharing her father's attention.

When their conversation finally began to wind down, Lee pulled out some prints and held them facedown on her lap. Theodore, politely deferring to his host on all subjects photographic, was acting like Man Ray was the only photographer in the room.

"Daddy, I've got some photos to show you, too. You know I've been modeling here, but I've also been doing a lot of work as a photographer. Man and I have spent hours in the darkroom together." Lee looked over at Man, whose lips were quivering in an attempt not to smirk. "And now I'm taking pictures for *Vogue* as well."

Excited about sharing her work with her father, her first mentor, she started off slowly, conventionally. Models in fashionable gowns, fragrance bottles reflected on a mirror. Then she took out her odder pieces inspired by the Surrealists' aesthetic: rats lined up on a wall, their tails hanging down; angry painted cows, trapped on a carousel; Tanja's face in the bell jar. Whatever the subject, he looked at them closely, marveling at the quality, at the fineness of the work.

"I must say, you're better now than your old man." With a warm smile, he patted her leg, then looked over at Man. "When she was a girl, I gave her a box Brownie. Even then, I was impressed with some of her photos: close-ups of the donkey, her friend Minnow covered in clover. She loved to watch me develop prints in the darkroom—she thought it was magic, that I was a wizard. But now the student has surpassed the master. As it should be."

"Someday she may even surpass me," Man said. He also gave her a proud, paternal smile. "I've never had an assistant who learned so quickly."

Glowing with their praise, she brought out the last few: three solarized portraits, each one more dramatic than the last.

"What's this?" Theodore stared down at the backward tones, the dramatic outlines. "It's completely new."

Both began talking about solarization at once; Lee about the accidental discovery—"It was all thanks to a rat!"—and Man the painstaking technique he had developed. They laughed excitedly, interrupting each other to add details.

"Really, I don't know who did what," said Lee finally, looking at Man with affection.

"It's magnificent. One of you will have to show me how it's done," Theodore said. "Elizabeth, are you up for some time in the darkroom today?"

"Actually, I have a sitter coming this afternoon. I would have canceled, but it's royalty." She gave them a humble shrug.

"It's the Maharani of Cooch Behar. She's lovely, always decked out in beautiful saris, silks, and jewels. She's the regent and a mother of five, but here she is in Paris, escaping it all."

"Lee's been getting a lot of calls for sittings since le Bal Blanc. I don't know what gave them the idea she was a photographer," Man said drily. He turned to Theodore. "I'll be happy to show you the technique in the darkroom. Then tonight, when Lee and Tanja are free, we can all go to la Coupole. And after dinner, why don't we go hear Kiki sing?"

"Wonderful!" Theodore nodded energetically.

Lee breathed out in annoyance.

Toward the end of the week, after a Seine river cruise, a trip to Versailles, and an inspection of the Paris sewers, Theodore Miller was itching to take some art photographs.

"Girls?" he began, fiddling with his camera and eyeing Lee and Tanja.

They were still in their pajamas, reading the newspaper in the double bed they shared. In fact, neither of them had gotten up yet; Man had brought them coffee and croissants on a tray. They looked up at Theodore at the same time.

"I was wondering if you two could model for me today. I'd like to take some compositions like the ones we made in Poughkeepsie. You remember?" He turned to Man Ray. "I find nude studies of two or three women *together* most preferable. The overcrossing limbs, the entangled hair. Using one body as a background for another's close-up. Such artistic possibilities . . ."

Man nodded his head, regarding his would-be father-in-law with awe. "I couldn't agree more."

"Well, girls, what do you say?" Theodore clapped his hands.

"I'm sorry, Mr. Miller." Tanja picked up a croissant crust and considered it. "I'm going to have to say no."

"That's too bad." Theodore looked like a child who had been given the wrong present on Christmas morning. "I hope there's nothing wrong."

"Actually, there's something very right." Tanja smiled shyly. "I've only told Lee so far, but you two might as well know. Henry has asked me to marry him."

"The young archaeologist?" Man said, surprised. "What, has he proposed by post?"

"Yes!" Tanja laughed. "We're getting married as soon as he gets back from Syria."

"Congratulations!" Man tugged her out from under the covers, propped her up and gave her a hug. "That's wonderful news."

"Best wishes, my dear," Theodore said as he shook her hand. "That's very fine indeed. But what does that have to do with you posing for pictures?"

"I just don't think Henry would be too keen on the idea."

"Is this fiancé of yours really such a prude?" Theodore asked. "That doesn't bode well, to my mind."

"Daddy." Lee scowled. "Let Tanja be. If she doesn't feel like posing, that's up to her. I'm sure we can find some other models for you while you're here. Right, Man?"

"In Montparnasse? If you throw a stone, you'll accidentally hit three."

A few hours later, Man and Lee went to the cafés in search of models. On le Dôme's terrace, they found the painter Pascin.

Over his clothes, he was wearing the long, checkered bathrobe he used for painting; a flop of dirty hair, which quivered when he talked like the tail of a nervous bird, was half-plastered to his cheek. He was drinking spiked coffees with two pretty girls, a blond Italian and a dark-haired Russian, both snuggled up in enormous wooly sweaters.

"Pascin! What a pleasure."

"Man. *Ma belle.*" He gave Lee a kiss flush with whisky fumes. "Join us."

They perched on chairs and got down to business. Theodore was waiting at Lee's studio, anxious to get started.

"We're looking for models," said Man. "Girls to pose for photos, not paintings. Just for the afternoon. Most of the women I work with seem to be out of town. Is there anyone around that you would recommend?"

"These two here have modeled for me." He gestured to the women at his side. "Don't be put off by these potato sacks they've got on." He pulled up a handful of knit-work from each sweater—"*Mon Dieu*, are *both* your grannies blind?"—then turned back to Man with a shake of his head. "They actually have nice bodies. And I can vouch for their skills. These dirty little bitches are limber." He gave his fingertips an appreciative kiss as the girls twittered with giggles.

Man looked them over. "I can offer you a day's wages—" he began. Without another word, they bounced off their chairs, ready to go. Pascin raised his coffee cup in a farewell salute.

When they walked in, Theodore bowed stiffly and greeted them in his formal, though limited French.

"*Je suis heureux de faire votre connaissance, mesdemoiselles.*"

They giggled again.

Lee began setting up her tripod.

"What are you doing, Lee?" asked her father, frowning in confusion.

"I'm going to take pictures, too. You don't mind, do you?"

"But, princess, I want you to model."

"Daddy, there're already two girls here—"

"And you're far prettier than either of them. It isn't right for you to be on the sidelines, taking pictures with us old men." He gave Man the wink of a comrade-at-arms. "Please, Li-Li?"

"If it means that much to you," she said sulkily. "I'll be posing, too," she told the other girls in French.

While the two photographers manned themselves with cameras, Pascin's friends kicked off their shoes, unfastened their stained stockings, and slid them down into silken heaps; with their bulky sweaters off, Theodore snapped a few candid shots of them unbuttoning each other's dresses. Silently steaming, Lee began taking off her clothes as well. After all the praise he had given her photographs during this trip, her father still thought of her foremost as his model, his beautiful little girl. Still a teenager on the sleeping porch in P'ok. She supposed parents never let their children evolve too much; regression was de rigueur.

"Elizabeth, I'd like to take a few shots of you and the blonde on the bed." He peeked down into his camera, adjusting the focus. "Side by side, like a reflection, an echo. Lovely. Now, bring your mouths together, as if you were going to kiss. That's right." He took a few more shots, then motioned to the brunette. "Could you join them, please?"

Lee did as she was told, nuzzling a neck, arching backward on the bed, propping her legs up on the wall. She could feel the excitement emanating from the men; she could hear the shutters snapping faster and faster, like breathing, like panting.

"Elizabeth, you're grimacing, darling. Just close your eyes. That's right."

As the afternoon light began to fade, the photographers decided to stop, satisfied with the day's work. Pascin's friends quickly got dressed and put on their hats. Lee watched them reapply their lipstick. Although she had been tussling on the bed with these two women for an hour, feeling their warm skin and smelling the bitter coffee on their breath, she didn't know them, their names, their stories. Modeling was such a strange business: women playing make-believe for the camera; men taking photos that told a nonexistent story.

"I'm going to get in the bathtub," she said to the two men, busy packing up equipment and going over the potentially best shots.

As she lay soaking, she imagined asking Theodore and Man if she could take a nude series of them. Just a few saucy poses—simple acrobatics, playful fondling, a love bite or two. She laughed aloud picturing their shocked faces.

The next day, before the boat train to Cherbourg departed, Man offered to take double portraits of Lee with her father. In a dark suit, the sixty-year-old sat up straight in Man's posing chair.

"Lee, where do you want to be?" asked Man. "Do you want to stand behind the chair?"

She plopped down on her father's lap. Nestling her head on his shoulder, she closed her eyes. She remembered falling asleep in those arms, warm, in front of the fire. How effortlessly, almost magically, they would lift her up and carry her off to bed. For better or for worse, Lee would always be his princess, his favorite, his girl.

She knew her relationship with her father was unconventional. Most fathers would turn their heads in shame from their daughters' nudity, would pretend they were asexual beings, even after they'd become mothers. But neither she nor her father were very ordinary. They both burned with curiosity, loved novelty and the outré. Their relationship, as singular as it might be, was the most important one she had. He'd always been her ally, her champion. With him, she felt safe.

"Now look at me," Man said.

She sat up and put her arms around her father's neck; his arms wound around her waist. When their brows touched, they looked at the camera. Neither one smiled. They were united, the photographer, an outsider.

At the train station, Theodore shook Man's hand warmly. "It's been a pleasure. Thank you for everything." He hugged his daughter and spoke into her ear. "I understand why you want to be here, in Paris, with him. This Man Ray is an extraordinary man." He looked her in the eyes. "But come see us sometime. We miss you back home."

"I miss you, too."

After the train pulled out of the station, off toward the Atlantic, Lee looked at Man with renewed admiration. His mind, his repute, his milieu, his skill and grace, his love for her— he *was* extraordinary. With a warm smile, she wove her arm through his and gave it a squeeze.

"Daddy likes you," she said.

XVIII

It was September. While Parisians were returning from their summer holidays, Tanja, newly married to her archeologist, went back to the States and Man Ray left for Cannes. His friend Picabia had managed to set up an exhibition for him there, and he would be gone a month. Most people did not consider photography a medium worthy of an art gallery, but Man had decided to try his luck; he knew from experience that his canvases wouldn't sell. Lee debated joining him for the late-summer sunshine on the Riviera, but opted for the time alone. Even though her relationship with Man had been on an upswing again since her father's visit, a romance this long—over a year!—was still a constant challenge.

As Paris came back to life after the summer, Lee's appointment book began filling up. While Man was away, she had a dozen sitters pose: a few royals, including the Duchess of Alba and that dapper divorcé, Duke Vallombrosa, as well as some American literati and wealthy Parisians. Most of the latter brought their children or—even worse—their pets. Apart from the private sittings, she also kept her hours at the *Vogue* studio, went to dance clubs with friends, and, when she wanted, had a fling. After three weeks of complete independence, meeting no one's expectations but her own, she was starting to look forward to having Man back.

By the end of the month, on a chilly, gray Sunday, she decided to go to his studio. For a few days now, she'd been feeling the blue jitters creeping in and wanted to stave them off with good thoughts. Memories of her first months in Paris, their artistic collaborations, their laughter. She let herself in—a faint smell of pipe tobacco was still in the air—put on one of his jazz records, then stood at a table, rearranging his building blocks. Instead of feeling better, she was overwhelmed with nostalgia. Was this longing what the poets call love? Did she really need him the way he claimed to need her? Or was this melancholy? Just passing boredom?

Suddenly, there was a knock at the door. Slightly startled, she answered it to find André Breton, the writer of manifestos, shaking his umbrella. He took off his hat in the entranceway; underneath, his hair was combed back in its perfect mold.

"Oh, hello, Lee. Isn't Man here?" He looked past her, into the room.

"No, he won't be back from Cannes until tomorrow or the next. Can I do anything for you?"

"I wanted to give him a copy of my new magazine, *Le Surréalisme au service de la révolution.* It's the first issue." He held up a thin, plain journal for her to admire. "Man was a great help getting it together—and he's got a few pieces in there, too. Make sure he gets it." He handed the magazine to Lee and replaced his hat. "That's a good girl." With a half-wave, he went back out the door.

Shaking her head at Breton's patronizing superiority, she

plunked down on the sofa and lit a cigarette, curious to see the latest from Man and his cronies: the charming poets, crazy painters, talented writers, and stuffy phonies; some, men of genius. Lee opened the magazine to a random page and there, scowling back at her, was her own face, trapped in a wire mesh. Rolling her eyes, she blew out a puff of smoke. Although she liked most of Man's ideas—even the most provocative or revealing poses—she'd resented putting that stupid thing on her head. Her hair and makeup done, she'd been about to go out when Man called from downstairs.

"Hey, Lee! Come here!"

She'd looked down from the top of the stairs. The corner was draped in black, and he was standing below, holding that filigree snare.

"Lose the dress, will you," he'd said, with an impatient wave of his cigarette. "I want to take a few shots with this."

"Can't it wait? I'm meeting George and Tatiana in a few minutes." She looked at her watch. "I'm already running late."

"Come on, Lee," Man jerked his head, motioning to the corner. "I've got a great idea. It won't take long. If you want you can just pull your dress down to the waist. Seriously, if you're late, those Russkis can keep each other company."

Lee sat in the corner and yanked down the top of her dress. Obviously, when *he* was inspired, saying no was not an option. She seemed to remember the muses of Greek myth as capricious, never at the artist's beck and call; yet hers was a full-time job. He stuck the wire mesh on her head and nodded, pleased with himself. From various angles and with different lighting, he'd proceeded to take a full roll of film.

She peered at the magazine reproduction. Underneath the wire, her features smoldered with resentment. Her eyes flickered down to the caption. YOUNG WOMEN: THE RAW MATERIAL TO POWER THE CREATIVE ARTS.

Lee poured herself a shot of whisky, then sat back down, sipping it slowly. She supposed many people would be flattered to think of their face, body, or character as the inspiration for an artist: that his work depended on their presence. Ah, the vanity of it. She stuck her tongue into the shot glass to lick up the last few drops. And such a poetic idea, she used to revel in it herself. But being a muse was not enough anymore.

With a pleasant buzz in her head, she picked up the magazine and leafed through the rest: an obligatory article boasting their alliance with the Soviet Union (*Vive le Communisme!*), an anti-clerical poem, muddy gray reproductions of paintings—dreamscapes and grotesque images. . . . Then, on the last page, she let out a gasp. There was her photograph of Tanja's head, trapped inside the bell jar. Had Man intended this as a surprise for her? Was she, then, part of their group? She eagerly read the caption underneath it: HOMAGE TO LE MARQUIS DE SADE. PHOTO: MAN RAY. She stared at the words, her head cocked, her mouth agape.

Remembering the tantrum Man had thrown after she'd reworked his discarded plate, she wanted to tear the magazine to shreds or stab it with a knife. Instead, she threw it across the room. The fucking hypocrite! How dare he steal her work, passing it off as his own? She gulped down another shot of whisky and paced, her stride too long and fast for the small studio. It was the first artistic photo she'd had published—her fashion shots didn't count—and she didn't even get credit. Her photo, his name. Did he think she'd never find out? He'd admitted to being envious of the shot. Had he swiped it, pure and simple? Forgotten to tell Breton it was hers? Or could it have been an honest mistake? Surely not. *Her* photo, *his* name.

Suddenly, she stopped pacing and smiled to herself. It occurred to her that the pompous bastards who esteemed this "original Man Ray" were in fact taken by her work, the vision of *Madame*. She'd hoodwinked them! Fury became pride as she picked up the splayed journal and looked at the photo again. It was a fabulous image, first-rate. Scanning it carefully, she looked for any changes; no, he hadn't retouched it. It was just as she'd developed it, just as she'd thrown it at him that night he lost his senses. The anger came crashing back. How shifty he was, how two-faced! She reread the caption, shaking her head. Her photo of Tanja—a tribute to Sadism? Who the *hell* had come up with that?

By dusk, she was tipsy and desperate for air.

She called her friend Tatiana Iacovleva. Since Tanja left—really, since she'd fallen in love and stopped going out—Lee had mostly been palling around with the sophisticated Russian model.

"Tata, darling?" Her voice was calm; she wanted to forget her anger, not dwell on it. Besides, Tatiana probably wouldn't understand how she was feeling—not that she did herself. "Sorry for calling so late. Do you have plans for dinner? I want to dress up and go out on the town."

"There's a soirée tonight, but it doesn't start until nine o'clock. Where do you want to go?"

"Let's go to the Ritz," Lee said. "I'm in the mood for the Right Bank tonight."

"All right. I quite like the Ritz now," Tata said, "since the Crash cleared out all the bores."

Seated in the middle of the room, Tata and Lee immediately drew attention from admirers who peeked at them through the palms and flower arrangements, or stared at their reflections in the mirrors. One stately gentleman, dining alone, sent over a bottle of champagne, but they couldn't be bothered to invite him to join them; Lee was not up for small talk just yet. Looking at the menu, she was suddenly starving. When her first course came—a borscht—she spooned on a heap of sour cream and dug in.

"Delicious." She offered some of the hearty soup to Tata, who had ordered a dainty crab salad.

"Very authentic. It's the fennels." Tatiana nodded, then took another bite. "It reminds me of my grandmother." She went back to her salad with a long sigh.

Lee glanced over at her friend. Although they were both expatriates who had chosen a life in Paris, she sometimes forgot that, since the revolution, the Russians couldn't go home if they wanted to (not that she would care if she were exiled from Poughkeepsie). She savored her last bite of borscht, thinking of Breton's love affair with the Soviets. Perhaps she should introduce him to Tatiana, surely she could give him a different point of view. She refilled her glass and sat back with a cigarette, determined to forget all about the Surrealists, photography, and Man Ray.

"So, where are you going tonight?"

"To Zizi Svirsky's place. Do you know him?"

"Zizi?" Lee grinned. In French, that was what little boys called their penis. "You've *got* to be kidding."

"No, unfortunately. He's Russian, too. Maybe it's short for Ziven?" Tata shrugged.

"That's even worse! 'I'm Zizi, but it's short.'" Lee laughed.

"Zizi is perfectly adorable," Tata said, pouring herself the last of the champagne. She glanced around the room, as if wondering who would provide the next bottle. "He trained as a concert pianist but suffers from such terrible stage fright, he's never been able to perform."

"Zizi has performance anxiety?" Lee's eyes twinkled.

"Yes, darling, I guess he was afraid he wouldn't measure up." Tata giggled, then dismissed the joke with a wave of her hand. "He works as a decorator, and his rooms are *gorg*eous. Do come along! What host wouldn't want the pair of us?"

They clinked glasses and finished the champagne.

They took a cab to Svirsky's apartment, in an elegant building next to Parc Monceau.

"You'll have a grand time," Tata said, reapplying her lipstick before getting out of the taxi. "Zizi knows everyone. I've told him to find me a title to marry, but I think he's too fond of me to get serious about it."

As soon as they entered the salon, Tata was swept off by a group of elegant émigrés; Lee went in search of the powder room. In one corner, a trio of black jazzmen—Americans, surely—played banjo, saxophone, and stand-up bass while an international crowd danced, chatted, or simply decorated the colorful rooms. Walking to the rhythm of the beat, her shoulders bobbing and hips swinging, Lee took in the eclectic collections of exotic rugs and statuary, antiques and Art Deco, modern paintings and naïf tapestries. Warm and worldly, innovative and chic, it made the Bal Blanc palace—with its rococo walls and pre-Revolution gilt—seem ridiculous.

Lee smiled graciously at several attentive young men—each one trying his best to latch on to her—before she finally found the lavatory. Waiting outside the door was a man of about fifty. Tall, fair, and impeccably dressed, he was not especially handsome, but looked vigorous and fun. Crow's feet danced around his blue eyes; a thin mustache twitched with contained laughter.

"I don't know if we've met," he said. His bow was formal yet slightly farcical. "Welcome to my home."

"You must be Zizi." Lee's smile was mischievous, but charming nonetheless. "Your home is one of the most beautiful I've seen."

Drinking vodka cocktails, she spent the rest of the evening with her host. He had none of Man Ray's gloom or temper; in fact, silly and carefree, he seemed his opposite. Lounging on the smile-shaped divan, he made her laugh with his frivolous talk and only became serious when discussing fashion and design.

"I've never met a model with such an eye for aesthetics, Lee," he said finally. "I'm impressed."

"I've studied art." She was tipsy enough to just come out and say it. "I'm more than just a model at *Vogue*. I'm a photographer."

"Now I'm doubly impressed. Beauty and talent both."

Lee took his hand in hers, tempted to tell him about the Surrealists' journal. About their adoration for his Stalinized country, about Man's fuming photo of her, and, most of all, her impressive bell jar photo, published under his name. No, she took a drink. To hell with that. And to hell with Man Ray. Leaning back on the cushions, Lee breathed out and looked at her host. She liked this Zizi. When the guests began to leave, and the son of a French viscount escorted Tatiana home, she stayed.

Later, when they got into bed, she blindfolded Zizi with her scarf. It excited him, but that was irrelevant. She didn't want him looking at her anymore. She pushed him down and got on top of him. This man would be the raw material to power *her* creative arts. For tonight, anyway.

"Lee, baby!" Man let himself into her studio, rushed in and embraced her. "I got in last night, but you weren't home," he said. His hands—one carrying a gift, a richly scented package—clasped around her. "I was beat, though, so I went back to my place. God, I missed you!"

She unwrapped his arms and stepped back. "I can barely look at you right now. You should probably just go."

"What are you talking about?" His face filled with dread; his voice quaked. "What happened while I was gone? Did you meet somebody? Are you with someone new?"

"No, but that sounds like a good idea. I need a person I can trust, Man. Someone who respects me."

His brow lifted and his smoking eyes began to clear. "Jesus, kid, I don't know what you've heard about me, but I wasn't with anybody else down in Cannes, I swear."

She looked at his mouth, tight but smug, resisting a smile—and wanted to slap him.

"I don't give a damn if you sleep with other women. But sneaking behind my back, playing me for a fool—"

"What the hell? I have no idea—"

"*This* is what I'm talking about, you son of a bitch."

She threw open the journal—she'd bought a copy for herself at the newsstand—and watched his face. He dropped his parcel on the table—colorful cakes of soap from Provence spilled everywhere—and grabbed the magazine. After giving the photo a cursory inspection, he looked back at Lee, his eyebrows arched in confusion.

"This is what you're all worked up about?"

"How could you put your name on my photo?" She felt like spitting.

He shrugged. "It's not such a big deal, Lee. Breton wanted to use a name people know. It's like the Old Masters and their workshops. Rubens, Rembrandt, Velazquez—they all had apprentices learning from them, painting in their style—"

"It's not the same. I'm not just making copies of your work or filling in the background. That photo was my idea—that's my print! How are people ever going to recognize my name if you sign my work?" Exasperated, Lee lit a cigarette and pulled on it hard. She didn't understand how he could act so faultless and unsympathetic. "And this title? 'Homage to le Marquis de Sade'? It's the stupidest thing—"

"The title's mine." He looked pleased with himself. "And the group loved it. I mean, suffering is the first rule of sadism and here we have a woman's head, trapped in a jar, unable to breathe. It's surrealistic sadism. Perfect, really." His manner was so cool that she had a mind to practice a little sadism herself—a nice cigarette burn should get his attention. "Why, what did you want to call it?"

"That's not important." Lee clenched her fists and glowered. She had to force herself not to raise her voice—Man stopped listening when the volume went up—because he needed to hear this. "What is important, and just wrong, is that we have two sets of rules here. It seems you can take my work and publish it under your name, but if I so much as rework a plate that you've *thrown in the trash*, you slit my throat." She took another long drag off her cigarette. "I won't have it, Man. I won't."

"I'm sorry, baby." He slowly walked toward her and put his arms around her. "I didn't realize it meant so much to you."

"Thank you." She kissed his cheek. It seemed he finally understood. She wasn't just his model or assistant anymore, but a fellow photographer. It was her profession, her ambition, too.

"But, really," he added with a knowing smile, "you should be glad. Everybody's just crazy about that photo."

"You bastard!" She pushed him away. His apologies were empty, just a quick way to end a row; he still didn't see any harm in what he'd done. She grabbed a handful of lavender soaps and started pelting him with them.

He ducked behind a chair. "What the hell? Stop it!"

"You treat me like a child. When are you going to realize

that I'm a photographer, just like you?" Soap bounced off the chair and clunked on the wooden floor. "We're colleagues, you idiot!"

He waited until she'd exhausted her supply, then put his hands up in surrender.

"I think I get it now, Lee."

XIX

It was Man's idea to go to the cabaret le Boeuf sur le Toit that night.

"Clement is going to be playing the songs from the new Cole Porter musical. I can't wait!" He attached his left cuff link, then looked over at Lee. "You ready?"

Lee looked up from blowing on her nails—she'd just painted them a brilliant crimson to match her lipstick—and nodded. She'd always like the Boeuf, the half-restaurant, half-nightclub where all kinds of people met and the latest music played at the loudest volume.

When they stepped into the crowded room, the maître appeared at once, exclaiming, "Monsieur and Madame Man Ray!" and the barmen, vigorously shaking their latest creations, called out hellos. As they were escorted to one of the coveted tables next to the piano, Lee dodged champagne buckets and waving cigarette holders, smiling at her various acquaintances. They quickly whispered their drink orders as everyone settled into the semidarkness, waiting for the first set. A saxophone player, his face nearly covered by a fedora, helped a scrawny French girl to her feet. She teetered in front of the microphone, then grasped it with satin gloves and, with her eyes closed, crooned "Love for Sale."

Her heavy accent in English and her youthful innocence—her thin body swaying artlessly, her lipstick a dull pink—made the lyrics even more tragic. A prostitute peddling her wares, a nighttime salesgirl. Lee shivered at the idea of a young girl using her body as currency. *Love* for sale, indeed.

When the combo took a break, Jean Cocteau came up to their table. Lee liked Jean, such a talented and charismatic man, but knew he got on Man's nerves. Artistic groups in Paris were always breaking into fractions and, currently, André Breton couldn't stand Cocteau—he called him an unctuous dandy—which had undoubtedly influenced Man's opinion.

"Good evening, Man, Lee." He bent down and kissed her hand. "Great music tonight, wouldn't you say?"

"Delicious," Lee said. "Lovely to see you, Jean. Won't you sit down?"

"No, thank you. I'm on a quest." He looked at them with an air of mystery. "Man, you know a lot of models. Do you happen to know any actresses? I need a real beauty to play a part in a film."

"You're making a film?" Man's look combined condescension and envy. "Have you found anyone to finance it yet?"

"Yes, of course." Jean's voice was velvet. "Viscount Charles de Noailles. I believe you made a film for him a year or two ago, didn't you?" He ignored Man's clouding brow and continued. "He approached me about backing a film. He wants a talkie this time. I've got a marvelous idea, but I need a beauty to play a Greek statue."

Lee nearly jumped out of her chair. "*I'll* do it, Jean!"

Both men stared at her. Jean gently took her chin in his hand and studied her face. "You are gorgeous, Lee. Yes, I think you'll be perfect."

"Fabulous." She kissed him on the cheek. "What's the title of the film?"

"*The Blood of a Poet.*"

"Ah, there will be violence?" She jiggled her eyebrows. "A terrible crime?"

"You'll find out soon enough. I don't want to spoil anything for you."

"This'll be such fun." Lee beamed, thrilled with idea of being in Jean Cocteau's first film, to work in his milieu, to meet his crowd. Ever since she'd arrived in Paris, she'd been under Man's wing; this time, she could fly entirely on her own.

"Shall we meet next Wednesday for a screen test? Give me your number and I'll call you with the details."

When he'd moved on to his next group of friends, she turned to Man excitedly, but when she saw his face—the dramatic pitch of his eyebrows, the scowl, furiously sucking on a wilted cigarette—her smile immediately drooped.

"Damn it to hell. What are you thinking, Lee?"

"What's the matter with you?" She looked into his eyes. "What's the problem? I told you I wanted to be an actress when I was younger. And this is even better than Hollywood. A Surrealist film—"

"Surrealist! That phony." He swallowed his drink whole. "Really, Lee, I can't believe you want anything to do with it."

She looked out into the crowd. *Here we go again!* She felt like a small child whose strict father—one very unlike her own—wouldn't let her play with the other kids.

"I just think it'll be fun," she repeated.

Man turned to Lee and exhaled a huff of smoke. She felt his eyes on her, but didn't look at him. She was sick of it. He couldn't even share her with another artist, couldn't let her go her own way. She felt him fuming next to her—would steam start rising from his suit?—and heard his groans and sighs, but ignored him. She glanced around the room, at the high heels on the dance floor, at the Picabia paintings on the walls, up at the chandeliers. After a few minutes' stalemate, he gently took her hand.

"Do whatever you want," he mumbled, then stubbed the butt to shreds.

"I will, *mon amour*." She closed her hand around his—a concession to his belated generosity—but repeated herself to cast aside any doubt. "I will."

Lee checked her watch anxiously. She was running late to the cast meeting. Man had wanted to play around in bed that morning—an amorous form of protest, obviously, as he was fully aware that she was expected by nine—and then pouted in silence when she finally got up. From stop to stop, she watched commuters getting on and off the metro; all of them—although half-asleep, bored, or grouchy—seemed absolutely certain of where they were going and what they were doing. She was neither. In the last few days, she'd begun to doubt her impulsive decision to participate in Cocteau's film. Did her community-theater roles prepare her for this? Her modeling? Her short stint as a chorus line dancer?

Lee popped out of the metro on the outskirts of Paris—the train's last stop—and got completely disoriented. Here was that odd, working-class combination of industrial and rural; this Paris was much shabbier than the one close to the Seine. Lee walked several blocks in the wrong direction until, finally, a cartload of farmers—Italian immigrants—gave her a lift to the studio alongside their onions. When she walked in the door, Cocteau had already given general instructions to the strange hodgepodge of characters there—amateurs and professionals, French and international—and many of them were readying to leave.

"Ah, Lee, there you are." His narrow face broke into a languid smile. "I was beginning to worry."

"Sorry, Jean." Nervous about working with a new artist, she breathed out, relieved he wasn't angry. "I've never been out this way before."

He took her by the hand to introduce her to the other main players.

"Mademoiselle Lee Miller," he said, "I'd like for you to meet our poet, Enrique Rivero. He's originally from Chile but has been making films in France for the last five years." Lee looked him over approvingly. Dark and well-built, he had black eyes, a straight nose, and full lips. He shook her hand warmly and gave her a wink. "And this is Féral Benga, the African dancer. He'll be our angel. Doesn't he look angelic?"

Ebony-black and muscular, Féral made a quick pose of a saint—eyes to the heavens, hands in prayer—then smiled at Lee with bright, perfect teeth.

"Wonderful to meet you both," she said, wondering which of the two might be better in bed.

"And Lee will be our statue. Her costume is going to take some work." Cocteau paused, reflective, then scratched his leg. Lee, who was also feeling itchy, suddenly noticed that most of the crew was absently scratching an arm or a side. Next to her, Cocteau pinched a flea from his white shirt. "What the devil is this?"

"I think it's coming from those old beds," said an older man, hired on to work the lights.

"You mean the soundproofing?" Cocteau said as he approached a wall. Discarded mattresses had been hung on the studio walls to block the noise from the street.

Curious, most of the cast walked toward them; they were crawling with fleas and bedbugs.

"Can't something be done about this?" Cocteau's shout was unusually shrill.

"We can try fumigating," said the lighting man. "Not making any promises, though."

"You do that," Cocteau said, raising his hands in disgust. "Lee, you come with me. We have to get your costume together."

He flicked on the switch in the women's dressing room and bare bulbs blinked on around a large mirror. There was a counter beneath it littered with a few leftover rouge pots and powder puffs, and a small sink in the corner. Behind a changing screen, she could see racks of old costumes—harem pants, petticoats, ball gowns, peasant clothes, even animal outfits—left stranded from other productions. From a cupboard, Cocteau pulled out two plaster arm fragments, one nearly to the elbow, the other little more than a shoulder, and began sizing them up next to her.

"I want the statue to resemble the *Venus de Milo,* a symbol of feminine perfection. Unfortunately, since we have to hide your arms somewhere, you can't have a bare torso."

He looked at her long, graceful arms with repugnance, as if he'd like to dispose of them, then took out a tape measure and began jotting down various measurements.

"We'll whitewash you, truss up your arms, then cover you with a toga." He reached out and touched her short bob. "I'll make a papier-mâché cast of your hair. We can't have this moving around. As a matter of fact, you won't be doing much moving at all. Imagine you are living stone."

Lee nodded unhappily. She didn't realize being a statue would be so uncomfortable. Living stone? Would she even be recognizable? Oh, what the hell! At least she was out of the studio, alongside talented people, trying something new.

"I think I can handle that," she said, game for anything.

"Fabulous." He gave her a preoccupied pat on the shoulder. "Come back in the morning for a fitting. If we have the bug situation worked out, I'd like to begin filming the next day."

Lee stood awkwardly, her balance thrown off, nervously awaiting her entrance. Her arms were bound around her ribs and waist as if she were hugging herself tightly. It was difficult to breathe. Her whole body was painted white, except for dark red lips; the two broken arms and the sculpted hair were smoothed into place with a mixture of butter and flour. Her skin itched all over; she suspected the tenacious fleas who managed to survive the pesticide had found new lodgings in her costume. Trying to ignore it, she peeked out from under her thick, white lids to watch the action. In the first scene, the poet was on his own.

Enrique walked out on set—bare-chested, wearing breeches and a powdered wig—to his place at the easel. Lee admired his looks, a handsome libertine straight out of *Les liaisons danger-euses,* but when Cocteau caught sight of his naked back, he realized his actor had a huge scar.

"What's this?" he asked, mildly annoyed but mainly curious. He ran his finger along the deep groove on Enrique's shoulder blade.

"I was shot by a lover's husband back in Chile," Enrique said, his words intensified by his musical accent. "A cuckold can be surprisingly dangerous."

Interested, Lee tipped her head back to see them better. She knew the perils of a jealous man. Having a lover shoot a man in the back, though, was beyond her experience.

"I see," said Cocteau, nodding slowly. "It's not bad. This is a story about the pain of the poet, after all." He cleared his throat. "Poets shed not only the red blood of the heart, but the white blood of their souls." He picked up a prop paintbrush from next to the easel, dipped it in black ink, and painted a swirl around the scar ending with a star. "Poets have scars that they turn into beauty. Continue!"

Enrique returned to the easel and filming started. He made a line portrait—or, rather, traced one Cocteau had drawn—and was shocked to see the mouth come to life (at least he pretended to be; the moving lips would be added later). When he tried to rub it out with his hand, the mouth became trapped on his palm. In a panic, he tried to rid himself of it, to toss it away.

Failing, he tried to meld it with his own mouth, in a long, suffocating kiss, then to rub it into his skin, a slow, licking caress moving from his neck down his torso.

Lee watched this scene of fearful auto-eroticism, trying not to smile lest she crack her makeup. She thought most men—Man especially—would love to have a working mouth on their palms. The possibilities! Watching Enrique pet himself—his black eyes flashing as he stroked his muscular chest—she thought perhaps she could use one as well.

The poet, desperate, then spied the statue on the side of his room, a Greek goddess, a Venus, his muse. Lee in plaster. He placed his hand over its mouth.

"Cut! Great job, Enrique. Lee, you're up."

A member of the crew carefully picked up the hollow sculpture made to Lee's likeness as Cocteau helped Lee to its place on the set, guiding her with a firm hand. The statue would now come to life. Her heart pounding, she stood straight, trying not to sway. In the lights, the rancid butter around her hairline started to melt. Her nose twitched.

"Now then, Enrique, put your hand on Lee's mouth. Gently; you don't want to smear the lipstick. Action!"

She felt his warmth for just a moment, then he briskly tore his hand away. Imagining an awakening after a long sleep, she fluttered her eyelids and took short, labored breaths. In that costume, she could scarcely do anything else.

"Lee! The muse is now alive." Cocteau's voice trilled with passionate energy. "You must egg the poet on, into the mirror, inside himself!"

Trying not to stammer, Lee said her lines in French, the

words she'd rehearsed a thousand times at home, worrying about her pronunciation as much as her delivery.

"There is only one way left. You must go into the mirror and explore. I congratulate you. You wrote that one could go into mirrors, but you didn't believe it. Try, always try . . ."

They did a half-dozen takes: Cocteau wanted her voice more lilting, more mysterious (even though a French woman would dub it later); Lee lost her balance and nearly fell; a light-bulb blew; Enrique accidently smiled. Finally, their director was satisfied.

"All right, now. We're going to take advantage of Lee's make-up—I daresay you don't want to put it on again—to film the statue's final scene. It will take place after the poet's trip into the mirror. Furious with his muse for sending him deep within his psyche, he comes out and, with that mallet, breaks her to bits."

The poet held the mallet menacingly—"Watch out, you!"—then winked at Lee. Again, they quickly cut to replace her with the plaster mold. Watching Enrique, wild and enraged, smashing it apart, she reflected drily on the fate of uncooperative muses.

"Well done, Lee," Cocteau said as he removed the plaster arm parts. "Although your statue scene is only a few minutes long, it is guaranteed to cause an impression. Armless, with marble skin, your dark lips curled into that sinister smile—it is truly unforgettable."

"I'm so glad you're pleased." Trying to open her eyes properly, she glanced over at the broken chunks of the plaster cast of herself. "Do you really think a muse could lead a poet to madness?"

"Of course. Think of poor Coleridge!"

"Who was his muse?"

"A muse need not be a woman, Lee." He looked down his long nose at her. "Or even a person."

When she and Enrique left the studio together, the white plaster glowing on their skin, Lee couldn't help but feel disappointed. As in Man Ray's photography sessions, once again she'd been little more than a prop.

"You say you've never been in a film before?" Enrique waited for the shake of her head, which caused bits of paint and plaster to flitter around her, then whistled. "Damn good job."

"Thanks," she said, but didn't believe him. All she'd done was try to stand perfectly still, make minimal expressions, and move her mouth correctly. The impressive part of her character was all in the costume, the makeup. On the other hand, his performance—sexy, strange, and intense—had impressed her. "And you—what stage presence."

The elderly hotel receptionist was startled to see two phantoms in coats appear at his window.

"What's this?"

"I believe Jean Cocteau has reserved some rooms? We're actors in his film."

"Yes. Monsieur Cocteau requested the rooms with baths. Here you are."

With keys in hand, they each hesitated in front of their narrow doors. Enrique turned to her as he unlocked his. "When you're ready, let's have a drink together downstairs."

"It may take a while," she said, pulling a bit of paint out of her eyelashes.

"I'll wait." Enrique kissed his palm like the poet in the film, then went into his room.

Soaking in the square tub, she thought about him: his accent, his bare torso and muscular calves, that scar. Lee had nearly suggested that they bathe together. Not only was he extremely attractive, but he could have helped scrubbing off the paint and getting the plaster out of her hair. But it was just as well—the bathtub was tiny.

After vigorously toweling her short hair, she put on stockings and a snug green dress, added some rouge and lipstick, then headed downstairs. Enrique was at a table wearing a dark suit and nursing a martini. She ordered one for herself, then joined him. He stood a moment as she sat down.

"You are much more beautiful as a woman than as a statue."

"Well, I sort of liked you as a poet." She smiled at him. "Tell me, what's behind the mirror that makes you want to smash me apart?"

"It's the Hôtel des Folies Dramatiques. All I know is that I go down the corridor, peeking in all the keyholes and behind each door, there's something strange."

"A voyeur, eh?" She looked into his eyes as she took a long sip from her drink. "And what do you see?"

"I'm not exactly sure. I've heard him talk about a Mexican firing squad behind one door, and a Chinese opium den behind another. I think the whole film—although it's completely mad—is about him. You know, his own father committed suicide when he was boy. In this film, I kill myself at least twice."

Lee twirled her olive stick around in her glass, wondering whether her life would have been different if her mother had succeeded in her suicide plans, if her father had not saved her. Would it torture her? Every time she got in a car, would she smell the fumes and feel the heaviness, the oncoming quiet? Would she set up photographs of such things—self-portraits of her dead body, still lives with guns or nooses? Would she contemplate suicide herself? She slowly pulled the olive off the stick with her teeth and chewed it, unable to imagine any of it, not even that depth of feeling for her mother. She shook the thoughts from her mind.

"Enrique." Lee's eyes sparkled. "Why don't we go around this hotel and see what we find? God only knows what there might be behind these doors."

"In a place like this? We'd be lucky to see some sad old man clipping his toenails."

"Maybe you're right." She looked around the room, empty except for a workingman at the bar, on his second round of pastis. "This place doesn't seem very promising. But hey, I still have my key. Why don't we go back to my room and make a scene?"

He stared into her eyes a moment, then quickly finished his drink.

"After you, mademoiselle."

XX

"That was a long day." Man rose from the small sofa in her studio to give her a warm hug. "I picked up some things at the charcuterie if you're hungry."

"Starving!" She plopped down on a chair and let him fuss over her. After opening various waxed-paper packages, he arranged cold cuts and cheese on a plate and cut a baguette. "A bit of wine?" He poured them each a glass, then sat down next to her.

She kissed him fondly. "Thanks, sweetie. I'm beat."

"So tell me all about it. How was your first day of filming?"

"Being a statue is not all fun and games," she said while chewing. "In fact, my costume was nasty. Plaster, butter, papier-mâché, paint, fleas . . . I could barely breathe and, when I could, I realized I stank." Lee laughed and cleaned the crumbs off her mouth with the back of her hand; she could still appreciate her clean skin—soft, warm, and no longer itchy. "It didn't require much in the way of acting skills either. I didn't have to move my limbs, open my eyes or anything."

"So how does the statue fit in? Is there an actual plot? Or is it just a series of images?"

"It's the story of an artist whose drawing comes to life. Well, the mouth does. And it gets onto his hand—in the middle of his palm—and he panics and tries to get it off."

She was about to joke with him about the erotic possibilities of such an aberration, but he broke in, changing tack.

"On his hand? That sounds like that scene from *Un chien andalou*. Have you seen it? One of its main images is the palm of a man's hand. There's a hole in the center and ants keep coming out of it. It's chilling—a really powerful image." His eyebrows pitched and his tone grew dark. "Sounds like Cocteau just stole it."

"I don't know. It seems very different to me. An ant hole and a living mouth? What does it matter if they're both in someone's hand?"

"I'd have to see it first. But Cocteau's always been a little magpie, picking up the shiny bits from everyone else's work, from here and there. Then he makes a lovely little nest for himself and everybody oohs and aahs." He shook his head in disgust. "He even looks like a bird."

"I don't know about that. You should see how he improvises, Man, how he solves problems right on the spot." She considered reinforcing her case with a word about Cocteau's friendship with Picasso, the longtime darling of the Paris art world, or Breton's obvious jealousy of him, but really, she didn't feel like arguing. Between filming and Enrique, she'd had a full, interesting day and now just wanted to rest. "Like you. A lot like you."

"All right, all right. What happens next? The artist has a mouth on his palm. Then what?"

"He gets rid of it by putting it on the statue's mouth. That's what wakes it up, you see. That living mouth breathes life into it."

Man stroked her lip with his thumb. "Is it your mouth, Lee?" he asked softly, pointing to the photograph of her isolated lips framed over the dresser. "That mouth?"

"No and yes." She understood his interest in that detail; her mouth was his. "It starts off as one of Cocteau's line drawings— you know, those simple Greek-looking portraits he makes— then, at the end, it winds up on me."

"And you are the muse." He got up and began to pace, each of his words louder than the last. "But, you're *my* muse, Lee. I don't like this one bit. It's like sharing your mistress!"

She ignored his shouting—indeed, the poet had shared his mistress as well—and tried to make light of it. "Well, you know what Cocteau does to this muse at the end of the scene? He smashes her to smithereens."

Man took a long drink of wine, then leaned into her face. "Perhaps all muses are ultimately meant to be destroyed." His voice was serious and thick.

"Or to destroy." She threw a piece of bread at him. "Jesus, Man, calm down. If it makes you feel any better, I've got a few weeks off from the film. We can spend that time together."

"Really?" His bitter mood quickly faded. "I've been waiting for you to have the time to work on a new project with me."

"That's grand. What is it?"

"I thought we'd make a film of our own. A little home movie, just for us."

"And what will this film be about?"

"Whittling pipes."

"My, my." Lee chuckled. After meeting Kiki in la Coupole, she'd never forgotten that French expression. "This promises to be a bit naughtier than Mr. Cocteau's film."

"And you won't have to worry about uncomfortable costumes." He grinned. "Or any costume, for that matter."

She laughed. "So I finally get to star in my own Man Ray film. Too bad it wouldn't pass the censors."

Two days later, Man was ready to start. He'd bought a long-stemmed pipe for blowing bubbles and, the evening before, had popped by his friend Brancusi's studio to borrow one of his sculptures. He arranged the lights in the bedroom and turned up the heat in the studio.

"Like I said, this is just for us. Just for fun." He pulled out the pipe. "Now, get comfortable on the covers. I'm going to take a few stills first before I start filming."

Lee lounged back on the bed and began blowing bubbles, excited about being filmed nude. It reminded her of when she first started posing for Man, their first months together when they could scarcely keep their hands off each other. After taking a few photos of Lee, he'd join her under the tungsten lights and, occasionally, the photo sessions would continue during sex. He'd grab his camera to take tremulous close-ups; moaning in pleasure, she'd arch her back or spread her legs wider, to give him a better shot. This time, it would be live action.

"I love the shadows the bubbles make on your breasts," he said, then quickly changed to the movie camera. "Here, look at me. That's right."

Lee gave him her most seductive gaze, with her eyes half-closed, her mouth half-open. She took a deep breath—making her chest heave—and blew a long trail of soft bubbles out of the pipe, then licked its stem, caressing it with carmine lips. She could see Man getting aroused and took another breath, this time while slowly stroking her torso.

"Here, Lee, now you film me."

They exchanged the pipe for the camera. Still looking at her, he took a drag off his cigarette, then blew through the pipe, making pearly bubbles. They wobbled, heavy in the air, then exploded, releasing the smoke.

"Nice," she murmured, zooming in on a bubble.

He put the pipe down and got up on his knees, exposing himself to her and the camera; she looked at his midsection through the viewfinder, remembering the Renaissance penises in Florence, those shy marble lumps, a lifetime before.

"I think this lens is too small for what you've got, Man," Lee drawled.

He laughed and took the camera back. "See that object wrapped in the corner?" he asked. "I want you to uncover it and discover it."

Lee walked over to it and dramatically pulled off the sheet. It was Brancusi's statue *Princesse X*, which, despite its title, was a stylized gold penis in full erection. Lee smiled back at the camera and, like an erotic harpist, caressed it up and down.

"Now that you're all heated up, come back to the bed."

She leaned toward the camera, pushed her breasts together, and put the bubble pipe down the hollow. Crouching down on the covers, she showed him her backside and waved at him from underneath. With a laugh, she flopped back onto her back and slowly began to spread her legs. He reached over and turned off the camera.

"Let's take a little break," he said, his voice strained. He straddled her hips then, on his knees, made his way to her face. "Blow my pipe now, Lee. Please?"

She took him in her mouth, surprised—and nearly disappointed—that he hadn't wanted to film it.

When they were both satisfied, they got up. She made some coffee while he poked around the kitchen, looking for something sweet. With nothing better at hand, he pulled out a tin of graham crackers, which Lee's parents—health-food connoisseurs—had sent her a few weeks before. He broke a cracker in two and dunked it in the café au lait. She took the other half of his cracker and popped it in her mouth. After weeks of tension, the happy mood, this camaraderie, was a relief, an echo of the enthusiasm they'd shared when they first met. However, she couldn't help but see the similarity of this home movie and *The Blood of a Poet*. This one was also about the artist and his muse. Man was reclaiming his property—and this time, it had to be on film.

"I know what I'll call this movie." He grinned at her. "*Self Portrait*."

"Does that mean that I am you?" she asked. "Or that you are me?"

XXI

Lee found Jean Cocteau in a corner booth at la Coupole, disheveled and bleary-eyed. He had sounded alarmingly urgent (and somewhat intoxicated) when he called from the bar telephone. She was surprised to hear from him—it was seven in the morning and, besides, she wasn't due back on the set for another week—but had dressed as quickly as possible.

She sat down across from him, ordered two coffees, and offered him a cigarette.

"What's wrong, Jean?" Was he back on opium? "Have you had bad news?"

"Haven't you heard? The scandal? The riot?"

"Which one?" In the Parisian art world, weeks were counted by scandals.

"What a dream world you live in, my child." His eyes flickered slowly for a moment, drifting, till he gave his head a quick shake and focused on her. "Really, I'd have thought Man Ray would have told you all about it."

"You tell me," she said.

"*L'Age d'Or*," he whispered, then wiped his brow with a large violet handkerchief.

"That new film by Luis Buñuel? Yes, of course I've heard of

it. Man said the premiere was a great success. I haven't had a chance to see it yet—"

"And you won't!" He was now fully awake. "Last night, right-wing fanatics, the dreaded Ligue des Patriotes, stormed the cinema, assaulted the audience, and threw ink at the screen." His hands flittered wildly. "Then they tumbled out into the lobby—decorated for the occasion with pieces by your Man, Dalí, Miró and the others—and destroyed the artwork. They ran off into the night. I daresay they'll never be found. Those types never are."

"That's terrible!" She grabbed his hand, wondering if Man had been there and if he was all right. "Why did they do it?"

"I'm sure those brutes didn't bother to watch the film— they never do—but they claim it's against all known values and mores. Family, church, society itself."

Lee broke into a little smile. "Well, knowing Luis, it wouldn't surprise me."

"Of course not! And who cares? What I'm concerned about is censorship." He looked at her gravely, his eyes yellowed and slick. "And you know who their producer is? Charles de Noailles. Lee, he's *my* producer! Without him, there is no *Blood of a Poet.*"

She frowned in disappointment. "Damn, Jean. Your first film, stalled by moral outcry—about someone else's work. It isn't fair." She was also indignant on her own behalf; it was her first film, too. "What are you going to do?"

"There's nothing I can do except work. I'm going to need you back on the set. Say, next Wednesday?"

"I'll be there."

He patted her arm, got up unsteadily, and headed out the door.

Lee sat in the almost empty bar—the smell of the night's festivities soured by daylight—and finished her coffee; Jean had left his untouched. How precarious the art world was. Film-makers, painters, sculptors, and photographers kept trying to push the limits, but most of the public just wasn't ready for it. Smiling to herself, she thought of her erotic home movie. What would the League of Patriots make of *that*?

Lee left a handful of centimes on the table, scooted out of the booth, and headed for the rue Campagne-Première. As ter-rible as it was to have a few of his pieces destroyed, she wanted to make sure that Man himself wasn't busted up. She let her-self in to the darkened studio and crept up the stairs to the bedroom; he was curled up in the covers, snoring peacefully. Lee took off her clothes and joined him, looking forward to his expression when he woke up.

The following week, hunched under a half-broken umbrella, the toes of her stockings already damp, Lee was on her way to the metro stop when a car pulled up beside her. The window rolled down.

"Lee?" a voice called from the backseat. It was Zizi Svirsky.

"Zizi!" She leaned in toward the window. "How lovely to see you."

"Get in. I can take you wherever you want to go."

She tore open the door, threw the wet umbrella on the

floorboard, and, after giving the address to the chauffeur, sat back on the seat, a veritable sofa. "What a miserable morning. Such luck you came by." She gave him a fond smile.

"What are you going to do out there?" he asked, surprised at Lee's destination.

"Act!"

As they snaked through the narrow streets and up the crowded boulevards, she told him all about Jean Cocteau's film and his preoccupation after the recent *L'Age d'Or* scandal.

"Sounds fascinating," said Zizi. "And a far cry from the Spaniard's film. Did you see it? I don't know how it got banned—I didn't understand a thing." He laughed. "I've always admired Cocteau, his artwork and poems. I'd wager he's one of the most interesting men in Paris."

"Yes, he's wonderful." It was a pleasant change to talk with someone who didn't dislike him. She wove her fingers through Zizi's long, fine ones, a pianist's hands. "But tell me, what's new with you?"

"Nothing as exciting as making a film." He gathered her hand up and kissed it. "I was on my way to the Duke Vallombrosa's house. He's hosting a big New Year's Eve party and wanted some fresh ideas for decorations. Would you like to be my guest?"

"Of course." Lee beamed at Zizi. "It's been ages since I went to a really good party. I like the Duke. I took his portrait a couple of months ago. Funny, he wanted it made with his hat and overcoat on."

"He'll need those today," Zizi said. Outside the foggy windows, it was now pouring. "What time do you think you'll finish today at the film studio? Shall I come and pick you up? You could drown out there if you're not careful."

"Thanks, Zizi. Could you come around five? If we're not finished, perhaps you'd enjoy watching for a little while?"

"You know I love to watch." He snuggled his face against hers and whispered, "That is, when I'm not blindfolded."

They dropped Lee in front of the studio and she made a dash for the door. When she walked in, she saw a group of people huddling around a large crate.

"What's this?" she asked Philippe, the head cameraman.

"Cocteau ordered a fancy chandelier for this next scene. Says it's crucial. It arrived today," he paused for effect, "in three thousand pieces."

"Damn." Lee looked over at the crew—three strapping lads used for hauling heavy equipment—and the boys from the snowball-fight scene; they were gently scooping handfuls of shimmering crystal teardrops onto a tarp, trying to organize them by size. "Do they need help?"

"I'm sure they will, but for the moment Cocteau wants to see you in the dressing room."

She found him and the costume designer looking at evening gowns, all long, white, and sleeveless. "Jean?"

"Lee, darling, how are you?" He gave her two kisses then studied her face. "Divine, as ever. How haggard we all must look to you. Have you heard the latest? De Noailles has been threatened with excommunication by the Pope. For a film! And, as the producer, he's withdrawn *L'Age d'Or* from public exhibition permanently."

"Man told me. The Surrealists are up in arms about it. They think he should go ahead and distribute it, no matter what."

"He claims he wants to avoid any further violence or vandalism, but I think he just wants to go to Heaven. The selfish bastard. How can one eternal soul compare to freedom of expression?" Lee chuckled at Jean's serious mien. "Who knows if our little film will ever be shown," he continued with a dramatic sigh, "but we must finish it nonetheless. It's been nonstop work here despite our fears."

"I'm delighted to be back on the job, for what it's worth," Lee said.

"Wonderful. And this time, I promise you'll be much more comfortable. You can use your own arms, you can wear your own skin . . ." He turned back to the gowns. "Here, help us choose the best dress to mimic a toga. I want to make it clear that you are still the muse, but in human form. After the poet's suicide, you'll revert to being a statue, your purpose fulfilled."

"That's my purpose?" Lee looked at Jean. "To get my artist to kill himself?"

"Not exactly," he began, weighing the question. "It's to force him to look inside himself, deep inside. If he can't accept what he sees, it's not the muse's fault."

"And I revert to the statue then?" Lee winced. "I thought we'd finished those scenes."

"Don't worry, there'll be no more plaster. The last scene is more of an echo. Instead of the broken arms, you'll wear long black gloves. The gown," he turned back to the dresses, "must flow like a toga."

"Here, why don't I try this one on?" Lee picked up the simplest of the bunch and went behind the screen. "Tell me, how's everything been going? I saw the chandelier. I hope there haven't been any other problems."

"A few days ago, Féral twisted his ankle dancing. Now we have an angel with a limp. But you know? That's even better." He shot her a mischievous look over the partition. "People will give it a symbolic meaning it doesn't have."

"You're terrible." Lee laughed, coming out from behind the screen.

"Ah, nearly perfect. I love the Empire style. It just needs a bit of altering." He pinched the fabric into folds, while the costumier put pins into place. Cocteau turned to his watch. "I don't know when we'll be able to start shooting. That damn chandelier!"

"Well, if you don't need me, I'll go help them. I've always liked puzzles."

She returned the gown to the designer for alterations, then joined the group of young men stringing baubles and hanging glass pendants on the metal frame. They looked up at her and their chatter immediately stopped.

"Good work, boys. What a lamp." She picked up two large crystal ornaments and weighed them in her hand. "It's so very well hung!"

They fell into titters of blushes and giggles. By lunchtime, the light fixture—a large, tiered structure dripping with prisms—was finally finished. And all of the boys were severely infatuated with Lee Miller.

. . .

That afternoon, Lee in her flowing dress met Enrique in white tie and tails on the set. Fluffy white asbestos snow covered the façade of an elegant building; in the street in front of it, the chandelier hung mysteriously over a table and two plush stools.

"Places everyone!" Cocteau clapped his hands.

Lee cleared her throat and sat stiffly on one of the stools. This time, without the plaster and paint, her acting skills—her facial expressions, movements, her *regard*—would be far more important. She looked at Cocteau, his greedy eyes taking in every detail, and slowly breathed out. He'd cast her as a society darling, an artist's muse, a femme fatale—really, how hard could it be?

As Enrique took his place on the opposite stool, a schoolboy, uniformed in short pants and a cape, lay down on the artificial snow next to the table. Cocteau bent down to retouch the blood on his face, then splattered a bit on the powdery ground.

"*Lucien, tu es mort.* Don't budge!" He shook his finger at the adolescent, who clearly found it difficult to remain dead, then turned to the other players. "In the previous scene, this boy was killed in a snowball fight—not that you can *make* a ball with this damn asbestos—and all of his comrades abandoned him. Pretend you don't see him there."

Lee winked at Lucien, one of her chandelier-assembling pals, as Cocteau began talking them into their roles.

"You two are playing a game of cards and the stakes are extremely high." His hands exploded in a grandiose gesture. "You're playing for your life. However, neither of you is nervous; if anything, this is a dull game to pass the time. After a few minutes, Lee will look at her cards and announce: 'You don't

have the ace of hearts, my dear. You have lost.' Completely in-
different to your fate, she pops open her compact and begins to
powder her nose."

"So like a woman," said Enrique. "In the end, this film of
yours is quite realistic."

"And so very like a man, Enrique, you cheat. Slowly, very
slowly, you pull the ace out of the dead boy's jacket. Although
you try to outsmart Fate, the boy's guardian angel will come
down those stairs—Féral, are you ready?"

The African dancer, his body gleaming with oil, dressed
only in a dark brown loincloth and stylized wings, waved from
the door at the top of the staircase.

"And will remove the boy—and the winning card." He
whisked the card from one hand to the next. "Lee, you look
triumphantly at the camera—I'll come in for a close-up—and
Enrique, you know it's all over. Your heart beats wildly. We can
hear it, like in Poe's 'The Tell-Tale Heart.'"

Cocteau produced a pump and arranged it under Enrique's
dinner jacket. When he squeezed it, the lapel moved in and
out.

"I'll signal you when you should start pumping. Slowly, me-
thodically. *Bum-bum, bum-bum.* That's right. And then, finally,
staring into the face of your muse, you pull a gun from your
pocket and shoot yourself in the head. Unlike the suicide behind the mirror—safe in the world of dreams—this time, you
will die. It's a silent shot. The heartbeat stops. Your head falls
onto the table, onto the bad hand you were dealt."

Cocteau made another sweeping gesture, then ran his hand
through his thick hair.

"Questions?"

Although the scene was only five or six minutes long, Cocteau had such a clear idea in his head that he demanded take after take.

"Cut! Enrique, what is this seductive look all about? I can accept wariness or even ennui—but we are not flirting, here! She is not some pretty girl you want to sleep with. She is deadly, man, deadly!"

"Spades? Cut! Lee, you have one line! One! It is the ace of hearts, not spades! I don't care if it's going to be redubbed, get it right this time."

"Féral, my angel, look otherworldly. Mysterious! *Putain*, don't smile! Cut!"

"Cut, cut, cut! Lucien! You are dead, goddamn it! Dead!"

"Pump, Enrique! Pump! No, no, I see your hand! *Merde!* Cut!"

After the nineteenth take, Enrique looked Cocteau in the eye and began ripping the cards in two.

"Christ, Jean!" he shouted. "You mean to edit it, don't you? Surely you'll find enough good acting in all those miserable takes to piece together this one goddamn scene!"

Cocteau glared at him. "Fine! Let's move on to this young man's *death,* shall we?"

Enrique had just shot himself for the fifth time when Zizi walked in. He stood silently in the shadow, fascinated.

"Cut! That one will do. Now let me paint on your bullet wound."

On Enrique's temple, Cocteau painted a five-pointed star, a smaller version of the one he'd put on his scar. With the film rolling, he dribbled on more red paint. Even though Enrique was older and had more experience than poor Lucien, he, too, struggled to remain still as the liquid dripped down into his eye.

"Cut! We are finished for today! Finally."

Zizi applauded the few minutes he'd seen. Cocteau glanced over and gave him a short bow.

"Now, Lee," he continued, "your final scene is tomorrow. I'll need you here early for makeup. Say, eight o'clock? Enrique, your contribution is over. A magnificent job!" The actor briefly stopped wiping blood off his face to shake hands with the director, their spat forgotten. "As for the crew—*à demain*."

Before going over to welcome Zizi to the set, Lee took Enrique's hand. "Perhaps we'll see each other again."

"I certainly hope so." He squeezed her hand with a glance at the older man, watching them from the sidelines as if they were still playacting. "It's been a pleasure working alongside you, *corazón mio*, even if you were my undoing." He made a gun with his hand and pointed it at his temple, still red from the paint. He kissed her twice on the cheeks. "*Hasta siempre*."

Lee watched him leave the set, off to his dressing room, then called out to her friend—"Zizi!"—motioning to him to join her.

Cocteau's head shot up at her exclamation. "Lee?" he asked curiously, wondering why she seemed to be calling the gentleman by his penis. Lee made quick introductions.

"We've met before, Monsieur Cocteau, I believe it was *chez* Charles de Noailles."

"Of course, Monsieur Svirsky." Cocteau patted him on the

shoulder. "Dear Charles." Just the name of his nearly excommunicated producer made him visibly nervous.

"I've taken the liberty to make dinner plans for Lee. Would you care to join us?"

"Maybe some other time, my good man, but now I must be off. Don't forget, Lee—eight sharp!" With a brisk wave at them both, he turned and left.

Alone on the set, Lee took Zizi's arm. "Walk me to my dressing room and tell me all about our plans. What are we doing tonight?"

"We're dining with Tatiana and her *vicomte*. He used his connections to reserve a table at Maxim's."

"Fabulous. But without making a trip back home, I don't know what I'll wear."

She wrinkled her nose; she didn't like the idea of going back to her studio in Montparnasse. Man was probably waiting for her, eager to hear about the film and criticize the director.

He held her out at arm's length and twirled her around. "You can just wear what you have on—a simple white evening gown. No one would imagine you've just walked off a film set. What am I saying? It's such a fantastic story, you must tell everyone!"

"No, this dress has to be perfect for tomorrow. It wouldn't do to wear it for a night on the town. What if I spilled a glass of burgundy down the front? Or at the end of the night, fell asleep in it?" Lee imagined Cocteau's intense stare, his bushy hair on end, as she came in for her last day's shooting in the gown, now a Crusoe-rag, stained, wrinkled, and torn. "He'd kill me."

"I sincerely hope I'll be able to tempt you out of your clothes before you nod off tonight, my love," he said lightly, as he strolled into the dressing room behind her. "At any rate, there must be something here you can use."

He rifled through the clothes rack and pulled out one of the surplus white gowns. "Try this one on. You can still claim it's the costume for the film."

She coyly went behind the partition to change dresses. She stood naked, carefully hanging the dress for the next day, when she felt Zizi's hands on her waist. "Reservations aren't until half-past seven," he whispered.

Lee turned around and kissed him hard. After the high emotions on the set—the worries, tension, and nerves—she could use a little nookie. They quickly made a pallet on the floor from the wardrobe on the rack. After they lay down, she covered them up with an old bear costume, made from a real skin. Falling into the rhythm of sex, her mind—so cluttered before with the film, her director, her mentor, and muses—went deliciously blank. She was a body, pulsing and alive, in the moment—and nothing more.

XXII

Stumbling in the film studio door, out of the morning haze and into the gloom, Lee nearly ran into George Hoyningen-Huene.

"You look like hell, darling," he said as a means of greeting.

"George!" She hugged his neck. "What are you doing here?"

"Michel thought that since you're taking time off to do this film, *Vogue* should get something out of it. We're doing a reportage on our girl's participation in *The Blood of a Poet*. I'm here to take photos." He lifted her chin with his palm, then ran his fingers through her limp hair. "I don't know whether to use soft lights or extremely harsh ones."

"I went out to dinner last night with Zizi, Tata, and her title," she said, as an explanation for the morning's looks. "Bottomless bottles of champagne at Maxim's accompanied by a few prawns and a wee bit of *confit de canard*. Then it was off in search of cabaret acts and dancing." Although she was suffering for it this morning, she'd had a wonderful evening. It was so easy to be with Zizi; there were no intense emotions—possession, jealousy, love—to muck up the works. At five in the morning she'd fallen into his bed; this morning, after sharing a pot of black coffee, he'd driven her back to the studio. "I only slept a couple of hours, so don't take any pictures until the makeup's been plastered on," she said. "Where's Jean?"

"He's in the dressing room. We're to meet him there."

She grimaced, hoping Cocteau hadn't noticed the make-shift bed on the floor behind the screen. George gathered up his equipment—"Shall we?"—and Lee grabbed a stray light on her way.

"Good morning, Lee," Jean said. He was making trials with base makeup, dabbing different shades of white on his hand. When he looked up at her, he frowned.

"Well, at least the dress is in perfect shape," she said in answer to his stare. "Will the makeup hide these dark circles?"

"Yes, you lucky cow. Can you believe this, George? *This* is my beautiful muse." He took a deep breath. "So, the Zizi kept you awake all night? Maybe I should have joined you two—and gotten you in at a reasonable hour."

Lee couldn't tell if he was truly annoyed with her or just joking. Behind the screen, she took off last night's dress, kicking the bearskin out from underfoot.

"I'm going to cover you with white powder." Jean Cocteau could have hired a makeup specialist, but he liked doing these things himself. It was rather like painting a human canvas. "Oh, and you'll wear the papier-mâché wig again, but I think we'll forgo the butter."

In the pristine white gown, Lee sat down on the bench in front of the mirror. Cocteau began coating her face a pure white, hiding the lines and shadows, erasing the night out. As she began to disappear and George to take photos, she wondered if Man had spent a sleepless night in her studio. On occasion, he stayed at his own place, working in the darkroom or on a painting, or indulged in a late night out with friends, to exhibitions, shows, or clubs. *No,* she thought, looking at herself in the makeup mirror, *he was there.* She could almost feel the weight of his presence—compact but heavy, like a ball of lead—waiting in her flat. Uncomfortably guilty, she fidgeted in the chair. She hated the constraints and limitations of being in a relationship.

"The most important part of the look is the eyes." Jean was talking to George, not to her. "I'm going to paint eyes on the lids. They'll appear huge, dark, unblinking. She'll move as if in a trance."

"Wait a minute," Lee interrupted. "You don't mean I'm going to do it with my eyes closed?"

"Yes." His face glowed. "This scene—the final scene of the film, you understand—will be its coup de grace. When it's done, the audience will wonder at what they have witnessed."

She thought of all the takes they'd made the day before to perfect expressions, gestures, the one line. Then she'd been using all her faculties. She could only imagine how many takes would be necessary today, especially working on very little sleep and a champagne hangover.

"You'll be barefoot—that'll help your balance—and at the very end, you'll be walking alongside a bull. You can hold on to its horn. It'll guide you."

"A bull? Jean, are you serious?" Lee grabbed her cigarettes out of her bag and lit one.

"A real, live bull?" George, uneasy, put down his camera and took a cigarette for himself.

"Oh, it's not dangerous. They'll be bringing it over from the abattoir in a few hours. It's just an old ox that we're saving from the slaughter—for a day, anyway."

They smoked in silence as Cocteau fixed the hard, white wig onto her head. He then pulled out a small palette and some very fine paintbrushes. Sitting still, she lost track of time as he dabbed paint on her lids with cool, damp strokes. It was almost hypnotic. She temporarily forgot her grogginess, acting, even the bull.

"Absolutely amazing," George said. "He's completely transformed you. Lee, I wish you could see it."

"Me, too." She opened her eyes to thin slits, trying to catch the effect. "I suppose I'll have to wait until opening night."

Jean put away the brushes, pleased with his work, then turned to her. "All right, it's time."

As George set up his tripod in front of the empty façade, Lee sat at the table under the chandelier.

"Pick up a hand of cards as if the game had just finished," Jean instructed. "I don't think Enrique tore all of them, damn him. When we start rolling, I want you to throw the cards into the air—a theatrical gesture—then stand up. Always, always with your eyes closed."

"Jean, you understand I'll be moving around like a blind person," Lee said.

"That's exactly what I'm looking for," he said. "Now, I'll be guiding you with my voice, telling you exactly where to move. Rely on me."

They took several takes of her throwing the cards until they made a pleasing arc, then, finally, she got to her feet. Nervous, she lifted her skirts and turned gracefully, and bumped straight into the stool.

"Ow!" Lee opened her eyes and blew out; she didn't realize she'd been holding her breath. "Sorry!"

When she was able to maneuver past the table, Jean called out instructions, directing her toward the door and down a few steps. Again, many takes were needed, as he wanted her to look as if she were gliding, an inhuman object, a mysterious presence who left no footprints behind.

"Let's take a break for lunch now," Jean said. "We have to wait for the ox anyway. Lee, could you stay in costume? I really don't want to redo all that makeup."

"Fine," she said, "if you and George will join me at that place on the corner. I'd like to shock the waiters."

Although she was chilly and uncomfortable in the street with her costume on, she enjoyed the startled reactions from the passersby, who stared in confusion at her long gown, the plaster wig, and thick makeup. Even on the street, she looked otherworldly.

She ordered lunch with her eyes closed, then covered herself with a large napkin to eat.

"You should have seen the expression on the waiter's face." George chuckled.

"That's the problem with this gag. I can't."

In a moment, the waiter was back to pour their wine. When he'd gone, Lee opened her eyes and raised her glass to Jean. "To the complete artist—painter, poet, novelist, film director."

"To every man's muse," Jean said, toasting her in turn. "By the way, how is Man carrying on without you?"

"He's fine," she said, her smile mechanical. "Jean, tell George about the other scenes in the film. It's going to be a grand success."

"I'll have to swear you to secrecy!" Cocteau cocked an eyebrow, reconsidering. "Well, I'll tell you which teasers you can print in *Vogue*. Now, in the beginning of the film . . ."

Barely listening, occasionally nodding, Lee nibbled at her food, catching the odd word about dreams, the unconscious, chance. It was no coincidence, of course, that her character was a muse; she'd been chosen for her statuesque beauty, after all. But, the muse in this film—an indestructible being, out for blood—seemed far removed from the roles she'd played in real life: Daddy's girl, fashion icon, the photogenic model willing to do any pose. This muse goaded her artist along, led him to his worst fears, dealt him a deathly hand, then watched coldly as he took his own life. What exactly did she do for Man Ray? Beyond excitation, passion, ire, and exasperation—was there anything more?

She was fed up with the muse role, its trumped-up responsibility, its creative tar pit.

When Jean had concluded his exposition, she smiled brightly at the two of them, tired of her own thoughts. "It's brilliant," she said. "Even the Surrealists won't be able to resist it."

"*If* it shows, they'll come, of course. To heckle." Cocteau made a quick gesture to the waiter. "My treat, everyone. We must be getting back to the set. The ox should be there by now."

Arms linked, Lee in the middle, they returned to the studio. The two men were still having a lively conversation, but she walked in silence. Lee was uneasy about the scene with the animal, but also about the one she'd have with her own stubborn ox when she got home.

The animal was waiting for them when they arrived. An

errand boy from the abattoir had delivered it, tied it to a pole, and left it in the care of the cameraman Philippe and two burly crew members. They stood a few yards from it, eyeing its enormous bulk. One horn missing, it was slowly rubbing its huge head on the wooden post; it had several mangy patches along its flank.

"What kind of half-rate ox is this?" Jean threw up his hands. "*Mon Dieu*! It's going to need more makeup than Lee."

He sent a crew member for a bucketful of asbestos snow while he went to look through the rubbish for cardboard; he immediately began shaping a horn from some thin packing material.

"Rub this snow on him. It should give him a mythical glow." Jean held up the paper horn next to the ox, tore off the end, and resculpted it. "Philippe, bring me some tape. Now, I've got to come up with something to hide this rash." He began pacing in front of the animal, staring it dead in the eye; it shifted on its feet—did the asbestos fluff itch?—but looked back at the director. "Bullfighting, the Minotaur, *toro bravo*, Taurus, the rape of Europa . . ." Cocteau stopped. "Europa. George, be a dear and run down to the stationer's shop—it's two blocks up, one block over—and get me all the maps of Europe they have. This will be perfect."

"Lee," he said quietly, taking her by the elbow. "It's going to take me a good hour to get this bull ready for shooting. Why don't you take a little nap? In the dressing room, there's a little pallet behind the screen. I daresay you noticed it when you were changing? You get some rest. I'll wake you up when it's time to touch up your makeup."

Too exhausted to blush, she squeezed his hand. "Thanks, Jean." He was as kind as he was clever. Why did Man Ray and his friends dislike him so?

When she and the bull were finally ready for filming, she stood in her spot, waiting for her cue. The animal was decked out in leathery-looking maps, the edges burnt to resemble the spots of its breed. When Cocteau called for action, Lee beckoned the ox—making a long, arrogant gesture in her black glove—but it did not move. She was lacking in mythical know-how, she could not control the beast.

"Cut, damn it! Get me some wire. I'll find a way to make him move."

They began filming again. This time, when Lee summoned the bull, the husky crew members pulled sharply on the thin wire from offstage. As it tightened across the animal's thick neck, the old ox let out a full-throated bellow. Lee's eyes flew open in time to see it buck and charge. It ran by her, bashing her arm with its flank, and knocked her over. It stopped in the corner, panting hard and eyeing them all furiously.

"*Putain de merde!*" Cocteau ran over to Lee. "Are you hurt?"

"I don't know." She stood up slowly, blowing out, rattled. Lee stroked her upper arm—it would bruise nicely—but found she was all right. "I don't know if I can do this, Jean."

"*Pauvre petite.* Sit down for a moment and collect yourself. Philippe! Get a herder from the abattoir. Someone who knows how to control him."

Lee gathered the long dress, now smudged, and tumbled into the director's chair. Shaking her head, she lit a cigarette and took a long drag. Why had she thought acting would be fun? Between Jean's perfectionism, the hot lights, the fleas, the plaster arms, and blinded eyes, and now a charging bull? It was very hard work and yet not very rewarding. Having someone else—the creative one—tell her where to sit, how to walk, which way to look, while she, covered in makeup and extravagant clothes, listened obediently and did as she was told? It was modeling all over again. To hell with that.

No, Lee wasn't cut out to be an actor. She didn't even think she was very good at it. She looked at the bull—a powerful beast in costume—and wished she had her camera.

Thirty minutes later, an old countryman, stooped and lacking teeth, walked shyly into the film studio alongside Philippe. Hands wedged into pockets, he went over to the ox— wrinkling his brow at the patchwork maps and the prosthetic paper horn—and spoke in its ear.

"Yanked you by a wire, did they?" he whispered, shaking his head. "Hurt you, I'd wager."

He rubbed the saggy folds under its chin, checking for blood. He did not seem to understand this animal would be sacrificed the following day.

"Now, my good man," Cocteau said pleasantly, "when I give the signal, I'd like the bull to move forward, just a few steps. You *are* ready to try it again, Lee, darling?"

She gave him a tired nod.

"Marvelous. Then our actress here will join him at his side with her hand on his horn, as if she has the power to control him. Then they will walk away together." His arm reached out in a lofty gesture, then he turned again toward the old man.

"Could you help me make that happen? Could you do it, say, from over there?"

The ox driver stood on the far side of the set, raised his arm as if he held a switch, and began to grunt, his toothless mouth moving wildly. The bull stared at him and then lowered its great head, as if nodding; slowly, it began plodding toward him. Lee breathed out in relief. Although she was its symbolic master, with bare feet and closed eyes, she was terrified of the animal's size, its unpredictable nature. To the sound of the old man's snorts and groans, they quickly finished the last scene.

"Lee, my dear." Cocteau kissed her cheek. "I'm so glad we had this opportunity to work together. You've been such a good sport."

"It's been an interesting experience, Jean. One I'll never forget. And now, I suppose, I must go back to reality."

"Reality in Paris? There's no such thing." Jean patted her lightly on the back. "Now, go take a long bath at the hotel."

After a few celebratory remarks on the closing scene, she gave brief hugs to Philippe and the other crew members. She left with a jaunty "*À la prochaine, les gars,*" though she doubted there would be a next time. She slowly crossed the street to the old hotel.

Makeup removed, hair clean, Lee sat soaking in the uncomfortable little tub until the water became lukewarm. Although it was a drab bathroom, depressing really (and lacking any intrigue without Enrique in the next room), she dreaded leaving, dreaded going back home and facing Man. She tried to add more hot water, but it came out freezing cold. Shivering, she quickly splashed out, but took her time getting dressed.

When the taxi pulled away from her building, Lee looked up at her studio window. It was dark. She breathed out in relief and took the rickety little lift up, thoroughly exhausted. As she threw her bag on the table, she saw the silhouette, the red glow of a cigarette tip. She gasped, startled, though she knew who it was. Lee turned on the lights, exposing him. He looked like he hadn't slept in days: unshaven, bags under reddened eyes, tousled hair, his shirt untucked and wrinkled. In front of him was a full ashtray, a plate with a discarded sandwich, and a brand-new bottle of whisky, a few fingers missing.

"Hello, Man," she said softly. She joined him on the sofa and poured herself a glass.

"I waited for you last night." His voice was gruff, unoiled. "And all day today."

"I was busy filming until late, then I went out with Tatiana and her friends. I had to be back in the studio this morning at eight, so I didn't bother coming home." Lee usually opted for the truth, but felt details were unnecessary.

He looked down at his hands, then up at her. "Your beauty, youth, freedom . . . it's what I most admire about you." He bit his lip, trying to stifle sobs. "I don't want to lose you, Lee."

She put her arms around him and held him close. He'd expressed those contradictory feelings before: what he loved about her—her headstrong nature, her independence, her sensuality—were the same things that drove him mad. Relieved he wasn't poised for a fight, she still hated to see him so needy and weak. She rubbed his back with a long sigh, trying to provide comfort, though part of her wanted to bolt out the door. To make an escape from this settled relationship with its duty-bound devotion, its accountability for bruised feelings.

"Listen," she said, pulling away, "my part of the film is finished now. I can go back to my normal life."

"So I'm no longer obligated to lend you out to Monsieur Cocteau?"

She frowned. "I thought you just said I was free."

He took a long drink of whisky. "Right you are. So tell me about the film. What have you been doing?"

"Today was a real nightmare," she began with a smile, glad to move away from such emotional ground. "I had to do all my scenes with my eyes closed. Jean painted wide-open eyes on my lids—"

"Fucking hell! You've got to be kidding me!" He jumped up and kicked a footstool. "I painted eyes on Kiki's lids in *Emak Bakia*. Doesn't the bastard have a single original idea?"

Lee listened to him go off. Although she was convinced of Cocteau's talent, she didn't bother contradicting Man. They both preferred him lashing out at a third party, however innocent.

XXIII

It was after eleven when Lee finally roused herself from the bed; Man still lingered under blankets. His passionate rant of the night before had eventually led to passionate lovemaking, their pent-up emotions—guilt, pity, suspicion, frustration—finding physical expression.

"What are you doing today?" she asked, flipping open her appointment book. She was ready to take sitters again and needed to make calls and update her agenda.

"Do you know Willie Seabrook?" he asked.

She marked her page with a bobby pin and sat back down on the mattress; the answer to her question was clearly not a short one.

"Seabrook." She scrunched her mouth to one side, thinking; she'd never been very good with names. "Why does that sound so familiar?"

"I've got some of his books at my studio. He spends a year or so in far-off places, living with the primitives—Bedouins, cannibals, voodoo worshipers—and then he writes about it."

"That's right. I read an article about him in the *Herald Tribune*. Didn't he say human flesh tasted like veal cutlets?"

"He says all kinds of outrageous things." Man snorted. "Not

only is he an avowed cannibal, but he's into the occult—he's pals with Aleister Crowley—and loves to brag about being a Satanist."

"Do you know him?"

"We met a while back—he's American, but he's in and out of Paris—and here lately I've been doing some work for him."

"What, a portrait for his dust jacket, tucking into a nice rump roast?"

"No," Man said slowly, then stalled a minute to light a cigarette. "I've photographed his fantasies."

"Let me guess . . . Did you have to hire nuns and a billy goat?"

"Nearly." Man chuckled, pinching a bit of stray tobacco off his lip. "He's a sadist. He explained to me what he wanted— shots of women in high heels and leather, torturing a naked woman, binding her in leather straps—and he was very satisfied with the results. Of course, no one was hurt. It was just pretend."

"Damn! What mischief you've been up to. I bet you loved every minute." She shoved his arm and he collapsed onto the covers. *This* was the Man Ray she was attracted to—the fearless photographer who did daring work for famous patrons—not the sniveling baby who wanted to argue. "You'll have to show me the prints."

He sat up, pleased with himself. "Anytime."

"So what does this Willie Seabrook have to do with today?"

"He's asked me to go to his hotel tonight," he said. "He's at that luxury place on Grande Chaumière. He specified from eight to twelve."

"Is it a dinner engagement?"

"Nope," he said. "That's the thing. He and his wife are going to a banquet in his honor. He just asked me if I could watch something at his place—it could be an alligator, for all I know. You want to go? Of course, he'll treat us to anything we want from room service."

"I wouldn't miss it."

That evening, Seabrook met them at the hotel room door. Despite his reputation, he looked like most of the other journalists Lee had met in Paris: brown moustache, a bit jowly, tweed jacket. He gave Man a firm handshake and nodded politely at Lee.

"So glad you both could make it tonight." He opened the door wide and ushered them into their extravagant two-story suite. "Marjorie will be down in a moment."

As Lee looked expectantly toward the stairs, she saw her. There, at the foot of the staircase, a young woman was chained to a post, like a martyred saint or the spoils of Viking warfare. Nude except for a soiled loincloth, her hair long and stringy, she sat awkwardly on the floor, her hands bound behind her back. She gave Lee a look of passive resignation, but didn't speak.

"Ah, yes," Seabrook said, following her gaze. "This is why I want you here." He went over and patted his captive on the head. "I've hired her temporarily. She's docile and willing and, really, she needn't bother you. I just didn't want to leave her all alone." He spoke in a kindly tone; Man and Lee looked at each other. "Release her only in the case of an emergency." He handed Man the small key to her padlock. "A fire, that sort of thing."

At that moment, his wife, the writer Marjorie Worthington— a handsome woman, elegant and slim—swept down the staircase. She didn't seem to notice the woman in chains.

"Good evening." She greeted them with a thin-lipped smile painted blood red. "Man, nice to see you again—"

"And this is Lee Miller," he broke in on cue.

"Delighted. Now, I must find my gloves." She walked into another room and her husband went back to business.

"Please order anything you'd like from room service— champagne, lobster, caviar—but under no circumstances is this girl to eat with you. If she gets hungry, cut up some food and put the plate on the floor next to her, like you would for a dog."

Marjorie joined him at the door, gloves in hand, and they put on their coats.

"Nice to be fawned over by the press," Seabrook said. "They're usually such a despicable lot. See you at midnight."

Lee and Man stood in silence, listening to the rattle of the elevator. As soon as it stopped, Man picked up the house phone and ordered dinner for three. As he spoke to the kitchen, she watched him. Man had a sadistic edge himself, which some-times came out in his work. With Lee, he generally emphasized her beauty—striking portraits, romantic postures, solarized profiles—but, on occasion, he had her do awkward, uncom-fortable poses. He seemed to delight in rolling her body into a tight ball, having her strangle herself, ensnaring her in a trap—whether she was in the mood or not. In the darkroom, he took things even further; she'd been decapitated, cut into

fragments, deprived of limbs. She usually agreed with his aesthetic choices—he had an unerring eye—but sometimes found
them unsettling. Outside of photos, however, Man was rather
shy around women. Was he on board with this game? It was
one thing to photograph make-believe torture scenes, but quite
another to be an accomplice to slaveholding.

"I can't believe you're worried about dinner," she said in
a nervous whisper, shaken by his nonchalance. Lee knew she
couldn't eat a meal while a bound woman licked from a plate
on the floor. "What are we supposed to do about her? You don't
mean to follow Seabrook's instructions?"

"Hell no," he said, handing the key to Lee; she gave him a
peck on the lips, relieved.

Lee undid the padlock. "Are you all right?"

"A little stiff." The girl rubbed her wrists. "But not bad."

"Would you like to go to the bathroom?" Lee asked. The
woman's face and hands were filthy. "And maybe take a bath?"

"One of his conditions is that I not wash. But I will take a
wee."

Lee watched her saunter off to the toilet, then turned to
Man. "What the hell?"

"Well, I knew Seabrook enjoyed images of bondage, so it
doesn't shock me that he keeps a *tableau vivant* here at home."
Man offered Lee a cigarette. "When we were devising the fantasy photographs, I asked him when he'd become interested in
sadism. He explained that when he was little he was coddled by
five doting aunties." He shrugged. "Somehow, that gave him the
desire to torture women."

"What a wicked boy." Lee blew a long stream of smoke

out as the captive—now with a small blanket draped around her shoulders—strolled back into the room. She didn't look upset or worried; it was as if she were a model from a life-drawing class, allowed to take a break and stretch her limbs. Lee couldn't understand it. "What's your name, honey?"

"Oh, you can call me Nana." Lee wondered how long it had been since she'd used her real name.

The bell rang and a waiter in a white coat and slicked-back hair entered, pushing a cart laden with domed dishes. Without registering the slightest surprise at the sight of a dirty, half-naked girl, he gave them a servile nod, then set the table for three. He uncorked a bottle of red, leaving the champagne on ice for later, then retired without a word.

Around the table, Man poured wine for everyone as Lee uncovered the various dishes: shrimp bisque, stuffed quails, prime rib. Lee served herself some soup, then looked over at their guest; obviously hungry, Nana was stacking her plate with thick slices of beef. The three of them began to eat, casually passing the salt, pouring more wine, cutting bread, as if the situation at hand were normal.

"Have you been working for Mr. Seabrook long?" Lee asked, finally breaking the silence. Though Lee always liked to appear at ease, absolutely unshockable, the Paris underbelly—the outskirts of bohemia—never failed to fascinate her.

"For about a week," she mumbled, then finished chewing her bite. "It's an easy job. He just likes to look at me. With a glass of whisky, a book, but mostly at his typewriter. He likes to see me there, chained up and miserable-looking. At night, he leads me to the bedroom and ties me to the bedpost. I sleep on the rug next to him. Sometimes he pats my head, but besides that, he doesn't touch me. I don't think he can, you know." She looked at them with big eyes and lowered her voice. "Do it, that is. As clients go, he's not too bad. And he pays well. But I don't see how his wife puts up with it."

"He doesn't beat you, then?" Man asked.

"Oh no," she said. "Other clients are much worse. I have a German businessman who comes to Paris for a week every year. He brings one suitcase just for whips and straps. I lay down on his bed and he chooses a whip. Sometimes it takes him a good five or ten minutes just to decide." She stopped for a quick gulp of wine. "With that whip, he gives me a single blow, then puts a hundred-franc bill on the table where I can see it. Then he chooses another. Watching the bills pile up, I can take more blows than I ever thought possible."

Although the girl seemed pleased at the idea, a hush fell over the table again. Lee shivered, wondering at how some people made their living. She glanced at Nana—a brunette with fine features and a nice figure—and tried to imagine what had brought her to this: being a professional object of men's fantasies, no matter how twisted. Was she orphaned? Abused? A hophead? And Lee herself? What if she was poor and alone? How many lashings would she be able to endure?

"Champagne, everyone?" Man pulled the bottle out of the ice bucket, interrupting Lee's train of thought.

"Is there dessert?" Nana asked. Peering over at the cart, she licked her lips like a little girl.

"Crème brûlée or apple tart?"

"Both?"

When the dirty dishes were stacked in uncertain towers on the cart, Man slowly rolled it to the side and pulled out a deck of cards. "Anyone up for some rummy?"

"What time is it?" Nana asked, looking toward the door. "I wouldn't want Mr. Seabrook to find me away from my post."

"We've got time for a couple of hands."

Lee watched Man deal the cards and thought of the game played in *The Blood of a Poet*. Arranging her cards by suit, she peeked over at Nana. Ragged, silent, tied up, she inspired William Seabrook at his typewriter, allowed his words to flow. How different this slave was from the powerful muse Lee had played! Or did Nana also force Seabrook to look inside his psyche? Was he pleased with what he saw?

Before the Seabrooks returned, they chained the girl back up. As a theatrical touch, Man left a plate with scraps next to her on the floor.

"Wonderful," Seabrook cried as he strutted into the room, finding everything in its place. "You had a good evening, I trust. No trouble out of this one?"

"It was our pleasure," Man assured him. "The restaurant service here is excellent."

"Yes, lovely." Lee studied Seabrook's insipid features as she smiled at him, trying to imagine his inner workings—cheek-pinching aunties breeding an impotent sadist—but soon gave up. "Thank you," she added.

While Man was helping Lee on with her coat, Marjorie murmured a goodnight and went upstairs. Seabrook quickly came over to them, his eyes flashing at Man.

"Tonight, during dinner, I had a brilliant idea. I'd like for you to design a collar for Marjorie that runs the length of her neck." He turned to Lee—"If you don't mind?"—and put his large hands around her neck, as if to strangle her; she grimaced and lifted her chin high, away from his touch, the bristling hairs and reek of stale tobacco. "Something about this size. Something that will constrict her movement—keep her head high and unable to turn—but not prevent her from breathing or swallowing." He let go of Lee's neck with a courteous dip of the head. "I saw some women in Africa wearing such things and the copper looked stunning against their dark skin. Well, what do you think?"

"I'm sure I could come up with a few designs." Man said. "You'd want it to work on a hinge?" He opened and shut his rounded hands like a clasp.

"Just so. And I want it to be a real piece of jewelry. Nothing cheap. Silver, perhaps. Like something from the king's own torture chamber." He was pleased at the idea of such a generous gift.

"I'll see what I can do." They walked out into the landing and pressed the elevator button. "Good night."

With a friendly little wave, he called from the doorway: "Thanks again for minding my slave."

Walking home, Man took Lee's leather-gloved hand and stroked it. "You know, they say ol' Seabrook was completely normal until he got gassed at Verdun."

Two weeks after she'd finished Cocteau's film, Lee's appointment book was already filling with sitters. She was putting newspaper on the floor as she waited for an English baroness, adamant about posing with her three greyhounds, when she heard someone bounding up the stairs. There was a quick single knock, then Man let himself in with his key.

"Lee? I've got something to show you. Oh, and I picked up your mail on the way up." He tossed a handful of letters on the table and handed her a black leather box. Inside sat a large silver choker, a good three inches high, studded with shiny knobs. "I drew the design, then got the silversmith who did my chess pieces to make it. Try it on."

"Hats off, Man," she said, removing it from the box. "It looks to be the very finest in slavewear this season." As she opened and closed the mechanism, which was very like a trap, her smile faded. She looked at him uncertainly. "I will be able to take it off again, won't I?"

"Ha ha. Here, I'll help you." He fastened it in place, then whistled. "You are stunning. Look in the mirror."

She looked at herself in the cold, tight brace; since her head was unmovable, she turned her body to different angles to see the effect. Her chin up and neck extended, Lee looked regal and commanding. It was a modern, kinky variant of Queen Elizabeth's starched lace ruff—also said to be extremely uncomfortable—which gave off the imposing appearance of arrogance, strength, and pride. The wearer, however, was on the verge of choking. Despite its grand illusion, Lee frowned at her reflection; she did not like being vulnerable, trapped.

"Truly impressive," he said, obviously delighted with his handiwork. "Damn it, I don't have my camera. Can I use yours?"

His eyes lit on the tripod, already set up for the sitting. Seeing the relish on Man's face, Lee knew at once that he'd want to do a full series. She'd need to get used to the idea.

"Take pictures later." Speaking was difficult; it was like slow strangulation. Skin prickling, she clawed up at the choker and tried to unclasp it. "Get it off me." With a chuckle at her panic, he took it off. She let out a gust of air. "It *is* a torture device." She rubbed her bare neck affectionately. "Do you think Marjorie will like it?"

"I think she'll like the attention. She can't stand the women Seabrook hires, but, then, she's not willing to take their place either."

"Neither would I." She started flipping through the mail. "I wonder if Nana's still there."

"Nana or someone like her." He looked over her shoulder onto the letters. "Anything good?"

"This one is from Elsa Schiaparelli." Too excited to think, she waved the letter—a personal, handwritten note from one of the most important designers in Europe—in front of Man. "She wants me to photograph her summer collection. She says I know more about fashion than any other photographer in Paris!"

He said nothing.

"Oh, Man." She patted his hand, then grabbed his cigarette case and lit one for herself. Lee knew this was sensitive ground; to his mind, she was still his novice assistant, not yet ready for prime jobs. But this assignment was ideal for her; there was no way she was going to hand it over to him for the sake of his fragile ego. "You must admit, after all these years at *Vogue*—as a model and photographer—I know a thing or two about fashion. She probably wants a woman's point of view. As well she should!"

"Right," he said shortly, knitting his eyebrows. "And I'm just a stupid sap. I don't know a damn thing about women."

"Well, you know how to get them hot and bothered—that's the important thing."

She laughed and went back to the mail, ignoring his sulk. There was nothing more to say about the Schiaparelli collection. Bills, a couple of unremarkable portrait requests, and, at the bottom of the pile, a large envelope made of thick, expensive paper. The return address was penned in a secretary's careful hand: Duke Vallombrosa. Man looked at her expectantly as she read its few lines.

"It's an invitation to a New Year's Eve party." This was the event Zizi had told her about that rainy day in the car, the seasonal to-do he'd been hired to decorate. He was expecting her there as his guest. She put the card down and looked at Man. The news of the Schiaparelli collection had completely doused his excitement about the silver collar. "Shall we ring in 1931 with the duke?"

"Are you sure I'm included?" he scowled softly.

"Aren't I Madame Man Ray?"

She was pleased to see his smile again. She'd nearly made a joke about him being Monsieur Lee Miller, but had decided against it.

XXIV

―――

On December thirty-first, as Man and Lee were ushered into the duke's mansion, they were struck by the smell of juniper and pine. It was as if, attracted by light and music, a forest had decided to join the festivities. Garlands of greenery were draped along the walls; branches and boughs, woven with silver strands of tiny bells, were artfully arranged on tabletops and mantels, with thin white candles and colorful nesting dolls— unstacked for the occasion—tucked into the foliage. Freshly picked wreaths of holly, laurel, fir, and ivy covered every door.

Lee breathed in. "It's like we're in the middle of the woods. We're like Hansel and Gretel."

"*They* were brother and sister," he whispered in her ear, grabbing her waist as she took off her coat. "No, Lee. I'm the Big Bad Wolf."

"If only I'd brought my red riding hood," she joked back, but removed his hands and walked into the main hall alone.

Lee saw Tatiana, spectacular in silver satin and surrounded by admirers. Someone had just made a toast, and they were all popping back shots of vodka. The circle immediately opened to include Lee; Man wandered off, looking for refreshments and familiar faces.

"Darlink." Tatiana embraced Lee, then swept her away from the others, leading her toward the fire. "Isn't this beautiful? We Russians are all getting very nostalgic tonight. New Year is the biggest celebration in Russia—well, it was until the blasted Soviets abolished it last year—and Zizi's decorated the place in a traditional way. Well," she said, eyeing the enormous wreath over the fireplace, "in my family, we never cut down this much trees."

"It's gorgeous. I love the smell." Lee looked around. "Where is Zizi?"

"I don't know. Dancing, perhaps? He was so pleased with himself when he told me you were his guest for party. He'll be disappointed that you didn't come alone."

"Yes, well." Lee shrugged.

At that moment, Jean Cocteau, elegant in gray pinstripes and juggling three glasses of champagne, joined them.

"I saw you ladies over here, empty-handed."

"Thanks, Jean." Lee took a glass. "You know Tatiana?"

"We've met." The three clinked glasses and took a sip. "I've just seen your friend Zizi and given him a good scolding." He turned to Tatiana. "For her last day of filming, Lee dragged in like she'd spent the night manning the trenches on the Western Front."

"As bad as all that?" Lee wrinkled her nose prettily. "Tell me, Jean, is there any news about the film?"

"Well, there's good and bad. The good news is I've finished filming the confounded thing." He blew out, wiping his brow. "But the bad news is that Charles de Noailles is postponing the premiere indefinitely."

"What terrible luck, Jean." Although nervous about seeing herself on film, Lee had been looking forward to the pomp and glamour of a premiere. "Just because of the other film? Has he even seen yours?"

"Not even snippets." Jean sighed. "But he's afraid of another scandal. Hopefully, in another six months, he'll have found his backbone."

"If not, couldn't you at least show it at a private party? Something like this?" Lee asked. She gestured to the well-dressed crowd. Aristocrats and Russian émigrés mixed with celebrated figures from the stage—opera singers and ballerinas—as well as a generous peppering of the Parisian avant-garde. She wondered how many of them were prepared to see a film like Cocteau's.

"Let's hope it doesn't come to that," he said.

"*Bon soir,* Jean." It was Man, back from inspecting the place. "I see you've got the monopoly on the most beautiful women here."

"Nice to see you, Man," he said, shaking his hand. "Are you taking photos tonight?"

"No." Man glowered at Cocteau. "I'm not always the hired help."

"Of course, of course." Cocteau smiled uncomfortably. "Well, if you'll excuse me. . . Lee, Tatiana." And he made his exit.

"Do you believe the nerve of that guy?" Man was just getting started, but Lee, who'd finally spotted Zizi hovering over the hors d'oeuvres, broke him off.

"It's nothing worth getting riled up about. You know, you

often *do* take pictures at these things." She kissed his cheek. "I'm going to get a bite to eat. Do you two want anything?"

Tatiana had also noticed Zizi at the table. "You go ahead. I wanted to talk to Man about taking a special portrait for my *vicomte*." She inched toward him until he could smell her perfume. "Unless it bothers you to talk businesses?"

"You could talk to me about anything, Tata. Your favorite buttons, Russian square-dancing, Léon Blum's mustache . . ."

Lee headed to the long dining table at the edge of the ballroom. Candles and braided greenery wrapped around platters of bone china, where artfully arranged finger foods, both Russian and French, were constantly replenished. She sidled up to Zizi, who was piling red caviar on a blini.

"Wouldn't you like some sour cream on that?" she said in his ear.

"Lee!" He abandoned his blini and took a step back to admire her. Elsa Schiaparelli had loaned her a fluid black dress that was deceptively simple: sleeveless, nearly backless, but not lacking a train. "You're ravishing. Pity you'll be taking that gown off so soon."

"Not so fast, you little lecher," she said with a laugh. "Did I mention that Man's here?"

"No," he drew the word out, scanning the crowded room for her lover. Finding him, his face fell. "But no matter. You're still going to have to take it off. You see, I want you to help me put on a little show. I would ask Tata—she's the logical choice, being Russian and all—but I thought it would be fun if we did it together."

Eyebrows raised, her gaze held an air of suspicious good humor. "Did what, Zizi?"

"Dress as Ded Moroz and Snegurochka!"

Her brow did not fall. "And who are they?"

"They are the traditional New Year's characters, Grandfather Frost and the Snow Maiden. We'll go around in costume giving out little presents. The duke loves the idea."

"Does he?" This was the kind of acting Lee really enjoyed: dazzling the elite (all potential clients) on the arm of a gallant courter. Man would survive without her for a bit. "Well, I suppose we should do it, then."

Zizi led her down a corridor; he'd stored the costumes in a ground-floor bedroom.

"Tell me, then," Lee asked, "who is this snow maiden?"

"In Russian folklore, she's the daughter of winter and spring. She is young, beautiful, and blond." He swept his hand before her. "*La voilà.* Some say she was raised by a human couple who weren't able to have children. They were told to keep her inside, but she fell in love with a boy she saw from the window. In his arms, she melted away after just one kiss."

"That's sad," Lee said. "It reminds me of *The Little Mermaid*."

"Yes, who can understand why these beautiful creatures want to be with lowly humans?" He stopped in front of the bedroom door and grazed her cheek with his. "Are you human, Lee?"

"I haven't melted yet."

Inside the bedroom, he pulled her close and kissed her, caressing her naked back. Although her body was tingling in delight, she thought of Man, a corridor away, gruffly charming as he mingled with the upper crust, the privileged rich who always made him ill at ease. This was not the time for a tryst. She gently pushed Zizi away.

"And our costumes, Grandfather Frost?"

"You sure you don't want to . . . ?" he whispered in her ear. She nodded and he shrugged, graciously accepting defeat. "Some say the Snow Maiden is Frost's granddaughter. Best not to cross family lines, I suppose."

He opened a wardrobe and pulled out two floor-length robes, both elaborately embroidered and trimmed in rabbit fur, and handed her one of silvery blue. Lee shed her silky black gown and stepped into the robe, buttoning it up to the fur collar, then looked in the mirror. Zizi stood next to her, all in red, hooking a long cotton beard on wires over his ears.

"And this is for my beautiful maiden." He crowned her with a five-pointed silver tiara, encrusted with fake pearls. "Counterfeit jewels, fit for a Romanov." He doffed a round cap and picked up a velvet bag filled with party favors. "Well? How do I look?"

She kissed his cotton-lined lips. "Santa Claus is eating his heart out."

The valets silenced the orchestra, then flung open the doors, ringing handbells to get everyone's attention. When Zizi and Lee marched into the great hall, smiling and waving, all the émigrés in the room burst into cheers and applause. Lee basked and beamed, enjoying the spotlight. Arm in arm, they made their way around the woodsy ballroom, giving Cuban cigars to the men and handkerchiefs to the ladies, and wishing everyone a happy new year. The delighted guests laughed and joked with the storybook characters, but the Russians were moved; most of them insisted on kissing them both. Tatiana was teary-eyed when they finally rejoined her and she gave Zizi a warm embrace.

"Your Russian New Year is ruining my makeup," she said, dabbing tears of kohl away with her brand-new handkerchief.

"I had no idea you were so sentimental, Tata." Lee smiled at her friend, then glanced around. "Have you seen Man? I swear, we've spoken to everyone but him."

"I think I saw him go out to the garden," Tatiana said.

"I'd better see how he's doing."

Lee found Man alone on the terrace. He was pacing the flagstones, slouched over his cigarette—as if it could warm him—shivering in his dinner jacket. When he caught sight of her, he puffed himself up to his full height and glared. Lee frowned. Lately, every time he felt insecure about other men, he tried to grow a few inches. At the moment, he was nearly standing on his tiptoes.

"Aren't you cold out here?" She gave him a lighthearted smile and adjusted her tiara. "For a snow maiden like myself, it's fine, but for you—"

"You are the cold one." He gave her a sharp look. "He's your lover, isn't he?"

"What?" Lee was taken off guard.

"I heard Cocteau teasing him about keeping one of his actresses out late. I was too stupid to think it was you—that you'd spent that night with him—until you walked in together, all cozy in your matching costumes. I can't stand the thought of you becoming one of those pathetic, ornamental women that flitter around Zizi Svirsky." He threw his cigarette butt down and rubbed his arms. "I know you sometimes see other men but, Jesus, Lee, he's older than I am." He paused. "And he'll never love you like I do."

His voice broke and he stopped talking; he stared at her, his chin trembling, his eyes wet. She returned his gaze in silence. She didn't know if she liked being loved with such intensity; the depths of his emotion, his visceral passions, were hard for her to understand. In fact, when confronted by the power of his love and desire—their crushing weight and stormy force—she felt their lack. An unpleasant emptiness. Lee had never been able to love like that; she doubted she was capable of it. The thrill of infatuation, urgent desire, simple fondness, yes, but love? Sometimes she wondered if there was something wrong with her. Maybe she was an ice princess, afraid of melting.

"Let's go home," he said, reaching out for her hand.

She did not take it. "Man, it's not even midnight. Let's stay and ring in the New Year—" But he had already turned around and was walking away. "Man," she called once, but didn't move.

Lee watched his inflated form as it retreated, barreled its way through the French windows and the crowd inside. She sighed, rooted to her spot on the terrace. She tried to work out her feelings for him—that familiar hodgepodge of affection and frustration, security and sameness—but couldn't deny the facts at hand. She had let him go.

When she walked back into the ballroom, Zizi immediately joined her.

"What's this long face?" He caressed her cheek. "There's a

saying in Russian: 'As you meet the New Year, so you will spend it.' You must enjoy yourself tonight—or you risk spending the rest of the year unhappy."

"That certainly wouldn't do." She put on a smile but wondered what 1931 would bring; would it be better? Worse? Because change, she knew, was coming. "More champagne?"

XXV

Dressed only in her kimono bathrobe, long, satin, and bamboo-green, Lee slipped down to the ground floor to fetch the morning post. Two thin letters were aslant in the box. Shivering with cold, she got into the lift; on the bumpy ascent, she took a quick look at the envelopes. She recognized the handwriting on the first one, though the casual characters were tighter than usual. It was from Man Ray, whom she hadn't seen since the New Year's Eve party. Today was January third.

In the warmth of her flat, she lit a cigarette and slit open the envelope. The letter was one long typewritten block, a series of half-finished thoughts outlining a list of reasons why he was a far better partner than Zizi. His passionate love, his position as mentor, the efforts he'd made toward her development. Lee pursed her lips, annoyed. He sounded like a whiny Adam reminding Eve about his missing rib. Man's letter babbled on: Zizi clearly did not care about her thoughts, achievements, or work; he just wanted her for her youthful energy, the way she looked on his arm. That Russian phony would use any means necessary to draw her in: diversions, introductions, money.

She read the letter twice, three times. However true his observations about Zizi might be, really, they were apt descriptions of Man himself: he, too, offered her financial help, contact with the best people, amusement. But his claim of a mentor's love, justified by her progress and capabilities? The interesting ideas he brought out in her? His Pygmalion hand in creating her? She shook her head, a twitchy feeling in her throat. She felt duped. It seemed that Man Ray, the man she'd been with longer than any other, wanted her as a complement to himself. Instead of loving her for who she was—with that huge passionate fire of his—he thought of her as his finest confection: his lover as his work of art.

She made a pot of coffee, stewing over the letter; it had certainly brought them no closer to reconciliation. Should she write him back? And say what? *As you meet the New Year, so you will spend it.* Did that mean that she and Man would spend the year angry with each other?

Back at the table, she swirled sugar into her coffee and picked up the other letter. It was from Elstree Studios, the British branch of Paramount Pictures. She opened it with a frown, uncomfortable with the idea of acting again. She skimmed the page—they didn't need an actress, after all—then read it again. The studio was looking for a photographer, and Michel de Brunhoff had recommended *her*. She grinned down at the paper. He'd called her an intrepid professional with a keen eye and excellent darkroom skills; he'd also mentioned her recent participation in a film, her insider's understanding of studios, sets, cast, and crew. They needed publicity shots of actors and stills of their new feature film, *Stamboul*, and would be delighted if she joined their team. Would it be possible for her to leave Paris for a few months to work in London?

She twirled around, then kicked out her legs, a ten-second Charleston. Yes! Here was a job offer, not for Man Ray's assistant, nor George Hoyningen-Huene's apprentice, but for a trained photographer, a professional in the field. An excellent career move, it also offered her the perfect escape hatch.

Lee had never liked decision making; in fact, she generally left things to work out on their own. And here was the perfect solution to her problems with Man Ray: time and distance. She could flee to London—far from him and these tiresome dramatics—and establish herself there as a photographer in her own right. Not Madame Man Ray, his muse and minion. With money coming in from Elstree Studios, she would no longer need his help. And perhaps, after being separated by the Channel for several months, they could start anew, relishing each other's company and collaborating on exciting projects. Working together as equals. Then again, after a long absence perhaps they would naturally drift apart. Lee had never liked messy breakup scenes. Up to now, when bored with a companion, she'd merely ignored him or behaved badly until he'd eventually gotten the message. With Man, she was sure that such subtlety would never do. She drained the last sips of her coffee, then nodded decisively. Either way, her stay in London would give her a new perspective; with time apart, her problems would fix themselves.

She threw off her kimono and got dressed. Regardless of what might happen in the next few months, she wanted patch things up as soon as possible. Burnt bridges were of no use to Lee. Especially not with Man. She hid his angry letter away in a drawer and snatched up the one from the motion-picture studio, heading out the door. It wouldn't be difficult to make up with him. Despite Man's fears, Zizi had never been a serious rival, but merely lighthearted fun. Really, he was a small sacrifice to allow Man to regain his security, his manhood.

They could spend a last few weeks together, and then— she'd be gone.

"I'm so proud of you, kid." Man sat on Lee's bed, smoking his pipe while she finished packing. "I can't get over it. Paramount Pictures!"

"It's just Elstree. Paramount's kid brother. It probably has buck teeth and pimples," she said, with a self-deprecating half-shrug. "And we know for sure there's no California sunshine in North London. Hey, throw me those stockings."

His pipe in his mouth, he tossed the shimmery stack of silk to her with both hands; she caught them in mid-air, the pile intact. They shared a smile. Ever since they'd made up, their relationship had been easy, with no arguments or accusations. Of course, he was thrilled to win out so easily over Zizi, to hear Lee's promise not to see him again; their lack of temper was also due to their incessant awareness of the months they'd be apart.

"What kind of title is *Stamboul?*"

"It's another name for Istanbul. The film promises to be a real melodrama, a gorgeous historical: a steamy love affair between a German countess and a French military officer set in the land of fezzes, hookahs, and Turkish delight. At least, a big painted backdrop of it." Lee gave Man an unabashed grin. "I love that stuff."

"Well, it was really swell of de Brunhoff to recommend you—"

"And how!"

"But doesn't he mind losing you at *Frogue*? Seems he'd want to keep his 'intrepid professional' in situ, working for him."

"He was just thinking of me." Fastening her trunk, she didn't look up. What was the Freudian term for what he was doing? Projection. That was it. "Michel thought it was a grand opportunity."

"Trading Paris for London? If you say so."

She stood up and clapped the dust off her hands. "I'm done. Let's go up to the boulevard for a drink. But just a quick one— tomorrow we're off!"

The Voisin packed with Lee's gear, they headed due north through the dense winter fogs up to Calais, the tip of France closest to Great Britain where the ferries ran. She was enthusiastic about everything: the low bridges over marshy flatlands, the naked landscape dotted with windmills, the passing architecture that became more Flemish as they went north. But she was especially thrilled about her new adventure and independence.

When they arrived late that afternoon, though the skies were gray and the sea a blackish-blue, they pretended to be on a romantic holiday to the shore. Hand in hand, they checked in to a small portside hotel and climbed the steep stairs to their room.

"How I love an ocean view." Lee turned around and beamed at Man; he joined her at the window and put his arm around her.

"This sort of reminds me of our rooms at Emak Bakia, down in Biarritz," he said. "Without the servants, mountains, and summer, that is."

"Well, it's the opposite end of the country, but the ocean's the same."

"And you'll be on the other side of it tomorrow."

"I'm just crossing the Channel, you dope, not the Atlantic."

"It's still too far to swim!"

She kissed his cheek. "I know." Man had been making an effort to be supportive, but she knew it was hard for him.

"You can call me whenever you want, day or night. Just reverse the charges, I'm happy to pay." He'd told her that a half-dozen times already; she kissed him again. "How long do you think it'll be before I hear from you? A couple of days?" He looked at her anxiously.

"I guess it depends on how busy I am. Don't worry. I won't fall off the map."

"And remember, you can tell me anything. I know you'll meet some fellas and all that. But you can be up front with me, kid. I'd feel better knowing what's going on over there."

"Whatever you say." She nodded, but knew it would be a huge relief for him not to witness her with other men; he didn't need to imagine any rivals. Lee would keep that part of her experience to herself.

He poked his head out the window and looked up the quay. "We need to find a quality restaurant for tonight. Get some good French cooking under your belt before you cross tomorrow. On the other side of the Channel, I hear it's all mushy peas and boiled meat."

"Mmmm, that's what I grew up on." She said, licking her lips and pulling him to her by his tie. "Tell me, what else can I get under my belt before I go?"

After a night of fine dining, champagne, and fondling farewells, they parted on the docks the next morning.

"Remember!" he called out. "I can arrange to come visit whenever you'd like."

With a brilliant smile, she waved down at him from the rails. Lee was reminded of her great good-bye to her father from the ocean liner decks on her first crossing to France at age eighteen, jumping up and down and waving like a castaway trying to flag a ship. Then, too, she'd been thrilled about traveling away, off on an adventure, (nearly) on her own. What a shame they didn't throw streamers and confetti on ferries. She looked around at the other passengers, the businessmen, soldiers, and students; for most of them, this was routine. At the sound of the horn, Lee headed to the lounge, ready to meet new people, to start her new life. As the ship left shore, however, it began to dip and roll. In just a few minutes, everyone, in varying tones of green, quietly moved to the window seats in desperate search of the horizon line. Lee spent her first hours of freedom begging her breakfast to stay down.

After the rocky crossing and a surprisingly unpunctual British train, Lee arrived at Victoria station in the late afternoon, wrinkled and exhausted. She was almost glad that the film studio had only thought to send a lanky, spot-ridden teen—surely, the lowest errand boy on their staff—to greet her. Straining under the weight of her trunks, he hailed a cab and accompanied her to the hotel. During the long taxi ride, he didn't try to make conversation, but gave her a note from the film director, Dimitri Buchowetzki. In polite, rather sparse English, he welcomed Lee to London and bid her settle in before coming to the set the following Monday.

The studio had booked her a hotel in a nameless neighborhood way up in the north of London—"a straight shot to Elstree by Tube"—which was no Bloomsbury, Kensington, or Chelsea. Disappointed, she went up to her small, clean room; she bathed, unpacked, napped, then, finding herself hungry, went to a nearby restaurant for dinner. She enjoyed being able to do exactly as she pleased—without demands or expectations from anyone—but it was strange being alone in this bustling capital, dining by herself surrounded by couples and clusters.

For the next two days, Lee explored the city center, but her excitement dampened along with her shoes. Ambling past street vendors and roller-skating kids—all seemingly unfazed by the drizzling cold—she restlessly ventured into places more for refuge than genuine interest: the Portrait Gallery, bookshops, churches, then, after five, pubs. She was hoping to meet interesting, artistic people, to find her niche. Where were the jazzy rhythms and creative energy, the risqué corners she'd known in Paris? Where was their Montparnasse? Hidden under umbrellas, Londoners seemed to rush back and forth, from work to shops to home.

On the third day, she decided to put in an appearance at *British Vogue,* confident that she'd feel right at home. Lee found their offices off Oxford Street and, before she went in, reapplied her lipstick and ran her fingers through her limp hair. How did anyone manage to look good in this weather?

"Good morning," she greeted the secretary, while trying to find a place to dump her dripping umbrella. "I'm—"

"Wait!" The secretary put up her hand. "Your face is so familiar. We've run pictures of you at least a dozen times. You're . . ." She knit her brow and frowned.

"Lee Miller." She filled in the blank.

"Of course! Are you going to be working here?"

"That depends." She looked over at the closed door beyond her desk. "I'd like to talk to the editor."

"Silly me! Let me tell her you're here."

Like Michel de Brunhoff before her, Alison Settle was delighted to meet Lee. When the secretary went to fetch tea, Lee could hear the buzz in the corridor (*model . . . Frogue . . . Man Ray . . .*), which led to a few staffers popping in to gawk. When they finally had the office to themselves, Lee explained why she was in town.

"Working for the pictures," Alison said. "How exciting!"

"Yes." Lee smiled at her and took a sip of tea. It hadn't been terribly exciting *yet* but, hopefully, it would all improve once she got started. "I still don't know my timetable, but I'd like to do a few shoots for *Brogue* while I'm here."

"We'd love to have you model for us. Have you ever worked with our crack photographer, Cecil Beaton? He's charming, and his work is divine."

"Actually, I was rather hoping to take the photos. That's what I'm doing in London—working as a photographer. At *Frogue,* I've been working alongside George Hoyningen-Huene for a year now. Setting up shots, taking pictures, developing, and printing. The whole bit."

"Oh right, I'd heard that you'd switched sides." Alison's eyes twinkled. "I'm sure we could use you. Whenever you have some spare time, we'll schedule you in. We'd love to have your byline."

During the long morning she spent at *British Vogue* touring the facilities and chatting with her British colleagues, everyone was friendly and flattering. When she suggested dinner or drinks to the perkiest of the bunch, however, they all declined with tales of part-time nannies, prudish parents, or how the husbands of working girls felt abandoned enough as it was. Back on the street, she headed to a pub and ordered a pint by herself surrounded by lone, silent drinkers.

Sunday night, Lee lay sleepless in the hotel bed, wondering what to expect from the big, almost-Paramount production. *The Blood of a Poet* was a poem, really, not exactly a normal cinema experience. She breathed out and turned on the light, trying to imagine the bustle of a large crew, various sets, expensive equipment, movie stars.

She picked up the issue of *Film Weekly* bought at the newsagent's the day before. Nearly lost among the lavish spreads on Greta Garbo, the Marx Brothers, and Gary Cooper, there was a small blurb about *Stamboul,* soon to begin filming at Elstree. Although none of the cast members were especially famous, Lee had heard of two of them. Margot Grahame, the star of the production, was younger than Lee—just twenty—but had already been dubbed the British answer to Jean Harlow. Warwick Ward, the handsome leading man, was in and out of the tabloids, the subject of romantic scandals. She peered down at the small photo of him, wondering if she might have a love scene with Ward herself.

The next day, she shyly entered the grounds of the large studio, her personal camera hanging neatly off the shoulder of her raincoat, and was directed to soundstage number nine. After a fifteen-minute walk past offices, workshops, the canteen, and a film laboratory, she found the right hangar. She tiptoed through the large door and waited nervously, wondering what she should do. Everyone looked so busy! Finally, the same spotty teen from the station noticed her and came to greet her.

"Good morning, Miss Miller." He looked half-awake. "Mr. Buchowetzki has asked me to show you around. He'll be with you later today."

With neither enthusiasm nor dialogue, the young man walked Lee around the modern studios. Here there were no flea-infested mattresses or broken-down oxen, but state-of-the-art equipment and an on-site darkroom bigger than any she had ever used. After the tour, he found her a chair to wait in and scurried off.

She smoked in silence, watching other people work: designers putting the finishing touches on various sets (including enormous panoramic paintings of the Istanbul skyline: day and night); cameramen moving their equipment; technicians checking lights; one actor discussing his costume with the seamstress, another arguing about his hair. Finally, after an hour of sitting ignored in a corner, the director appeared.

"Hello, there." She stood up to accept his firm handshake. "Thank you for joining our team. I want to introduce you to Robert Mann, our head cameraman. I thought that, as well as taking stills, you could operate a motion-picture camera." Lee gave him a delighted smile, always happy to learn new techniques, but he didn't seem to notice. "Once you've got the hang of it, you can shoot stand-ins and backgrounds. Here's Robert now."

After minimal introductions, Buchowetzki disappeared again. Lee spent the rest of the day next to a cameraman so reserved, he preferred to see life through the camera lens and used more gestures than words.

Hours later, back on the underground, she slumped in her corner seat and made a balance of the day. Even though the work itself had been satisfying enough, Lee couldn't shake a vague feeling of disappointment. At the film studio, she was not the leading lady she'd been in Paris, but rather a sideline member of the crew who held no status or glamour. She looked at her shadowy image, reflected in the window by the darkness of the tunnel, and compared this production unfavorably with her last. Buchowetzki was less involved, less intense than Cocteau, whose filmmaking was art, not work; the *Stamboul* crew was polite but standoffish. Warwick Ward had none of Enrique Rivero's charm—at least, she didn't think he did. He hadn't said two words to her. There was no sense of community; after work, everyone had left alone, rushing back to their lives.

Chugging along in the stale-smelling tube, she felt homesick for Paris, where, in many districts and nightspots, she was well-known and celebrated. As a good-time girl, as a capricious beauty, as a grade-A photographer, as Madame Man Ray. Here in London, she was nobody.

Back at the hotel lobby, Lee closed herself up in the telephone booth and called Man, reversing the charges.

"What an angel you are for calling so soon," he gushed.

Her spirits rose immediately. "Miss me?"

"Are you kidding? Last night I went to dinner with Breton and the others, down by the Seine. On the way home, I walked along the quay in the moonlight, imagining we were arm in arm. I hadn't felt so romantic since I was a teen."

For an instant, she tried to imagine Man Ray—with his widow's peak, his stocky frame, his downturned mouth holding a pipe—as a fresh-faced teenager. It was nearly impossible.

"And the bed," he went on, "it's so big and empty."

"My bed is empty, too, but it isn't so big." She stopped smiling to light a cigarette.

She told him about her promising day on the set, playing around with the big movie camera. He gave her technical advice about composition, camera angles, and lenses, then told her a few problem-solving anecdotes from his filmmaking days, clearly delighted to be her teacher once again.

After a long talk with her faithful admirer, Lee got the boost she'd needed; her self-confidence was fully restored. She went into the hotel bar and ordered a sidecar. As she was leafing through the *Times*, the barman whispered discreetly, "The gentleman at the end of the bar would like to treat you to your drink, Madame."

Lee looked up from the paper and raised her glass at the stranger. That was more like it.

The initial feeling of being out of place soon faded away and Lee began enjoying herself in London. After a couple of days on the job, she took a photo shoot of the main actors for a film magazine—melodramatic stills that had them all in stitches—which led to lighthearted friendships. She didn't find them as interesting as Cocteau's international cast—and Warwick Ward didn't give off the faintest spark—but they were fun to pal around with. The shy cameraman also came round and stopped squinting through the viewfinder to talk with her, lovingly and in detail, about his craft: light and shadow, movement and sound. Going to the studio every morning had become a pleasure; instructive and rewarding, social and fun.

After she'd been in town a month, visitors started arriving, eager for London theater, museums, ales, and pork pies: Yalies she'd known in New York, George and Tatiana from Paris, her brother, Erik, in town for three weeks. And then Lee kept meeting new people, mostly men, some local, others just passing through. When she wanted, she had a fling, occasional one-nighters, others that became irritatingly more serious.

Through it all, Man wrote and called. He spoke of his adoration for her, he outlined his future plans for them, he got his passport renewed in case she needed him, he begged her to tell him about her every move. Sometimes Lee would skim an ardent love letter while reapplying her makeup, then put on her coat and go out with someone else. At other times, however, when she was alone in her yellowy hotel room, tired and melancholy, she missed him, too.

That promising combination of time and distance hadn't been able to make her decisions for her; she still didn't know what she wanted from Man Ray. Entertained and busy, she kept putting off her return. When the *Stamboul* production was finished, Lee did a few photo shoots for *Brogue*; after that, she wandered up to the Lake District and Edinburgh. Finally, after six months away, she decided it was time to go back to Paris.

"This is wonderful news!" Lee pulled her ear away from the telephone; Man was nearly shouting.

"There's a new train service that goes straight from Dover to Paris. I can't imagine how they cram a train onto a ferry-boat," she said, incredulous, "but they say it's the quickest way."

"Wonderful! I'll be waiting for you at the Gare du Nord."

"You'd better be. If you're not, don't be surprised if I get lost and end up in the wrong man's studio. I haven't been to Paris in so long, anything could happen."

XXVI

On a muggy afternoon in late July, Lee lit from the train, delighted to be surrounded again by French conversations, even
the most banal. Walking down the platform at the Gare du
Nord, she breathed in deeply—the diesel steam of the trains
nearly masked the ubiquitous smell of tobacco and perfume—
wanting to immediately retake Paris. Due to a mix-up in the
timetables, she was fifteen minutes earlier than expected.
Whisking through the station, she scanned the faces around
her, wondering if Man was already there. Suddenly, she caught
sight of him on a bench, stopped short—the porter with her
trunks almost slammed into her—and stared.

Man's body was drooping down, his hands—carrying an
exaggerated bouquet of lilies—folded between his legs. Although he was sharply dressed for their reunion, he had put on
a few pounds and sported an unfamiliar haircut that was not
to his advantage. His face was both puffy and lined, his body
soft and slack, his enormous eyes those of a tragic baby, pre-
maturely aged. In a single glance, Lee knew. This was not the
alluring stranger who had magically risen up the spiral staircase
in the Bateau Ivre, not the gruff gangster that she'd chained
herself to, not the famous photographer who she had to have

in the darkroom. No. She was no longer attracted to him. And, despite what she'd occasionally told herself alone in her English hotel room, she did not love this man.

Suddenly, he felt her presence and looked toward her. He shot out of his chair and enveloped her in a tight embrace. He kissed her again and again. She hid her face in his hug; he murmured superlatives in her ear. What was she going to do? The time away hadn't helped. His feelings for her had not slackened, and her resolve to leave him had not strengthened. She sighed in frustration, disappointment, exhaustion.

"It's swell to see you, too." She managed a big smile as she pushed him away.

He chattered happily en route to her studio on rue Victor Considérant, deaf to her silence. In the tiny elevator, he took her by the waist. "Ah, it's so great to have you home. Your place is just the same as you left it." He opened the door and set her bag on the floor; her trunks would be delivered later. "I sometimes slept here while you were gone. The bedsheets are dirty, I'm afraid."

"Man?" What had he been doing in her studio?

"They still smelled of you." He gave her a sheepish look. "I couldn't bear to wash them. Now that you're back, though, I'll change them. I don't have to rely on any sad pillowcases anymore. I can smell you anytime I want."

She drew water into a vase for the bouquet. An exuberant, unlikely mix of pink, tiger, and calla lilies—not *all* funeral flowers—which he had doubtlessly put together himself. "It's gorgeous. Thanks again."

Why couldn't she be satisfied with this man? For all his abilities, for all his adoration, why couldn't she just love him? If not him, who? Would she always be unable to return affection—the Snow Maiden, the stony, destructive Venus—drifting from one set of arms to the next? She bit her lip. And when she was no longer desirable or attractive, when her beauty could only be found in old photographs—what then? Why was Man Ray not enough?

As she arranged the flowers, he came up from behind and nuzzled her ear. He unzipped her dress and led her to the sofa. He combed her hair with his fingers, then let them slide lovingly down her neck to her back. He wanted to greet each part of her—her shoulders, breasts, stomach, thighs—and welcome it home. She closed her eyes, yielding to his warm, silky touch. Not one of her lovers in London had taken such care.

During her first days back in Paris, she felt as awkward and green as she had that first week in London. On her own, she made the rounds to see her friends to find that almost everyone she knew was off on holiday. George was in Deauville, presumably doing a shoot of beach fashions; Tatiana was planning her wedding at her viscount's chateau; Zizi was in Geneva, reportedly infatuated with a new, younger beauty; Cocteau was in Provence. Most of Man's friends were also away, except for Kiki, who was still holding court at the Montparnasse cafés, now filled with foreign tourists. It seemed that Man was the only person who had eagerly awaited her return. The only one who had missed her.

Stay or go? Trying to make a decision was giving her a serious case of the blue jitters.

Unconsciously avoiding him, Lee began going to bed early, quickly rapt in restless sleep, and rising at dawn. She quietly dressed and slipped out, leaving Man alone in her bed. She stole away from Montparnasse and had coffee among early-morning workers—omnibus drivers, vegetable vendors, pre-mass priests—then ambled the warm, waking streets, the song "Love for Sale" stuck in her head. She stopped at parks and squares and leafed through newspapers or novels, scarcely reading a word. Through strangers and unknown *quartiers,* after a week she felt once again like she belonged in Paris. But where, exactly? And with whom?

One morning, after coffee and brioche in the din of les Halles marketplace, Lee slowly strolled across the river and up the long boulevard Saint-Michel to the Luxembourg Gardens. Past statuary and fountains, she made her way to the pond and fell into an iron chair, slightly softened by innumerable coats of thick green paint. She propped a book open on her knees. Man had loaned her William Seabrook's *The Magic Island*, about his adventures in Haiti; Lee flipped through it, stopping only for il-lustrations, grotesque charcoals of voodoo rituals and zombies. In one, hollow-eyed natives walked in a trance. Was that what she looked like this morning? She dropped the book on her lap and glanced around her. It was almost eleven and the park was filling with children.

All around the basin, boys in short pants were prodding model sailboats with long sticks. One boy gave his bright-red craft a vigorous poke; it was caught by the wind and went off to sea. Hands on his hips, he watched as it stalled in the middle of the pond, lost to him. Mildly curious, Lee waited to see if he would burst into tears or take off his shoes and wade in to fetch it. But instead, after a moment eyeing the bobbing red boat, the boy lost interest and, with his pole, began digging around in the pond slime. Lee liked the determination on his round, rosy face, the effort he made as he tried to lift up a bunch of dead leaves plastered to the bottom. How serious he was, dragging the small lake, looking for God-knows-what. Suddenly, Lee's hands went cold. Harold, she thought. Oh fuck, poor Harold.

Lee had met him at age nineteen. She'd recently been dragged back from France and was grieving the loss of her Parisian freedoms: the wild parties, sodden with drink; nights dancing at cabarets; the long string of lovers. She was profoundly unhappy back at her parents' farm in rustic Poughkeepsie, and to make matters nearly unbearable, her childhood gonorrhea had flared up. Her pinch-mouthed mother had begun the daily acid douches again; the cure gave Elizabeth cramps and forced her into a state of chastity. Whenever out, she flirted recklessly—she cared little for those provincial boys' feelings—and received scores of declarations of love. Harold, however, she liked.

Like her, he was fun, lively and audacious, and together they took off on all sorts of little adventures. They loved taking the train to New York City to pretend they were part of the avant-garde scene. Lounging around bohemian cafés in Greenwich Village, they acted like poets; they went to art galleries and theater productions. There was a spark between them; although she couldn't have sex with him, she liked talking dirty to him over the telephone, which never failed to arouse them both.

In July, on a cloudless summer day not unlike this one, they went rowing on Upton Lake. When they were far enough from shore to enjoy a little privacy, he brought the oars in. After a few steamy kisses, he began to take off his shirt.

"Harold! What are you doing?" She watched in disbelief as he yanked down his suspenders and shook off his pants.

"What do you think? I get so damn hot when I'm near you . . ." Stripped down to his underclothes, he bent over and kissed her again. She was about to protest when he stood up in the rowboat and added "that I guess I need to cool down."

He balanced himself on the seat, then made a perfect dive into the water. Elizabeth laughed and shouted, "I never told you to go jump in a lake!"

Chuckling, she scanned the lake's black surface, waiting for him to pop up. Would he try to push the boat over? She clutched the rim of the boat, grinning down at the water, staring first at one side, then the next. After a minute went by and then another, she grew cold, unable to move, frantically eyeing the water. Where the hell did he go? Was this a joke? Was he hurt? Should she jump in? Could she save him? Finally, she screamed, long and loud.

Much later, from the shore, her father's arm around her, Elizabeth watched them dragging the lake. When his body was found, they hauled him in, chalky white in his undershorts, thin, and so, so young.

She rarely thought back on Harold, on their innocent

romance, on that day at the lake, but when she did, her insides froze. It wasn't so much the picture of his death she avoided—the sudden, achy still of the silent lake, the nightmarish consequence of the harmless prank: the unnatural color of his skin, the odd position of his wiry legs—but the horror of loss. The emptiness that followed. Although she didn't return his love, he had been her friend. A boy she not only flirted with, but talked to. A playmate whose company she enjoyed.

Was that what she had with Man? Was he a real friend, almost family? Was he the only person in the city who really cared about her? If she left him, would she regret it? Would she feel that loss, that emptiness?

Lee wondered if all long-term relationships were like this, filled with highs and lows, enjoyment and animosity, desire and disgust. Her mother, for example, had a complicated tangle of reasons for being with her father—but love was not among them. Did Tanja ever doubt her feelings for her beloved archaeologist? Did Tatiana sometimes want to run away from her viscount, hide, never see him again? Was it normal, this indecision, this uncertainty? She thought of all the heroines from books and films—the passionate countess from *Stamboul*—primed for sacrifice, all unshakably convinced of their love. Lee had never been very feminine—in fact, she took it as a great compliment when her detractors said she had a man's attitude toward life—but this cold inability to love sometimes made her feel half-human.

She heaved herself out of the uncomfortable metal chair and

turned away from the pond, away from the plump, pink-faced boys. Staying with Man made practical sense. That she knew. Not only was he very generous but their work was linked: she often appeared in his images and they shared a similar style. In fact, upon her return he'd announced that they had both been chosen for upcoming group exhibitions in New York, Paris, and Brussels.

She'd looked up him, ecstatic, her first moment of real enthusiasm since being back with him.

"Really? Oh, Man, that's wonderful! My work, in the Surrealists' shows!"

"And you know what they're calling you?" he'd added, grasping her hand, pleased with them both. "A photographer in the 'Man Ray School.'"

Her smile had faltered. "Does being in your school mean I'm still your student?"

"Well, I guess it means you were, that you've learned my technique. Like 'in the School of Rembrandt.'" He smiled at the thought.

"Yeah, those people are generally referred to as 'Anonymous.'"

"Hey, hey, don't work yourself into a lather. Your name'll be up there, big as anyone else's."

"It irks me that, even after a half-year working in London, I'm still Madame Man Ray."

"Aren't you, baby?" He looked at her nervously.

"I've got a name, just like you."

God, she was tired of being in Man's shadow, professionally and personally. Paris was bigger than him, his artist friends and Montparnasse. Even if it wasn't the most practical decision, she had to leave him; she could manage just fine on her own. Lee headed out of the garden gates, thinking again of Harold. He had drowned at nineteen. Had he had any regrets? Was she one of them? Life was too damn short—even if you lived to be a hundred—to spend it with the wrong person.

Walking back to the studio, she tried to think of the best approach. Nothing too dramatic, nothing too final. Perhaps something about being just friends? Or, she could make a bid for sincerity and explain her inability to provide what he needed. Or warmly tell him that she loved him, but was not "in love." Whatever that meant.

She let herself into her flat and heard him in the bathroom; he hadn't gone back to his place since her return.

"Where were you, kid?" he called out.

Man strode into the living room, rubbing the stubble on his face, a cigarette clamped in the corner of his mouth. His legs emerged from shorts, as thin and white as Harold's. She put the zombie book away with a shiver.

"Where do you keep disappearing to these days?"

"Disappearing?" she repeated. That was a trick she'd liked to learn. She took a deep breath, steeling herself for the necessary words. They were no longer a couple. She wanted to be on her own. He needed to leave. She turned to him and opened her mouth.

"I've just talked to Max Ernst." He rubbed his hands in delight. "Everyone is back from holidays, so there's a big Surre-alist party this weekend. Costumes, jazz, art, the works! What shall we wear?"

Her mouth stayed open, but Lee was swallowed again by doubt. In another instant, she managed a quirky half-smile.

"I think I'd like to be a gypsy. Telling fortunes and predicting the future."

XXVII

———

"Move that light to the left. *Oui, c'est ça.*" Lee nodded at her assistant, on loan from Coco Chanel, then looked back through the viewfinder and smiled to herself.

Sworn to secrecy, she was in a windowless room, shooting Chanel's first *haute joaillerie* collection, diamonds dripping in innovative designs: celestial bodies, feathers, ribbons, knots. Lee wanted to take photos that would be as original and startling as the jewelry. As an inside joke—to amuse herself—she decided to use wax mannequins with arms cut in the style of the *Venus de Milo*.

She carefully arranged a choker on a dummy, delighted at its ingenuity. The comet's star was nestled on one side of the neck; its long tail—six thick diamond strands—wrapped around the back of the neck, then shot down the chest, leaving the throat bare. Lee moved a mirror behind the mannequin to catch its reflection, then turned the body to a better angle; she added a tiara, then critically looked at the shot.

"Could you please find me a strapless black gown?" she asked the assistant. She covered the mannequin's breasts tightly with her navy jacket, trying to get an idea of the look. "It doesn't have to be from this season. Hell, it doesn't have to be a real dress. I just want some black satin to hang this brooch from. Right here." She jabbed her jacket. "Then the picture will be complete." She fished her cigarette case out of the jacket pocket and lit one. "When did Mademoiselle Chanel say she'd be back? In an hour? Let's move along, then."

Waiting for the assistant to find something suitable, she set up the next shot: two bodiless mannequin arms. Remembering the zinc tray at the Sorbonne medical school—the one used for discarded parts—she arranged a pair of black opera gloves alongside them with a smile. This was much more elegant than cutlery. To decide which jewelry to lavish on the wax hands, Lee tried it on: platinum bracelets, dazzling with five-pointed stars, a chic gold ring tied up in a bow, diamond fringe, hanging finely off her wrist. It was exquisite, all of it. She admired herself in the mirror, making histrionic high-society gestures to make the gems sparkle—ooh, it had been too damn long since she'd dressed to go out!—and then slid her favorite rings onto the lifeless fingers. She looked through the viewfinder and added the star bracelet. No, better, the fringe.

After finishing the hand shots, she took a close-up of the mannequin's head, looking calm and demure in her tiara, an obscene display of diamonds in these Depression years. Lee got on a chair to take a shot from above, to emphasize the riches and make the mannequin's eyes humbler, more downcast.

How easy it was to work with these mannequins—so quiet and complaisant—with their motionless hair and perfect wax teeth. Most people, even some professional models, felt uncomfortable in front of the camera. Trying to look their most attractive, they twisted their mouths, stretched their necks, or stared until their eyes bulged. Lee had to relax them, to coax away those unnatural grimaces. Man had always made it look so easy. Standing there without a word, he distracted his sitters with his indifference. Then there was George, who intimidated them with his moody temper. Her sessions tended to be much more difficult. Perhaps, having modeled herself, she was too understanding.

She looked at her watch. Fashion designers were often worse than models. Living off of high levels of stress and tobacco, they were perfectionists by nature. They usually hovered behind her during a shoot and insisted on redoing it, even before they'd seen the results. Hopefully, Coco Chanel would be pleased. At least she'd felt confident enough to let her work alone—for a few hours.

After a long day shooting diamonds—various combinations and rearrangements, with and without Miss Chanel—Lee was happy to get home and soak in her tub. When she'd announced her return from London at the end of summer, her agenda had immediately filled; famous fashion houses wanted her to shoot their winter collections, and portrait sittings were booked weeks in advance. She'd thrown herself into work, giving herself no time for creative pieces, very little time for *Vogue,* and the bare minimum for her waning relationship with Man Ray. Lee was trying to maintain the independence she'd had in London, keeping her own schedule instead of behaving like half a couple. Work provided the perfect alibi for her absence. It was the only one he respected.

Suddenly she heard the studio door open, the sound of a man's shoes. He would have walked by and seen her lights on. She breathed out, making bubbles in the water.

"Lee?" Man called.

"I'm in here."

"Ah, that's how I like to find you—in the buff!" Man smiled as he plunged his hand into the water and squeezed her upper thigh. "I've brought—"

"Stop." Lee cut him off, pulling his hand out of the water. With a pitiable look—a boy who'd just been scolded—he let his arms fall to his sides. "Look, I've had a long week." She softened her tone. "I'm just trying to relax."

"I know you've got a lot of work, but that's a good thing nowadays. Lucky, even. You've been over at Chanel, right?" He remembered her assignments almost as well as she did.

"Yep. Her new jewelry collection. Amazing stuff. I could use a few pieces—"

"Is that a hint?" He gave her a wry look. "Speaking of work, I've done a few good pieces myself this week. Solarized self-portraits of me with my camera. In it, I'm adjusting the focus ring, making the viewer my sitter. Clever, huh? It turned out really well. I almost look handsome."

He helped her into her bathrobe, obviously waiting for a reply, some reassurance. She caught his expectant gaze. "I'd love to see them," she murmured.

"Reminds me of the day we discovered the technique." He raised his eyebrows suggestively. "If the walls of that darkroom could talk . . ."

"If your rats could talk, you mean." She gave his arm a sisterly punch and strolled out of the bathroom. "Can I get you some coffee? Or would you prefer a glass of wine?"

Lee had taken to treating Man like a guest, not a roommate,

in an attempt to establish some distance. She'd still not found the right words to end their relationship, but was trying to let him know in every other way.

"No, doll, make some coffee. Look what I've brought."

A pink pastry box sat like a birthday present in the center of the kitchen table.

"Have you been to that new bakery on Raspail?" he asked. He snipped the ribbon, opened the box, and swept it under her nose. "Their chocolate éclairs are to die for. Here, try one."

The last thing she wanted was sweet gooey pastry, but she daintily extracted one from the box. Man watched her chew a small bite.

"So? What do you think?" He beamed at her. "Do you think they're as good as the ones we had in Biarritz? On the Wheelers' terrace? I thought I'd never find a better éclair until I tried these."

"I think that was less about chocolate and more about the view." Lee shrugged, but understood this sudden enthusiasm for pastries.

Since she returned to Paris, he'd been harking back to the beginning of their relationship, to that honeymoon stage when, with fairy dust in their eyes, they couldn't see each other's faults. He'd been waxing nostalgic about Biarritz as well as their first six months in his studio: their outings, art poses, nights together, the darkroom—the éclairs, she thought, were a bit far-fetched. It seemed Man was trying to lull her back to the time when she depended on him, when she was smitten with him, when she wanted him. These reminiscences did nothing, however, to make her feel closer to him. On the contrary, she felt mollycoddled and manipulated—and annoyed past patience.

"Man, I'm going to get dressed now." She was walking him to the door, her hand flat on his back, the coffee unmade. "I've got plans for tonight, but I'll see you again soon."

"What is this?" He jerked around. "Are you kicking me out?"

"It's not that." She racked her brains for a plausible plan, something innocent, but not a place where he could tag along. Nothing occurred to her. "I've got things to do."

"Busy, busy Lee." He spit out. "You've always got things to do. And, these days, it appears I'm never included."

"All I do is work." It wasn't even a lie.

"Let *me* take you out, then. Damn it, you're *my* girl!" His eyes pleaded. "Come on, Lee, we could dress to the nines, have dinner out, go dancing. It'll be fun. Like old times."

"Old times." She swallowed hard. "I can't tonight, baby, but real soon."

When he'd finally left, she went back to the bedroom, took off the robe, and snuggled under her covers. She had a ton of developing to do in the morning.

"Miss Miller? I was wondering if you'd have time to do my portrait this week. My name's Charlie Chaplin."

Lee's mouth dropped open and she gazed into the phone. After a second, she shook her head and responded, surprised to find her usual voice, warm and confident. "Of course I have time. When would you like to come by the studio?"

"I was hoping you could come to my hotel. I'm over at the Scribe. Does tomorrow morning work for you?"

"Yes, it does. Shall we say half past ten?"

The next day, Lee dressed carefully, but not extravagantly, in velvet trousers and a pearl-gray jersey. She chose flat shoes, remembering his stature. She'd caught glimpses of Chaplin at several New York soirées and had even been introduced to him once. But usually at those affairs he'd be clowning around, center stage, putting on a little act while Irving Berlin played impromptu refrains on the piano. Either that or he was besieged by his hosts or the evening's other shining stars: Dorothy Parker, George Gershwin, the Vanderbilts. She wondered if he even made a connection between the Paris-based photographer he'd called yesterday and the tall blond model from those Manhattan parties.

She gathered her equipment and headed across the river in a cab. Would he be a difficult sitter? At parties, he always seemed like such fun, but she'd learned how unexpectedly demanding some people could be.

At the Scribe, Lee was sent up to his suite. Her knock at the door was immediately answered by a silver-haired man in an elegant suit. She'd almost been expecting the Tramp, but today there was no black mustache, no bowler hat. He kissed her hand with a shy smile—the only remaining part of the character.

"Delighted to see you again, Miss Miller."

"I'm surprised you remember me, Mr. Chaplin." She tried not to grin. "And please, call me Lee."

"I'm good with faces—and yours is not so very difficult to remember." He led her to the sofa, where a tea service waited on a silver tray. "And you can call me Charlie. Or, here in France, perhaps Charlot is more apropos?" He said this last with a thick French accent, emphasizing the silly rhyme. "Tea?"

She watched his graceful gestures as he poured—the motions of a conductor during a pianissimo movement—then peeked up at his face. He was about forty, Man's age, but his face was completely unlined. No bags under the eyes, no sagging skin; it was as if a young man's hair had gone white.

"I must say," he began, handing her a cup. "You've come a long way since those get-togethers at Condé Nast's place. One of the snappiest photographers in Paris?" He raised his eyebrows with a nod. "Impressive. I also hear you acted in a film by Jean Cocteau. When will we be able to see it?"

"Who knows? There's been this ridiculous public outcry about morality—"

"God, have I had my fill of that." He breathed out, letting his lips flutter. His divorce a few years before—and the numerous charges of infidelity—had been a tabloid staple, a media sensation. "I hope it comes out soon, though. It's a Surrealist film, isn't it?"

"Yes, but it's not just a bunch of meaningless images. It tells the story of a poet and his muse." She thought back on that early conversation with Man Ray, when he had proclaimed the death of cinema. How pompous he'd sounded—and how impressed she'd been! What absolute rot. Movies with plots—like Chaplin's work—were by far the best.

"And you must be the muse."

"That's right," she said, ready to change the subject. "Are you in Paris working on a new film?"

"No, I'm on holiday. After *City Lights*, I needed a rest."

"So you came to the City of Lights?" she asked with a little laugh. "I positively loved that picture. How I cried at the end!"

"Me, too! Of exhaustion!" He fell back on the sofa, eyes closed. After a moment, one striking blue eye opened and peered over at her. "I'm curious what kind of portraits you have in mind. I've never worked with a Surrealist photographer."

Lee smiled at him, taken off guard. She had assumed that he would want straight shots—that was certainly what most sitters wanted, to look their best—not anything artistic. She took her camera out of its case while scanning the room, looking for inspiration. Her eyes lingered on the shiny tea service.

"Let's use this tray as a mirror." She removed the pots and cups and quickly rubbed it down with a handkerchief. "Hold it up next to you."

Holding the tray at different angles, he moved his body onto his back, his side, and looked up at her while she took the different shots; she made double portraits in some and let the tray cast an interesting glow in others. Through the viewfinder, she was able to stare at him, study his features, his real face—without makeup. He was handsomer than she'd thought.

"You're a real natural in front of the camera. Who would have guessed?" she joked. "I bet I could get you a job at *Vogue*."

"Evening gowns or bathing costumes?" He turned on his belly, crossed his hands under his chin, and stuck out his bottom.

Lee laughed. "Whatever you want."

Tired of the tray, she looked around again. "Hey, I wonder if I can get that chandelier to spring from your head? Stand over there. With your imagination, you don't just have one-light-bulb ideas—you have a half-dozen bulbs at once!"

"How about if I stand on a chair? Like this?"

"Perfect! It looks like you're balancing it on your head. Talk about your *City Lights!*" She lay down on the floor and squinted through the camera, then adjusted her settings. "Let me see what it looks like from this angle."

He cocked his head to the side and looked at her from the corner of his eye.

"Finished?"

Chaplin jumped down from the chair, joined her on the floor, and planted a kiss on her mouth. It was something she'd seen him do so many times on screen: kissing with that funny combination of bashfulness and determination, that exquisite shy passion. Then he gave her another one. And another.

In the cab back to Montparnasse, Lee couldn't stop smiling. Chaplin had said that he'd never had such fun at a sitting, that her *surréaliste* photography was wonderful indeed. She chuckled to herself. Since she'd gone behind the camera, this had been her favorite sitting to date.

XXVIII

—

"Darling!" Man pulled her into a hug; Lee gave him a series of maternal pats. "Why didn't you just use your key? This is your place as well as mine."

"I didn't want to interrupt you. In case you were busy."

"Nonsense. I asked you to come."

He took Lee's coat, then offered her a drink with a quick gesture. As he chipped the ice, she looked around his studio; she hadn't been there for weeks. Searching for new work, Lee found little had changed since she'd lived there: early nudes of her were on every wall. He handed her a sweet vermouth, then led her to the sofa. He was almost trembling with excitement.

"I've got some amazing news, kid."

"What is it?" His mood was contagious. Were they in a new show?

"I've heard from Dr. Agha, Condé Nast's new art director. He's tired of the Steichen school and thinks my work is the new thing. He says you and I should get ready to take over the U.S. market."

"Man, that's fabulous!" She creased her brow. "But what does he mean? Is he talking about exhibitions, or what?"

"He says Americans finally understand my work. They like

it." He was beaming. "It's time to relocate to New York and open a studio there. You and me."

"Go to New York? That's crazy. We can just send our work over by courier. It would be much easier than moving."

"No, he says now's the time for my return." He took her hand in his. "This could be the end of any money problems—ever—and the start of a new life for us."

She glanced at his hand, perched on hers like a crab, then took a quick dose of vermouth.

"But we both love Paris. We're happy here." She faltered at her unfortunate use of the coupling pronoun, took her hand from his, then continued. "I can't believe you really want to leave Montparnasse and all your cronies. Have you even thought this through?"

"Things could be even better there. Sitters, magazines, advertising, film. We could go to Hollywood, too. You'd like that, wouldn't you?" His eyes shone. "We can pool everything together—our skills, resources, connections—and be a team."

She pulled a cigarette out of her case and packed the tobacco, tapping it deliberately on the tabletop. "Things are going so well for me here," she started slowly. "The Schiaparelli collection, Chanel jewelry, the new Patou line. Like you said, I've been lucky. And I don't think I'm ready to leave yet."

"Oh, Lee," he said, fishing her hand off of her lap and kissing it. "I know you have doubts about such a big step, but we could do it as man and wife. We could get married."

In wide-eyed surprise, she barked out a laugh; with a fallen face, he popped off the sofa to refresh his drink, to have his back to her.

"I'm sorry, Man. But you know I'm not interested in marriage."

"Forget about it," he grumbled. "It was just a thought."

He turned back around to give her a casual shrug, but his eyes were red-rimmed and watery. Seeing him so dejected filled her with pity, but not enough to make any regrettable sacrifices.

"Listen, why don't you go to New York first?" Lee suggested innocently. "Test the waters and see how it goes."

"Nah. I wouldn't want to go without you. Now is our time. 1932 will be our year." He sat back down and caressed her cheek. "You know what I'd really like?" He lowered his voice to that lusty whisper, the one she once found so appealing. "For you to spend more time modeling for me. Some artistic shots, erotic poses. Like we used to."

She looked him in the face—the canine begging in his dark eyes, the hope in his half-smile—then sighed.

"I don't have the time," she said flatly. "I've got so many—"

"Who the hell do you think you are?" A flash flood of anger washed over him. "What an uppity little b-b-bitch you've become! You're nobody without me."

"That's what you'd like to believe. But, the fact is, I'm not Madame Man Ray anymore. People call *me*. Just last week, Charlie Cha—"

"D-do you think you'd have been included in those Surrealist shows if I hadn't pulled a few strings? The hell you *aren't* Mrs. Ray!"

"You fucking bastard!" She jumped up and grabbed her coat. "My work stands on its own, and you know it. That's why you've put your name on it a time or two."

"Jesus, will I ever hear the end of that shit? One or two good photographs and you think you're too good for me. Good luck with that c-c-career of yours."

She slammed the door behind her and walked quickly back to her own studio, annoyed by his arrogance, but marveling at the fact she had outgrown him. Her mentor, her guide, her companion. Now he seemed to need her far more than she needed him.

Man immediately sent Lee a long letter—an angry justification bleeding into a nervous apology, with an addendum reiterating the New York plan—but she didn't reply. The next day, she left for the Swiss Alps to spend the Christmas holidays away from Paris and Man Ray.

Charlie Chaplin had invited Lee to join his entourage at the Palace Hotel in Saint Moritz, the most fashionable ski resort in Europe. And she was delighted to be able to live it up in her best clothes and jewels, away from the darkroom and the newfound stutter in Man's deep voice. Amongst royalty and movie stars, she threw herself into the glamorous social life. Skiing, toboggan runs, and skating filled the days, while at night, the beau monde mingled at chic restaurants and jazz clubs, dancing the latest steps while getting tight on newfangled cocktails. George Hoyningen-Huene was also there, on assignment, happily taking snapshots of his friends while enjoying himself at Vogue's expense.

One night, Lee and George joined Chaplin for dinner with a group of his friends, which included a wealthy Egyptian couple, Aziz Eloui Bey and his wife, Nimet, a celebrated beauty.

"Good evening, Mr. Bey." The man on Lee's right was classically good-looking and elegantly dressed, probably in his early forties. To provoke him slightly, to see what he might say, she decided to compliment his wife. "Nimet is the most beautiful woman in the room."

"She should be," he said, his accent more British than exotic, "she spends all her waking hours applying makeup and skin creams."

Lee laughed; she was already his confidante. "I know she's sat for George and Man Ray. I wonder if she'd allow me to take her photo?"

"I'm sure she'd be flattered. But you'll have to schedule a time that doesn't interfere with her beauty regime: baths in Vichy water, strolls, long naps . . . Truly, I wish you the best of luck."

"Oh, my darling girl," Chaplin said suddenly to Nimet on the other side of the large round table. He looked at her teeth through a spoon, then wrapped her head in a napkin. "I'm afraid that molar is going to have to come out. Luckily, I am a graduate of the Grand Canard School of Dentistry." He pulled up his sleeves and put her head on the table. "Open wide!" Using a pair of butter knives as forceps, he pretended to tug and pull, until he finally extracted a sugar cube from her mouth.

Everyone at the table shook with laughter. Lee peeked over at Aziz. She liked the way his eyes sparkled, his teeth shone.

The next morning, they ran into each other at the door of the coffee shop.

"A pleasure to see you again, Lee."

The night before, by the end of dinner, they had insisted on first names; in the daylight, the clipped sound of her nickname caught her by surprise. She took his arm—finally, a man taller than her—and returned his familiar tone.

"And you, Aziz. Would you like to join me for hot chocolate? I recommend it with a touch of Grand Marnier."

"Sounds delightful."

They sat together at a window filled with snowy mountains and ordered cocoa and croissants.

"Are you on your own this morning?" Lee asked him.

"As usual. I wasn't joking about my wife's strict routine." He looked at his watch. "At this moment, Nimet must be having her facial. That's the curse of marrying a peacock, you know. You spend all your time alone." He gestured to her with his hand. "And you, Lee? A woman as lovely as you surely has a trick or two."

"Mine is an anti-regime. Late nights followed by a hearty mix of darkroom chemicals, tobacco, and cocktails. Perhaps I should write an article about it for *Vogue*? It could start a whole new fad."

"Whatever you're doing, it's working like a charm." He leaned back, allowing the waiter to serve them. "Plus, it leaves you free to have breakfast with me."

Unlike the scores of ski-resort flatterers, Aziz seemed perfectly sincere. Blowing on her chocolate, Lee watched him drink, his elegant movements, the dapper mustache disappearing behind the cup. He glanced back at her, nearly startled to find her staring at him.

"Tell me. What other things do you do with all this spare time?"

"I'm an engineer," he began.

"No kidding." Lee smiled at the handsome Egyptian, warming to him by the minute. "So is my father."

"I took a degree from Liverpool. Since then, I've worked in both business and diplomacy. We usually spend half the year in Cairo and half here in Europe."

"Is that so?" Lee dunked her croissant in her spiked cocoa and took a bite, trying to imagine Nimet's life: luxury, travel, and utter leisure. What might it be like to be spoiled by a gentleman—one who gave her room to breathe and money to spare? To be the only artist in a pair? A photographer who didn't have to do endless sittings, but could concentrate on creative work—for galleries and shows, not rent and electricity. To have complete security, to never worry. It sounded perfect to her, ideal. Nimet was lucky to have such a husband, such a marriage.

"What are your plans for today?" Lee asked him suddenly.

"I haven't made any."

"Why don't we go sledding?" She looked so excited, like such a small child, that he broke into a grin.

"Excellent idea!"

They changed into sports clothes and met on the run, opting to share a large sleigh instead of using two singles. Deferring to her childhood spent in northern climes, Aziz let Lee steer. They bumped down the hill, rosy-cheeked and laughing, until they hit a stump and fell into each other's arms. He scooped her up and kissed her. His arms were youthful and strong, his mouth still tasted of chocolate. In the snow, she felt herself begin to thaw.

XXIX

—

Lee and Man stepped out of the taxi, in front of the Théâtre du Vieux-Colombier. She smoothed down her new dress—although it was late January, she wasn't wearing a coat—and smiled at the crowd around her. A photographer's flash went off, momentarily blinding her; she took Man's arm.

After her holidays in Saint Moritz, she'd headed to his studio, ready to make a clean break; smitten with Aziz, she'd no longer felt the need to carry on with the charade of being Man's girl. Puffed up with pride, he'd greeted her casually, almost coldly. She supposed that her refusal to go to New York—to marry!—had been clear enough. They'd spent a half-hour together, saying nothing. Did that mean they could just be friends? As a token of her goodwill, when she heard about the premiere of *The Blood of a Poet,* she asked him to be her escort. She felt she owed him that.

"It's finally showing!" She'd told him on the phone, their first conversation since the awkward meeting three days earlier. "Jean's asked me to invite all my friends. The *beautiful people.*" She said this last imitating Cocteau's nearly unintelligible English, making them both chuckle. "I thought, since you're my oldest friend here, you should accompany me."

"You know, Breton's boycotting it, so the Surrealists won't be there," he said, obviously torn, but flattered, hopeful. "But, don't worry, Lee. I'll be there, at your side."

Lee and Man made their way through the packed theater. Aware of the Surrealist ban, Cocteau's friends had come out in full force. Lee spotted Picasso, André Gide, and weren't those the musicians from the Boeuf sur le Toit?

In slinky beige silk with scalloped fringe, she glided down the aisle like a bride, nodding and smiling at everyone she knew. Her *Frogue* family, friends from the émigré community, influential clients, neighbors from Montparnasse, the actors and crew members, all their faces were aglow with encouragement and anticipation. She was walking at a luxurious pace, savoring the moment, but nearly tripped when she saw Aziz Eloui Bey. Handsome in tails, he was seated on the groom's side, an amused look on his face. She shot him a longing glace, wondering if the wrong man was on her arm.

She sank into her chair as the theater went dark, reliving the experience while seeing something new. When she came onscreen, she barely recognized herself, especially with the redubbed voice. A beautiful, powerful muse? Hardly! She was hideous, really, with no arms, albino-white skin, and a mouth like a lipsticked monkfish. Lee fidgeted in her chair, watching her own image—its sniveling smile, its failed attempts at stony stillness—and wondered what the others thought.

When the poet fell into the mirror, she lost herself in the picture, in all of the mysterious scenes behind the hotel doors. But when her likeness returned toward the end of the film, she bit her lip, doubting her performance again. She seemed so uncomfortable, so wooden, especially compared to Enrique, a real actor. Lee glanced around—she peeked over at Cocteau, Man, the others—but no one was frowning or stifling laughter. They were completely engrossed in the film, the artist's suicide.

She turned back to the screen—it was the final scene—and saw her form gliding along with large, painted eyes. She didn't stumble or look nervous, but was commanding, hypnotic. It was a miracle. She *was* a Cretan goddess able to tame a beast. A triumphant muse who had left her artist behind. Lee stared at her image on the screen. That was exactly what was happening with Man. What was she still doing with him? She needn't destroy him nor leave him cold and lifeless, but she had to go. And she didn't need a bull to guide her.

When the screen flashed *FIN,* Lee breathed out and the audience roared with applause. "*You* were amazing," Man said into her ear, hugging her close.

She murmured in assent—in the last scene, it was true—surprised to find Man so cheerful, so pleased. Hadn't he understood? Didn't he see what happened?

At Cocteau's urging, Lee took a bow with the other actors—the crowd jumped to their feet—and dipping down, again and again, she suddenly felt free.

At the party after the film, Lee went from one group to the next and was kissed, toasted, and fêted wherever she turned. At one point, she turned from a group of admirers to see Man and Aziz standing next to each other by chance. Each was silently watching her with a drink in his hand. Aziz, casually elegant in his formalwear, raised his glass to her, his smile shining with wonder and delight. Man stood uncomfortably erect, his chest swollen, his mouth a thin line of nervous disapproval.

Perhaps he was beginning to understand after all.

At the end of the party, after midnight and plenty of cocktails, Lee ushered Man into a cab and slid in after him. She gave the taxi driver instructions to go to rue Campagne-Première.

"You want to sleep at the studio?" He smiled with surprise. "You haven't—"

"No, I'm taking you home."

"You're getting rid of me? Then what, you're going out with that Egyptian guy? I saw you flirting with him and—"

"No, I'm going to my place." She gave him the key to his studio. "I'd like my key back, too."

"What the hell are you saying?" The words came out slowly as his large eyes nearly closed in anger. "You're leaving me? Why? What haven't I done for you, Lee? I've given you everything."

They'd had this discussion before. With a brisk nod, she interrupted him before he started counting things off on his fingers.

"I know, Man. And now it's time to give me up. It's time to say good-bye."

"Here you are, milady." He yanked her key off his ring and pressed it hard into her open palm. The cab pulled up in front of the looming Art Nouveau building; its doorway looked nearly Gothic in the dark. "Don't expect me to wait around for you. I might not be here when you come back."

As the taxi circled back to her place, she stretched her arms across the back of the seat, taking up the entire space. How simple it had been. Why hadn't she done it six months earlier?

. . .

"Lee, are you there?" Man pounded on the door to her studio.
"Lee!"

She froze in her chair. When was this going to stop? It had
been two weeks since their last cab ride together. Despite his
bravado that night, Man had not taken the breakup well.

"Lee!" He tried the locked door; it jangled frantically. She
stared at the knob—would it open? Although she wasn't really
afraid, his bellowing made her heart race. His shoes scuffed outside. What was he doing? She imagined him on his knees, peeking under the door—would he be able to see anything through
the crack?—and silently drew her feet up onto the chair, out
of a mouse's-eye view. Suddenly, a paper slid under the door,
a white stain on her wooden floor. She heard the pounding of
his feet, the rattle of the elevator, and blew out. She let a few
minutes go by, then picked up the paper, as quietly as possible.

My dearest Lee—

*I know that your infatuation for the Egyptian will soon fade
away, like it did for all the others before him. When it does, I'll
be waiting for you. I am here for you. I love you.*

Yours always,
Man

She squeezed the paper, crushing it soundlessly, then let it drop
into the bin.

After the premiere, Lee had begun seeing Aziz Eloui Bey

more seriously, taken by his foreign sophistication, his charming intelligence. Surprisingly broad-minded, he had a lover's passion, yet he never tried to control her. Like her father, he accepted her contradictions and gave her freedom and security both. Man Ray, however, had not given up. As a painter and a Surrealist, he had always been a firm believer in liberty, a staunch advocate for independence. As a lover, however, he could not let go. As Lee tried to begin her new life without him, he stepped into her path at every turn.

Phone calls, impromptu visits, messages stuffed under the door, letters through the post; she ignored all his attempts at communication. Frustrated by her silence, after another month he broadened his campaign, keeping vigil outside her house. Lee peeked out her window before going out. Man was often there, leaning on a street lamp and smoking a cigarette like a Dashiell Hammett private eye. Feeling trapped, she stayed home to avoid him, receiving sitters, working in the darkroom, reading, but mainly pacing. If she had to go out, he would spring to life, often drunk and always glowering, and call out to her.

"Hey, Lee! Come talk to me. You still with that Arab?"

"Man, give it a rest. Go on, now. Go home," she'd say, gentle but firm. In her mind, however, she was screaming *Get the hell out of here! Leave me the fuck alone!* She was careful around him, wary of what he might do; she had not forgotten the photograph with the slit throat. She hailed cabs to get away, making the beckoning gesture from Cocteau's film, the arrogant goddess summoning the beast.

Neither caution nor panache were enough. Jumpy, stressed, sleepless, dark circles grew under her eyes, she lost her appetite. Lee began avoiding her studio—and Montparnasse—altogether. Taking time off work, she went on excursions with Aziz, or stayed with him at Right Bank hotels.

One spring evening, finishing dessert at the Ritz, Aziz popped his last chocolaty raspberry into Lee's mouth and calmly said, "You ought to know, darling. I'm leaving Nimet."

Wide-eyed, she quickly swallowed and blurted out, "Aziz! I never meant for you—"

"Don't panic." He held up his hands with a smile. "I'm not putting any demands on you. I just thought since you'd left Man, it was only fair. And truly, since you and I have been together, I've found it impossible to be with her. The beauty regimes, the lotus-eating, holding court from her sofa bed. What a waste of time."

"How did she take it?"

"She actually found the energy to threaten suicide, but she wasn't serious. It's fashionable nowadays. Absolutely de rigueur for jilted parties." He lit her cigarette, then his own. "She quickly tired of that idea, though, like everything else. I'm not worried about her. She'll have a line of admirers at her door soon enough. She always has. We're getting divorced."

"So, what does that entail exactly? Do you just say 'I divorce thee' three times fast?"

"That's for Muslims, you goof," he said. She smiled at his attempt at American slang. "I'm just a Francophile."

"So how does your religion handle divorce?"

"There's a bit of paperwork, but not much. Since we never had children, you know."

"Tell me, how does it feel to be free?" she asked, then

frowned. With Man popping up on street corners, weeping on the telephone, and shouting her name outside her studio, she had yet to experience that sensation.

"Fabulous. It's like a weight's been lifted off me. I feel like I could fly." He raised his champagne to her. "Thank you, darling."

"Me? But I——" Lee shook her head vehemently. She had never wanted the responsibility of someone else's breakup. Would he expect her to stay with him forever now?

"Relax, *ma petite*! I know you are a wild colt, ready to run fast and play hard. I love that about you." He took her hand. "All I meant was that you've made me see what life can be like. The alternatives to a lonely marriage, a dry desert land, to becoming old too young."

She leaned over and kissed him, suddenly glad he'd left his legendarily beautiful wife for her.

"Of course, I've had to move out of the flat. I bid farewell to Anatole France's lovely house and got new rooms."

"Where are you staying?"

"Upstairs." His eyes twinkled. "Would you like to come up to my suite? Have a little nightcap?" He ran a finger along his mustache. "Or shall I take you back to Montparnasse?"

"Are you playing hard to get, Monsieur Eloui?" She squeezed his upper thigh and ran her hand down his leg. "On your first night of freedom?"

"Just giving you choices, Lee. I always want you to have choices."

"To your rooms, then."

XXX

Lee bounded down the stairs in her kimono, eager to start her day. Before getting dressed, before having coffee, she wanted to check the mail. It was still a novelty that she could look forward to the post, to fetch it without worrying that anyone was lurking in the lobby. Man had finally stopped bothering her. Gradually, as the weather became warmer, he had slowly given up his crusade. Except for the odd late-night telephone call—the emergency in the ring, always startling—she didn't hear from him anymore. He'd abandoned his corner, his scribbling, his door-pounding. For the last several weeks, she'd felt comfortable in her home and in her neighborhood, free from harassment and worry.

She poked her hand in the box and brought out a short stack. A picture postcard from Tanja (she'd taken to sending Lee the worst ones she could find; this one was the First National Bank of Tuskaloosa, the "tallest building on a dirt road east of the Mississippi"), a thin aerogram from her father, various business requests and—yes! A fat envelope with an Egyptian postmark.

When Aziz had been obligated to return to Cairo at the beginning of summer, she was taken aback by her own disappointment. Fortunately, she'd quickly discovered that he was a wonderful correspondent, a charming letter-writer guaranteed to send at least two long missives a week.

Back in bed, Lee read his letter: his daily news followed by the compulsory entreaties for her to visit (this one included a lovely description of a desert oasis) and, tacked on to the end, an innocent inquiry on whether he should buy a chalet in Saint Moritz. "Wasn't it wonderful? We could spend next winter there." She sighed. Next winter seemed a lifetime away. Aziz signed off with a simple "I adore you." Somehow the exaggerated *adore* was less threatening than the homespun honesty of the word *love*.

She tucked the new letter safely away with his others in a black leather hatbox, then looked in her wardrobe for something to wear. Narrowing her eyes critically, her lips pursed, she pulled out various frocks and suits—held them up under her chin in front of the mirror—then discarded them on the bed. She wanted to look her best, but shunned anything too conventional. She decided on her flowered crepe de chine; it had a flattering tailor-cut, but the illusion of carefree youth. Pinning on her new straw hat, she remembered the collage exhibition. (A straw hat? Picabia's absurd nonpicture had questioned.) That was when Tanja was still in Paris, when she and Man were together, mentor and student, a passionate couple. Everything had changed since then.

Grabbing her portfolio, she headed to le Dôme; Lee had a meeting with a gallery owner who wanted to see her work. At just twenty-five, Julien Levy had his own New York art gallery and was intrepid enough to fill it with work by the Surrealists. On the telephone, he'd said her pieces would undoubtedly fit nicely in two different group shows. She could hardly believe it. Her career, even without Man Ray, was definitely going places.

On the sunny terrace, she ordered a café au lait and looked at her watch. Ten minutes early. Humming excitedly to herself, she glanced down the street; her song was immediately stifled by a blossoming frown. Kiki and her friend Jacqueline, Man's long-haired model, were walking up the boulevard arm in arm, square handbags bouncing against their hips. Lee pulled a cigarette out of its case and looked away, but soon felt their shadow on her, heard the scrape of iron chairs on the pavement. She moved her portfolio and bag onto her lap and looked at them.

"Good morning," she said without enthusiasm. She hoped they'd be gone before Julien arrived; Kiki had a way of stealing thunder, of making men forget why they'd come in the first place.

"Lee Miller." Kiki sat down. She was not wearing her characteristic grin, but a somber expression; her brow creased under the wide arcs of her penciled eyebrows. "We've just come from Man's place. He looks like shit."

"Like he hasn't slept in weeks," Jacqueline added, using the same accusatory tone as Kiki. "He said he's on a liquid diet, to purify himself."

"Makes you wonder what liquids he's drinking," Kiki said, inviting herself to Lee's cigarettes. "Even worse, though"—she blew the smoke out through her nose—"he's carrying a revolver around. When I asked him why, he glared at me, shrugged, said it wasn't my business."

Lee's head jerked up, wondering if Man had gone completely crazy. Had he spent the weeks of silence planning murder? She squinted down the street in the direction of his studio, half-expecting to see his silhouette coming toward her, pistols raised, outlaw-style. Kiki followed her gaze with a caustic smile.

"I'm not worried about you, honey, I'm worried about him. I've never seen him this blue. He'd turn that gun on himself before he'd shoot you with it. Even in the best of times, the idea of suicide fascinated Man."

"He never told me that," Lee said, wondering if Kiki had always known Man Ray better than she did.

Was he really contemplating killing himself? First Nimet and now Man. Aziz had said it was de rigueur for jilted parties, but Man Ray had never been one to follow the crowd. Lee remembered her mother's failed attempt—her feeble revenge against Theodore's unfaithfulness—but couldn't imagine Man doing it. He was too strong, too self-assured—or at least he used to be. Perhaps Kiki was lying and the gun was for her.

"He probably never told you a lot of things." Kiki stubbed out the cigarette, half-smoked, and got to her feet. "I just thought you should know."

Itching to go, Lee flagged the waiter to bring her the check, then watched the two women disappear down the stairs into the Vavin metro stop. Oh, Man. She resented being held responsible for another person's happiness, for his well-being.

Ever since Lee could remember, men had wanted something from her—her body, her approval, her devotion—had declared their love and pined for her, desperate for her attention. When she didn't return their affections, they called her cold, pitiless, unfeeling, *la belle dame sans merci*. As if she could control how they felt—as if it were her fault! She couldn't understand why Man refused to let her go. He had always been possessive of her, of her body, her person. Would he rather kill her than give her up?

Gazing at the dark passage into the metro, she suddenly saw a thin young man in a double-breasted suit taking the stairs two by two. Julien had finally arrived.

"Great to see you!" She gave him a kiss on both cheeks. "Now, let's get the hell out of Montparnasse."

"Anything wrong?" He took her portfolio and offered her his arm.

"I don't want to run into Man Ray. I've just heard he's packing a gun."

"In that case, I certainly don't want him to see us together." Julien laughed, but immediately put out his arm for a taxi. "I went by his place yesterday to look at his work. I didn't see a gun, but he looked half-dead." He slid into the cab beside her. "Where do you want to go?"

"It's such a pretty day." Lee began, trying to shake thoughts of Man and guns out of her head. "Let's go to the Île de la Cité. To that tiny park at the tip of the island. It should be cool under the trees next to the river."

"Perfect," he said, repeating the instructions for the driver. "Then we can have lunch at the Henri IV at the Place Dauphine."

On the quay, between an old man serious about fishing and an amateur painter crouched on a camp chair before an easel, Julien and Lee sat on the warm stone, letting their legs hang down like children, staring up at the sun with closed eyes. Lee began to relax, away from Montparnasse. A *quartier* filled with the same old faces, it made the bustling French capital into a village, made Paris intolerably small. Finally, Julien turned to look at Lee.

"Another thing about Man." He had obviously not stopped thinking about him. "When I was at his place, he showed me a new readymade. It's a photo of your eye on a metronome. It even comes with instructions. It says to cut the eye from a portrait of a former lover, then, after clipping it to the pendulum, regulate it to the desired tempo." Julien pulled a piece of paper out of his pocket and read out loud. *"Keep going to the limit of endurance. With a hammer well-aimed, try to destroy it with a single blow."* He looked at Lee while stuffing the paper back inside his jacket. "It's called *Object of Destruction*. It's a powerful piece. I'm going to show it in the gallery."

"If he doesn't destroy it first, that is." Lee breathed out, reminded of the scene in *Blood of a Poet* when Enrique smashed his muse with a mallet. It seemed Man Ray wasn't above copying ideas from the little magpie.

The hammer, the crushed statue, the gun. In the film, the poet tried to destroy his muse but, in the end, she led him to his fears, to madness, to suicide. She'd watched his demise coldly, her purpose fulfilled. She shivered, thinking of Man's revolver. As his muse, had she dealt him a deadly hand?

Like the metronome in his *Object of Destruction*, Lee's feelings about her former lover swung back and forth, from dread to pity, from revulsion to guilt, from resentment to exhaustion. She wanted done with him. Lee changed the subject, fleeing from Man Ray and his suffering.

"Speaking of the gallery, I've brought the photos you asked for."

She handed him her portfolio and watched as he looked through the thirty-odd prints she'd chosen from her three-year stint in Europe, from wryly observed encounters—labyrinths of architecture, living statuary, surreal glimpses of urban mystery—to original portraits of the famous and the anonymous both.

"They're wonderful," he whispered, gazing into her in the eyes, as if astounded.

"Which show do you see them in? The Surrealist show? Or the modern photography one?" Lee didn't really mind—both would include Man Ray—so long as he took three or four.

"Lee, you've got plenty of pieces here, all high-quality prints of interesting subjects. What I'd like to do is give you a one-woman show."

"Really?" Her mouth flew open and her eyes lit up; she flung her arms around him in a warm hug.

He held on too tightly and, as she pulled away, kissed her on her mouth. Confused, she studied his face; a cavalier smile played on his lips. Would she be given the show if she were plain? Was this an elaborate gesture to get her in bed? Did it matter? Lee wasn't sure. She popped up from the cobblestones and pulled him up by the hand.

"Let's go celebrate."

At the wine bar in the Place Dauphine, Lee ordered champagne and escargots.

"I've been wondering," Julien said, "why don't you take any self-portraits? It would be a great asset to the show."

"My photo has been taken too much as it is. When I'm behind the camera, I prefer to look at other things." The waiter served the champagne, and they clinked glasses. "I hope the people that go to the show will be more interested in the photos than the photographer. Who knows? They might imagine

Lee Miller is a little old man from Intercourse, Pennsylvania, or a soldier boy off on leave. I'd like that."

"As much as you may like the idea, I think you're already too famous for that."

He locked eyes with her again. She found him good-looking, despite thin lips. Debating the idea of a fling, Lee grabbed a shell with tongs, pulled a snail out of its parsley-butter cocoon, and chewed slowly. While Aziz was in Egypt, their relationship was on hold; Julien was married and would not want a commitment. She licked her buttery lips, then took another sip of champagne. Perhaps they could both get what they wanted.

"Am I?"

"You are." He smiled broadly. Could he sense that she was considering it, that she was tempted? "In fact, I know a few businessmen who would be more than happy to finance a Lee Miller photography studio if you ever decided to move back to New York."

"Now, that one's hard to believe." She looked him in the eye, trying to decide if this was real information, or more well-timed flattery.

"Claire Luce's husband, for one. He's the heir to the Western Union fortune, you know. Loved the portraits you took of her." He soaked a piece of bread in the snail butter, obviously unsettled by the contents of the shells. "With the gallery show and a financed studio, it'd be a great time for you to come back to New York. I know I'd love to have you around."

Had she learned everything she could from Paris? From Montparnasse and *French Vogue*, from the avant-garde art scene, from the city's most famous photographer? Had she gotten what she came for? She looked up at Julien; he touched the tip of her finger with his.

"Maybe it is time to go," she said slowly. As they slid out of her mouth, the words surprised her, but she knew it was true.

Only a half-year had passed since Man Ray had suggested the very same move. How preposterous it had seemed then. She wondered how he would react when he heard the news, that *she* was going, that New York was ripe for *her*. How bitter would that irony taste? She hoped it wouldn't be the final blow, the one to make him pull a trigger. Lee, however, was finally making a firm decision about her life, and not Man Ray, Paris, or future winters with Aziz Eloui Bey could make her change her mind.

The next morning, before dawn, her telephone rang. She bolted up in the dark, instantly ousted from sleep. She tiptoed over to answer it, but didn't hesitate; she knew who it was.

"*Oui, âllo?*"

"Lee?" Man's voice was a dried husk, pleading and desperate, but this time she didn't cringe or slam the phone back on its cradle. "Don't hang up! Listen to—"

"No, Man. You listen to me. I'm leaving Paris. In another month or two, you won't have to see me anymore."

"Wha?"

"I'm going back to New York. I'm leaving."

There was a muffled silence on the line—she thought she could hear him deflating.

"Good-bye, Man."

She quietly hung up and went back to bed.

· · ·

That fall, Lee closed her studio and booked passage to New York on the *Ile de France*, set to cross on October eleventh. The evening before her trip, as she was getting ready to go out, she found a gnarled envelope that had been pushed inside the door. The handwriting—although loose and wild—was still familiar. It was the first message she'd had from Man in months. He must have heard about her imminent departure.

Inside was a page torn from a notebook; he had drawn her eyes and lips—a simple outline, a vacant stare—then covered it, from top to bottom, with her name. *Elizabeth, Elizabeth, Lee* . . . She imagined his voice calling her—not that of a gangster, but that of a spoiled child—and nearly tossed it in the bin. She stopped herself and tucked it away in her handbag instead. Maybe the next time she saw the drawing, she wouldn't find it so cloying, so filled with self-pity. Perhaps she'd remember a time when they were equals, a pair.

She slipped her fur coat over her satin evening gown. Michel, George, Tatiana, and the others were all waiting at the Ritz for a farewell dinner. She could hardly believe she was leaving tomorrow, that three years had passed since she'd been in the States. After refusing Man's entreaties to return, she was the one going back to New York—with contacts, a show, studio backers—and he was staying in his same cluttered old studio near the boulevard Montparnasse.

Lee headed out into the night under her umbrella. Her heels clicked on the wet pavement as she got into the cab. As the driver took off, Lee gazed out at the people, the lights, eager to enjoy Paris one last time. She'd long lost the habit of examining every corner for Man Ray, worrying what he might do. In fact, she'd already forgotten the note in her bag.

EPILOGUE

———

"When exactly was the last time we saw Man?" Lee asked Roland.

He turned from the window to give her his attention. "It was before the war."

She snorted. "I knew *that*." For Lee, the past fifteen years were inescapably divided into pre- and postwar: the before and after of that five-year parenthesis when everything they had once thought normal had abruptly stopped.

From the back of the taxi, she peered out the window and into the glare of California, a clean, modern place, untouched by conflict. The long snouts of shiny automobiles inched along the wide boulevard lined with palm trees and telephone poles; the neon and lights of the cinemas and restaurants were pale in the summer sun. When would Europe look like this again? Had it ever? The last time she'd been to the States was in the "before" category. Not that it mattered—the only thing changed here was the rise in its own prosperity. Lee fidgeted with the clasp on her handbag, remembering when she'd returned to

New York in 1932. Even before the war, her life had not been without danger. Though most of it, she admitted, was of her own making.

After Paris, she'd spent two wildly successful years in Manhattan: she had all the uptown socialites coming to the studio, the best accounts—Saks, Macy's, the fashion rags—her solo show, and *The Blood of a Poet* running ad nauseam on Fifth Avenue. But it had worn her out. Not the photography—soulless commercial work—but her frenetic social life. The relentless dinner parties, all-night poker games, the weekends on Long Island. The drinking, always drinking, with everyone so blotto that nothing ruffled them: a Rolls-Royce diving into a swimming pool, nearby gunshots, the smell of burning hair, a boathouse split by lightning . . . Nothing.

Lee's fevered pace—the constant outings and nonstop fun that did nothing to make her happy—had finally caught up with her. She was exhausted, unhealthy, perpetually cranky, on the verge of losing her looks. When Aziz Eloui Bey came to New York on business, they spontaneously eloped. She was ready; it was time. Lee had always needed change, novelty, motion . . . Ecstatic, she returned with him to Cairo; it took only a few months in Egypt to soundly squelch nearly all that enthusiasm.

It wasn't so much the god-awful heat, the mosquitoes, the typhoid injections, the crazy traffic, or the persistent odor of camel dung, as it was the boredom. On occasion, her intense longing for Europe would surface and overwhelm her like nausea, her idleness would paralyze her until she could scarcely get out of bed. Everything was so colorless in the desert, all ochre, tan, and bone. She became plagued by dark moods—the

Plagues of Egypt! But instead of frogs, locusts, and darkness, it was insomnia, depression, and recklessness. At times, Lee tried to combat the blue jitters with danger and excitement. She took lessons from a snake charmer, rode camels and a wild horse, swam with sharks in the Red Sea. And there was more drinking. Often and excessively. After a few years, Aziz, perpetually understanding, encouraged her to go off on holiday by herself, to spend the summer in France with old friends.

That was in 1937, two years before Hitler began invading everything, still during that enchanted time people now called the "Interwar Period." And suddenly, for the first time in five years, Lee was in Paris.

Her first day in town, Julien Levy—who had evolved from lover to friend after their short-lived affair—whisked her away to a Surrealist ball. Although excited, she was nervous about bumping into Man Ray. Would he be hostile, icy cold, or filled with nostalgic longing? Would he still want to photograph her? Sleep with her? Would he follow her around Paris?

None of it. At the party he'd smiled and given her a wan kiss on the cheek. She was taken aback by his lack of passion. The maddening jealousy, the tireless arguing, the drunken stalking with a gun in his pocket—in five years, it had all been erased. They stood side by side, polite as strangers. Lee's relief was tinged with profound disappointment. Man Ray no longer cared.

He had then introduced her to the man next to him. A tall Englishman, barefoot and bare-chested, his hair painted green. It was Roland Penrose, an aristocratic Quaker, a modern art collector, curator, and painter. She looked at him now, sitting by her side. Was it ironic that Man Ray had casually introduced them? Roland was the one who finally propelled her out of Cairo; the one she wanted to be with when war broke out.

"It had to have been *before* the war. The war just ended last year," Lee said with a slight hint of derision, but truthfully, she could barely believe it was true. Although the war itself had passed slowly—the Blitz, the blackout, and the food rationing had seemed interminable; her three-year stint as a war correspondent, the work of a lifetime—ever since, she felt as though she'd been trudging through mud. No, mud was the currency of war. Noise, chaos, constant movement had all turned into the silent stillness of peace.

"Well, if you want precision," he said, his accent refined, "I believe the last time we saw Man was in southern France, August 1939, a week before Hitler invaded Poland. Right before we ran screaming back to London."

"That's right." She frowned, remembering that last visit. It had seemed their common past had never existed. No longer his mistress or muse, she'd been demoted to little more than his friend Roland's lover. One of the women. Six years later, what would this visit to Man Ray bring? Was it a mistake to come?

At the crosswalk, Lee eyed the long-haired girls in their high-heeled sandals and flowered skirts, smiling at strangers, each one a Hollywood hopeful. She crossed her legs in the roomy backseat, feeling dowdy in loose-fitting slacks.

"I can't believe Man lives here," she said, running a hand through her frizzy halo of hair. The cab turned right off Sunset and onto Vine. "It seems the polar opposite to Paris."

"Didn't you fancy coming here as a girl?" Roland teased her. "To get your start in the pictures?"

"Not for long. I was always more attracted to the Atlantic than the Pacific."

The cab pulled up in front of a narrow redbrick apartment building with an arched gate: Villa Elaine. Two steps inside the quiet courtyard—a tame jungle of palms, hibiscus, and ivy—and the street seemed far away.

"Nice." Roland nodded his approval. "Perhaps Man's found a corner of Provence here in Los Angeles."

When they rang the bell, Man flung the door open. Although in his mid-fifties, he didn't look remarkably different from when Lee lived with him. His hair, still dark, had stopped receding years before; he was stylish, quick and slim. His big, curious eyes had not lost their glow—they seemed almost darker, more intense—though they were now framed by glasses. Remembering that magnetic pull that had attracted her at twenty-two, she smiled at him shyly. Lee had changed far more than he; almost forty, she was no longer slim, fresh, unlined. Bags hung under her slanted blue eyes, her fluffy blond hair needed re-dyeing. War and lifestyle had taken a toll on her looks.

"You made it." After giving Lee a warm embrace, the kind reserved for favorite sisters and special friends, he shook Roland's hand in delight. "It's wonderful to have you. It's been too long."

He ushered them in. The studio, with big windows, high ceilings, and a balcony, had a similar air to his old place in Montparnasse. Paintings and pipes mingled with books and old rayograms; a long piece of driftwood twirled up a standing lamp. In a nook of one wall, Lee noticed a small version of *Observatory Time,* the enormous painting he'd done, postbreakup, of her red lips dominating a gray sky. This one was a mere memory, a shadow of the original, obsessive piece. She sighed—of course, she no longer merited monumental proportions in his life—then noticed the new harvest of photos, all portraits of an exotic-looking brunette. As Lee turned back to face Man, the model herself walked in from the bedroom. Dark, with sculpted features and a graceful frame, she was at least five years younger than Lee.

"And here's Juliet," said Man. "Darling, I'd like for you to meet some old friends from the Paris days. This is Roland Penrose, an English Surrealist, if you believe in such things. And Lee Miller. You've heard of her, of course. She used to be my assistant and model. You might recognize her from some of my earlier work."

"Pleased to meet you both." Juliet gave them a dazzling smile.

"And you." Lee smiled stiffly, wondering why she felt so awkward. "Man, I can't believe you're in Hollywood. Are you working for the pictures?"

"Hell, no," he said with a chuckle. "I'm doing what I've always done. You know, when I came here in 1940, I only planned to stay a week. I was off to Tahiti! I wanted to be as far from the war as I could get. But on my first day in town, I met Juliet." He took her by the hand and gazed at her dotingly. "That decided it for me. We've been together ever since."

Pleased, Juliet looked down, demure and docile. Lee raised

her eyebrows. Man's new muse was nothing like her or Kiki. Maybe this was the kind of woman he could hold on to and grow old with.

"Can I get anyone some coffee?" Juliet asked, smiling around the group. "Or tea?"

"I wouldn't mind something a bit stronger," Lee said. "Isn't it about cocktail hour?"

In mild distress, Juliet looked over at Man. "Cocktails? I don't think we have anything. Of course, I could run to the market and get something. What would you like?"

"I don't want to be any trouble," said Lee.

"No, you're right," said Man. "We should celebrate with something more exciting than coffee. Champagne? Or vodka and orange juice? That's very California."

"With lots of ice?" asked Lee. After years in England and the Continent, she'd been overly warm since they arrived to the American southwest. "Sounds like heaven."

"I'll be back in a little bit," Juliet said, picking up her purse.

"I'll go with you," said Roland. "We can leave these two to reminisce. That way, they won't bore us with their old stories when we get back."

As Man and Lee settled on the couch, they both sought tobacco. Man lit her cigarette, then puffed on his pipe.

"How long have you been in the States?" Man asked, preferring safe questions to talk of old times.

"We arrived in May. We visited friends in New York—I saw my family in Poughkeepsie, too—then we went to Arizona to see Max Ernst. He's doing great work." She put on a happy face.

Although she'd been taking lots of photographs—mainly

portraits of artists—she hadn't felt passionate about working since the war. Their friends' artwork, shows, and lives all seemed so inspired, so fulfilled. Compared to them, she didn't feel talented or driven. Lee was just going through the motions.

"So are you thinking about coming back to the States?"

"No." She shook her head. "I've been away so long, it doesn't feel like home anymore."

"I think of Paris every day. Now that the war's over, I'm dying to get back. Not only do I want to live there again—Lord knows, there's nothing interesting about being an *américain* in America—but I want to see if my work survived. I only brought two suitcases with me. You wouldn't believe how hard it is to pack when you think you might never return. I filled one valise just with artwork, but my big canvases, archives, and readymades are still in France. That is, if they didn't get destroyed."

"I was there at the liberation of Paris," Lee said, wistful. "It was such a beautiful thing. I saw Picasso, Louis Aragon, Cocteau . . . Everyone was thin but well—and so happy to have done with the Nazis. Picasso told me that you'd left France."

He took a quick puff on his pipe. "Although I'd lived there for nearly twenty years, once the Germans stomped into Paris, I couldn't take it. The Resistance hadn't been organized yet, my friends were out of town, I couldn't work. Finally, I made the decision to leave."

"Probably for the best."

"Could have saved my life." He looked over at Lee. "Six weeks after I left, the Vichy government passed a law allowing foreign Jews to be interned—and we all know what that means. I'm not a religious man, but I don't think the Nazis would have cared."

Lee's mind suddenly began swimming with images from the death camps. An abandoned cart piled high with bodies; the overwhelming smell of uncontrolled bowels and rotting flesh; her combat boots covered in white ash: "Fucking hell!" she turned to a green-faced soldier as she tried to wipe it off, "this isn't from the ovens, is it?" Her eyes darted back to the pile. She stood up and stared down into her Rolleiflex camera, just a foot from the cart. She began taking photos to make the men real: the clutched hands, making baby fists; the open eyes, some blue, some blank; mouths wide as if in song; the extraordinary thinness, bones that had made bodies move. Zooming in on one face, her cold terror. There was a dark-haired man with dramatic eyebrows and a hawk nose. No, impossible. Picasso had assured her that Man had left—"on the same steamer as that idiot, Dalí"—but this cadaver looked so familiar, she'd wanted to touch it. Her former lover, mentor, companion.

Lee reached out for Man's soft, warm hand; in slight surprise, he gave hers a quick pat.

"When I went to get my traveling papers," Man continued, "the Nazi officer recognized my name. He said that I could be their photographer, that I would be well-paid. So perhaps I could have saved my skin by being a toady. Though I would have jumped off the Eiffel Tower first."

"But they gave you the papers?"

"Yeah, they let me go. I locked up my place on Campagne Première, and before I left, I took a long stroll around the old neighborhood. Past the cafés and bars and even the places that didn't exist anymore—where ol' Rosalie dished up spaghetti when I first got to town, the Jockey Club, your studio in front of the cemetery—"

"That's funny. Last time I was in Paris I must have taken that very same tour. I had quite a lump in my throat by the end." She took the last drag off her cigarette, then stomped it out.

He relit his cold pipe. "But you! When Juliet showed me one of your stories in *Vogue*—was it about a *siege?*—I couldn't believe it was the same Lee Miller I used to know. It was only when I saw the photo of you—in a helmet, no less—that I was finally convinced."

"Now I can hardly believe it myself."

"And the frontline reports! The field hospitals, the Siegfried Line, the head-shaven collaborators, then on into Krautland! I was bowled over by the writing. The three years we were together, I never saw you write anything more than a letter."

"My dispatches were sort of like that, I suppose. Long letters to strangers."

"True." Man nodded. "That personal tone."

"And, Man? What did you make of the photos?" Lee asked shyly. Her former teacher's opinion still mattered to her, after all those years.

"Well, I knew you were a great photographer. That didn't surprise me." He gave her a wink. "Seriously, bearing in mind the conditions—the photos were excellent. They put you right in the scene. I could hear the bombing and smell the smoke. An old studio-bug like me never could have taken such shots."

"Thanks, Man." She blinked back tears, then struggled to

smile. She'd been so sensitive lately, not herself at all. She lit another cigarette and looked at the door. Although she was enjoying their conversation—one-on-one for the first time in years, she finally felt comfortable with him again—Lee was ready for that drink. More than ever before, she'd gotten in the habit of having a drink nearby, to calm her nerves, to chase the blue jitters away.

"So, tell me," he said with a tinge of irony, "how have you been passing the time since Hitler killed himself?"

"After a year of riding around in jeeps, muddy and flea bitten, listening to soldier-talk and avoiding artillery fire, I found I missed it. Can you believe it? I didn't really know what to do in postwar London. What kind of journalist I should be. Would *Vogue* want hats, recipes, sewing tips?"

"That's a laugh," Man said. "I used to sew *your* buttons on."

She smiled at him, remembering those happy-go-lucky Montparnasse days. Since then, Lee had owned an upscale Manhattan photography studio and been an upper-class Egyptian housewife. A Surrealist and fashion expert. But her life as a wartime photojournalist had been the most fulfilling one yet. Her pretty young self—so cocky and self-absorbed—would have had a difficult time imagining her roughing it with soldiers—not in their beds, but by their sides, a comrade, a friend—and taking honest photos of destruction and death.

"Even though the war in Europe had ended, I wasn't ready to call it quits," she said. "By August, I was already back at the Press HQ—the Scribe Hotel, you know the place—trying to map out a trip to the east. Truth was, I could barely organize my room." She tried for a lighthearted chuckle, but it came out

as a cough. "But I had *Vogue*'s blessing, a few letters of intro-
duction, and an old Chevy, so I packed some clothes and my
cameras, got my jerry cans and took off."

She didn't mention that her medicine bag had also become a
vital part of her kit. In the morning, with a black coffee chaser,
she often took Benzedrine to get herself going; in the evening,
along with a few stiff drinks, she calmed down with sleeping
pills. Since Dachau, she'd gotten into a secretive pharmaceu-
tical routine. But that was not material for carefree reunion
chats.

"I was on the road for five or six months—Austria, Hun-
gary, Romania—taking photos, interviewing people, shooting
the breeze with the other leftover correspondents still hanging
around. In Budapest, I even got arrested. A Soviet soldier took
me in for taking pictures without the proper papers. That story
made it into the *New York Times!*"

Lee was trying to tell her tales with élan, like she had on
other occasions, but was having a hard time pulling it off. Truth
was, she didn't really know how to describe those travels. After
the fighting stopped, she'd taken a handful of prize photos, but
most of her days were just frittered away.

"I went back home in February." She shrugged. "I suppose it
was finally time for my war to end."

"Sounds like that would be a good thing. I saw those pictures you took at the concentration camps." Man shook his head
and whistled. "Not everyone could have taken those."

"We felt like our cameras were weapons; that with a few good
shots, we could change the way people thought, maybe even end
the war," she said. "That sounds awfully noble. But now, I think

of those pictures." She looked him in the eye, her speech became low and halting. "And realize that, when I was there, I was just making compositions, framing, checking light and shadow. I almost never thought of them as bodies, as real human beings."

"They are powerful pictures, Lee. You did what you could to make others react to them. Even if, at the time, you were unable to. It was all too overwhelming. I think I understand that."

"One thing I haven't forgotten, though, is that smell. Sometimes, when I'm walking in a city street—or just sitting in my living room—I catch a whiff of bodies."

Lee swallowed, half-nauseated at the thought. At the Dachau camp, trying to get the best shots, she'd gone into railway cars, half-filled with corpses, the cramped bunkers, where men lay rotting, the ovens, which had run out of fuel to burn the piles of wasted cadavers outside. In every corner, she was constantly attacked with the stench of shit, body odor, putrefaction, and death.

"Maybe it's garbage, sewage, I don't know. But it fills me with panic. I think I might scream."

She bit her lip. The horrific daytime smells. At night, nightmares intermingled with insomnia.

"Lee." This time, he reached out to touch her hand. "You've seen more of the world than most of us. Than most of us would ever *want* to see."

"The crazy thing is that now, with the war over, my work has no focus. Without an enemy and a front, I feel lost." She lit another cigarette, but it just made her thirstier. "I've come to realize that the war was my muse. The noise, the danger, the movement, the cast of thousands. Even the horror and death. It gave my work meaning—made it come alive."

She stared at Man. To feel inspired, he only needed a beautiful woman—all the better if she loved him and slept in his bed—whereas she'd needed a theater of destruction, madness, the possibility of death. Even after the war had ended, she had gone looking for it, unable to stop. He was squeezing her hand when they heard the door. Bottles jangled inside a paper bag. Lee sat back with the anticipation of relief. Before they walked into the room, Man leaned over and whispered in her ear.

"A great muse is like a fast-moving train. Don't let anybody tell you different."

AUTHOR'S NOTE
AND ACKNOWLEDGMENTS

The Woman in the Photograph is a work of fiction inspired by the lives of real people. Lee Miller was a complex woman, not entirely of her time. Although the feelings, thoughts, dialogues, and many details in the novel are entirely of my invention, most of the events are based on published biographical information about Lee, from the truth-is-stranger-than-fiction chance meetings she had with Condé Nast and Man Ray to her photographing the liberation of the Dachau concentration camp in World War II (though in some instances, in the interest of narrative flow, the order of events has been altered). At times, when only a bare-bones account of an event has survived—for example, in the case of her childhood rape—I have tried to imagine a more detailed story. As for her relationship with Man Ray, I have tried to create a plausible version of their romance, based on the information available.

The photographs and films described in the novel are based on Lee Miller's and Man Ray's work from the time, with the notable exception of the photographs of Coco Chanel's jewelry collection. Although those photos do exist, there is no indication they were Lee's work, although to my mind they were very "her."

In writing this book, I perused countless sources regarding Lee Miller, her contemporaries, and their times. For anyone interested in learning more, the following sources would provide an excellent starting point: *Lee Miller: On Both Sides of the Camera* by Carolyn Burke; *The Lives of Lee Miller* by Antony Penrose; *Self Portrait* by Man Ray; *Man Ray: American Artist* by Neil Baldwin; *Kiki's Paris: Artists and Lovers 1900–1930* by Billy Klüver and Julie Martin; *Bohemian Paris* by Dan Franck; *Jean Cocteau (Critical Lives)* by James S. Williams; *Paris Was Yesterday 1925–1939*, by Janet Flanner, *Julien Levy: Memoir of an Art Gallery* by Julien Levy and Ingrid Schaffner; and *Memoirs of Montparnasse* by John Glassco (which included the anecdote that inspired Lee's excursion to the transvestite club in Montmartre).

On a personal note, I would like to thank my agent, Michelle Brower; my hawkeyed editor, Kate Dresser; our lovely publisher, Jennifer Bergstrom; and the entire Gallery team. Special thanks also go out to Alex Lewis and Kathy Sagan. Lucky for me, I've also had the help of many talented friends during the course of this novel. My utmost gratitude goes out to the photographer Elise Smith, the artist James King, and the web designer Colleen Tully, as well as my amazing reader friends: Mary Dansak, Frannie James, Judith Nunn, Peggy Stelpflug, and, most of all, my sister, Lynn Gynther. As always, kisses go out to my entire family, especially to my husband, Carlos, my girls, Claudia and Lulu, and my mother and biggest supporter, Ruth.

This novel is not affiliated with or authorized by the Lee Miller Archives, the Man Ray Trust, or the heirs of either Lee Miller or Man Ray.

The Woman in the Photograph

—

DANA GYNTHER

INTRODUCTION

Model and woman-about-town Lee Miller moves to Paris determined to make herself known amid the giddy circle of celebrated artists, authors, and photographers currently holding court in the city. She seeks out the charming, charismatic artist Man Ray to become his assistant but soon becomes much more than that: his model, his lover, his muse.

Coming into her own more fully every day, Lee models, begins working on her own projects, and even stars in a film, provoking the jealousy of the older and possessive Man Ray. Drinking and carousing is the order of the day, but while hobnobbing with the likes of Picasso and Charlie Chaplin, she also falls in love with the art of photography and finds that her own vision can no longer come second to her mentor's. *The Woman in the Photograph* is the richly drawn, tempestuous novel about a talented and fearless young woman caught up in one of the most fascinating times of the twentieth century.

QUESTIONS AND TOPICS FOR DISCUSSION

1. Early in their affair, Lee notes that "from the outside" she and Man "looked like opposites: old and young, short and tall, dark and light, serious and gay" (p. 33). While these are superficial differences based on Lee's first impressions of the other artist, discuss the deeper chasms that separate Man and Lee. Do you think that they were a mismatch from the beginning, or is there truth in the saying that opposites attract?

2. Man and Lee's love for each other and their love for art are entwined from the beginning, while modern workplace romances are often frowned upon. Do you think they would have been smarter to disconnect their work from their affair after their initial meeting?

3. Though she leaves New York in search of a less conventional life, one of the things Lee says that she loves about *French Vogue,* or *Frogue,* is that "relationships there were simple" (p. 86), while her time in the studio with Man is anything but. What keeps Lee tied to her complicated life with Man? Can you relate to her reasons?

4. Were you shocked by some of the descriptions of the erotic photos Man and Lee take? Do you think viewers of the 1930s would have had similar reactions?

5. Gynther notes that Lee had "few close female friends" (p. 116), but a few key female figures feature prominently

in Lee's life. Discuss her relationships with Tanja, Kiki, and her mother. How do these women shape her story and sense of self?

6. "It was actually the art history class that made me want to quit painting. . . . I thought, what could I possibly do that was new? Then I came here and saw what Man and his friends were doing. Turning art upside down and on its head. . . . And I think it's more than just interesting, funny, or what have you. It's necessary" (p. 125). What do you think Lee means when she talks about "necessary art"? Do you think art is necessary?

7. Would you describe Man as Lee's muse? Why or why not? What inspires her most?

8. Compare the ways that men "use" Lee to the ways Lee "uses" men—whether sexually, socially, or professionally. You might examine her relationships to Man, her father Theodore, de Brunhoff, Jean Cocteau, Zizi, and Aziz Eloui Bey.

9. Lee is infuriated at the art world's double standards when she sees the caption of Man's photo of her in *Le Surrealism au service de la revolution* ("Young women: the raw material to power the creative arts") and laughs at the notion of her father and Man being asked to kiss and fondle each other in erotic photos as she and her fellow female models do. Why do you think sex and women are such important themes in Man's art? What do they add to his art that men cannot?

10. How do you think Lee's early sexual trauma relates to her views on sex and relationships? Did her constant fear of being "tied down" to a man strike a chord with you?

11. Lee compares herself to the Seabrooks's slave girl, remarking at how different she is from the muse she plays in Cocteau's film. What do the women have in common? What separates them, other than their appearances?

12. While sex is an important part of Man and Lee's relationship, in what ways does it keep them from seeing eye-to-eye?

13. In the end, Lee wonders whether all artists need either extreme pleasure (sex, love, beauty) or extreme pain (madness, war, death) to create their most meaningful works. Which do you relate to more?

ENHANCE YOUR BOOK CLUB

1. Man mentions the music of "Django Reinhardt, tango, and Strauss" that he used in his films, and Lee connects to the showtune "Love for Sale" by Cole Porter. Use these mentions as inspiration and create an avant-garde playlist inspired by the novel to provide a soundtrack for your book club.

2. Display photos of Lee by the artists mentioned in the book like Arnold Genthe, Edward Steichen, and Man Ray, as well as photos taken by Lee, both in her surrealist days and as a groundbreaking war photographer in Europe.

3. Learn more about the author and her other works of historical fiction at her personal website, http://danagynther.com